AT THE
HANDS OF
ANOTHER

A RINEHART SUSPENSE NOVEL

BOOKS BY ARTHUR LYONS

OTHER JACOB ASCH NOVELS

All God's Children
The Dead Are Discreet
The Killing Floor
Dead Ringer
Castles Burning
Hard Trade

NONFICTION

The Second Coming: Satanism in America

A RINEHART SUSPENSE NOVEL

AT THE HANDS OF ANOTHER

ARTHUR LYONS

HOLT, RINEHART AND WINSTON
NEW YORK

FOR JAMES W. GRODIN

Lawman
Gunman
Madman
Friend

*Published by Holt, Rinehart and Winston,
383 Madison Avenue, New York, New York 10017.
Published simultaneously in Canada by Holt, Rinehart and
Winston of Canada, Limited.*

*Library of Congress Cataloging in Publication Data
Lyons, Arthur.
At the hands of another.
(A Rinehart suspense novel)
I. Title.
PS3562.Y446A8   1983   813'.54   82-21315*

ISBN: 0-03-059616-5

*Designer: Kate Nichols
Printed in the United States of America
1 3 5 7 9 10 8 6 4 2*

ISBN 0-03-059616-5

ACKNOWLEDGMENTS

I would like to give special thanks to
Dr. Lawrence Cone, for his medical
expertise and his diabolical mind.

AT THE
HANDS OF
ANOTHER

A RINEHART SUSPENSE NOVEL

1

Any hopes I'd had for Farrah Fawcett-Fats died in a splash of light from the door.

She was wearing a black silk blouse and white slacks and her long blond hair was pulled back and tied, making the effect of the weight she had lost even more startling. Her cheekbones jutted out of her pale, triangular face, giving her an almost gaunt, fashion-model look, but whereas that kind of weight loss can give a dimension of hard inflexibility to the beauty of some women, in her case it did nothing to diminish her softness. She broke into a wide smile when she saw me, and I stood up and grinned stupidly, annoyed and at the same time confused by my reaction.

It had been five years, for chrissakes. Much too long ago for all this high school, pulse-pounding crap. Especially after what she'd done to me.

Which was why I'd been hoping she would be fat. Designer-jeans-by-Orson-Welles fat. The fantasies had long ago faded of her crawling in on bloody knees begging forgiveness, but it would have been nice to think that she'd fallen apart, at least a little. Aside from making it easier to make a clean getaway, there would have been a measure of satisfaction in it, the kind that must go along with divine retribution.

1

The only reason I'd agreed to meet her when she'd called and said she had to see me, that she needed my help, was a mixture of curiosity and ego gratification. The fantasies might have faded, but the questions remained. I'd waited five years for the answers. The answers and a good gloat if I was lucky. At least that was what I kept telling myself.

"It's good to see you," she said, extending her hands to grab mine. As she did that, I noticed the ring. A minor detail she had neglected to mention on the phone. It looked like whomever she had finally landed was well fixed, anyway. At least four carats, with good fire. After giving me an appraising look, she said, "You look absolutely great."

"So do you."

She smiled weakly. "I look horrible, but thanks for the lie."

I had forgotten how beautiful her eyes were, like aquamarines that changed color with the light. Now they were the deep-violet color I'd liked the best, but they looked tired, and I could see where she had tried to cover up the dark circles beneath them with makeup. As if noticing that I had noticed, she turned away self-consciously and waved a hand at the room.

"Your choice of meeting spots was very romantic."

"It was the first place that came to mind," I said, trying to sound casual.

"It used to be our favorite place."

I nodded. "Now that I think of it, I'm glad I picked it. It sort of lends a note of symmetry to the reunion."

She lowered her head a little and her tone turned serious. "I really debated about whether to call you. But when I said you were the only one I could trust, I meant it."

I took her arm, saying, "Let's get a table," and we moved away from the bar.

The dining room, a glass-enclosed wood-plank patio built over the beach, had a ceiling of canvas strips that flapped noisily when the breeze hit them. On the other side of the glass, over the ocean, was a narrow balcony occupied by five small tables. I asked the hostess if we could have one of those, and she took us outside.

2

A strong breeze blew off the ocean, but the sun was hot for October and it was not chilly at all. The sky was cloudless and looked washed-out, as if all its color had bled into the sea. A few surfers straddled their boards beyond the breakers, waiting for one big enough to ride. The beach was deserted except for a matronly-looking sunbather probably trying to escape the drudgeries of housework for a few hours.

After we both ordered Bloody Marys, I leaned back and studied Sharon's face. There was something missing besides the weight, I decided, a lack of animation in the expression, as if something had burned out there. That and the pale, feverish glow on her cheeks gave her a strange and special beauty, like that taken on sometimes by the critically ill.

My silent stare seemed to make her nervous. She rummaged around in her purse and pulled out a cigarette and a lighter. I took the lighter and struck a flame. The hand holding the cigarette trembled violently as she leaned across the table.

"You've got the shakes."

"I've always had the shakes," she said, snapping her purse shut and depositing it on the floor. "You used to comment on it quite frequently, remember?"

"Not this bad."

She shrugged and tried to smile. "It's been a bad year."

The waitress came back with our drinks and by the time she took our order, Crab Louie for Sharon and snapper for me, half of Sharon's drink was gone. I wondered if that was part of the reason for the shakes. Schick Center was out, but I could still hold out for Raleigh Hills. She had never been what you would call a timid drinker, but then I was one to talk. That had been one of our problems, but just one. A person's strengths can compensate for another's weaknesses, but weaknesses together are logarithmic.

She looked at me earnestly and said, "You know how many times I've wanted to pick up the phone and call you?"

"Not really."

"Lots."

"So why didn't you?"

3

She took a drag from her cigarette. "I don't know. I guess I felt guilty. I was afraid you'd hang up. Or worse, of what you'd say if you didn't. Then, after a while, I said, 'What's the point?' I don't know, I guess it was just easier."

"The last word I got from you was that letter saying, 'Dear Jake: I'm in Kansas City with a pitcher from the Boston Red Sox. I'm sorry, but things weren't working out with us. I'll explain later. Sharon.' After a year, I gave up waiting for the explanation."

She shook her head. "I know it must have sounded cold, but I couldn't get up the nerve to face you and I didn't know what to tell you, except the truth. I knew I was blowing whatever we had going, but at the time, it really didn't seem like it was much. I honestly didn't think it would matter much to you."

"You were right. It didn't. I just wandered around for a month or two listening to the canned goods in the market and hyperventilating a lot. I lost about eight pounds, and lived on Valium and whites and one-fifty-one rum. It was a fun time."

"That surprises me. It really does."

"Why?"

"Just the way you were acting the last couple of months. I thought you might even be a little relieved that it was over."

My mouth may have gaped a little. "Where in Christ's name would you get that brilliant idea?"

Her eyes were icy blue now, and a little hard. "Remember the night when I drove up to L.A. and told you I was pregnant?"

"How could I forget?"

She stubbed out her cigarette and pushed the ashtray away roughly. "Well, maybe I was just a naïve little girl living in a romantic fantasy world, but I really thought you were going to ask me to marry you. I was totally prepared for it. I was going to settle down and have the kid, and we were going to live happily ever after. When you got on the phone to your friendly doctor and proceeded to get everything neatly and clinically arranged, it really blew me away."

"You never said anything," I said weakly.

"What was I going to say? That I had visions of white picket fences dancing in my head? You obviously weren't in the mood to listen to anything like that. All you knew was that you had a problem that you very efficiently had taken care of."

"What would you rather have had me do? Let you make the decision? You weren't exactly in the emotional state to make a rational one."

She shook her head and said, "I don't know, Jake. All I know is that I was a basket case after the abortion. I was filled with a lot of self-doubt and guilt and I needed you with me to tell me that you loved me and that everything was going to be okay, but you were nowhere in sight."

I looked up from the beach, where a tanned and shirtless boy was tossing a yellow Frisbee to a big red setter.

"What are you talking about?"

"How many times did you come down in the two months afterward?"

"Hey, I was backed up with cases," I said defensively.

She stared at me. "You were scared."

She was right, of course. The closeness of that scrape and the responsibility it represented had scared me shitless. I had loved her deeply, but after just coming through one Poseidon Adventure of a marriage, the thought of going through another—with a prepackaged family on order—had sent me into cold sweats. So I'd stayed away, to get some breathing room and to do some heavy thinking. Only, by the time I'd regrouped and the sweats had passed, she was gone.

When I looked back now, I could see how stupid I was not to have seen it coming. But then maybe I hadn't wanted to see it. Maybe I'd been unconsciously trying to kamikaze the whole relationship, although I wasn't sure about that either. The only thing I was sure of was that I'd handled it like a total klutz. I felt myself becoming annoyed. At me, at her, at the situation. "So along came Sir Galahad of the baseball circuit and struck you out with fastballs," I said.

"He was *there*," she shot back. "You weren't. I was feeling ugly and fat and unwanted. Sparky made me feel as if I were the most beautiful girl in the world."

I choked on a swallow of Bloody Mary. "*Sparky?* How in the hell could you fall in love with a guy named Sparky, for chrissakes?"

A chalky line appeared above her upper lip.

"Sorry," I retreated. "Go on."

"I needed Sparky then. I'd been crying too damned long and he made me laugh again. He made me feel beautiful and special. He gave me baths in cases of champagne. He even stole a chandelier for me from the lobby of the Waldorf-Astoria."

A chandelier. Christ. "So you married Sparky?"

"No," she said. "I married an attorney."

I nodded. "Better choice. Sparky will probably just wind up pushing insurance when the arm goes." I was beginning to feel the effects of the drinks. I took another gulp and said in a tone approaching nasty, "So what happened to the old Spark? You blow him off, too, or is he still in the bullpen, warming up?"

It was a cheap shot and I really had no idea why I said it except that this whole thing was not working out like I'd planned. She was the one who was supposed to be feeling guilty here, not me, and I resented it.

She snatched her purse from the floor and stood up. "This is obviously not going well. It was probably a bad idea on my part. Good-bye, Jake."

She started away from the table and I sat there, feeling suddenly like a complete heel. I thought for a good ten seconds before I got up. I caught up with her as she reached the stairs to the bar, and grabbed her arm. She would not turn to look at me.

"I'm sorry, Sharon. I'm acting like a jerk. You didn't come here to rehash old times. Come on back and sit down. Please."

She hesitated, then the stiffness drained out of her arm and she followed me placidly back to the table. I looked around for our waitress, to order more drinks.

"On the phone you said you needed help. What kind of help?"

"I want to hire you," she said quietly.

6

That momentarily halted my waitress-scan. "To do what?"

She paused. "It's my husband—"

Here it comes, I thought. I should have known. Jealous wife wants private detective to follow errant husband and provide proof of infidelity. I really needed that drink now, and felt myself getting angry as I looked around the room. Waitresses are like cops— never around when you need them.

"What about your husband?" I asked.

"He was killed last month in an automobile accident."

I stopped looking over her shoulder and looked at her. Killed. The word sank in and I felt like more of a heel than ever. "I had no idea. You didn't say anything on the phone."

Her eyes grew faintly misty and she said thickly, "No. I probably should have."

"I'm sorry, Sharon. I really am."

She cleared her throat and dabbed at the corner of one eye with the heel of her hand. "That's the reason I called you." She looked at me and smiled faintly. "One reason, anyway." She sighed. "Five months ago, Hugh took out a life insurance policy with Transcontinental Life for two hundred thousand dollars. The company is refusing to pay off. They're saying that it wasn't an accident, that it was suicide."

"How did it happen?"

"You know the Ortega Highway?"

"The old highway that runs over the mountains from Capistrano?"

She nodded. "Hugh's car left the road and went into the ravine. There was a bottle in the car and the autopsy showed he'd been drinking."

"What is the official cause of death?"

"Cerebral hemorrhage and internal injuries."

Our waitress finally materialized and I caught her attention with a wave and pointed to our empty glasses. "So how did the insurance company come up with suicide?"

"Their investigator says that evidence at the scene proves that Hugh's car was parked before it went over the edge. Something

7

about the tire tracks, I don't know. And now, suddenly they've come up with a witness who swears he saw the car parked at the exact spot it left the road, shortly before the accident."

"That's it?"

"It seems to be enough for them."

"What about motive?"

She bent her head forward and touched the back of her neck. "They're saying Hugh was despondent about his health and financial problems."

"You obviously don't believe them."

"Not about Hugh committing suicide, no." I was about to ask her what she *did* believe them about, but she sidetracked me by saying, "Hugh was more optimistic during the past few months than he had been in a year."

"What happened a year ago?"

She looked down at the beach. The setter and the boy were gone. The matron, her heavy, rippled thighs bulging out of the bottom of her one-piece bathing suit, was shaking the sand out of her towel, preparing to leave.

"Hugh got involved in a business deal with some bad people and lost a lot of money. It nearly wiped us out. But lately he'd begun to turn things around, and he'd really been up. Especially the day he died."

"Why? What happened the day he died?"

She fidgeted with the ashtray on the table and touched her neck again.

"That's something I'd like to know."

"What do you mean?"

She stopped fidgeting and we locked stares.

"He called me from the office that afternoon to tell me that he wouldn't be home until seven-thirty or so because he had some work to finish up, but that I should get dressed up because we were going to the Balboa Bay Club for dinner. He said there was a party there he didn't want to miss. I asked him whose party, but he just said I'd find out when I got there, that it was a surprise. He said he'd gotten some news he'd been waiting for for months and that he was going to announce it at the club. He sounded ecstatic."

"Did he say what the news was?"

"No. He was very mysterious about it. Well, not mysterious exactly. More coy, like a little boy hiding a surprise. All he said was that he'd tell me about it when he got home and that I'd really love it."

"What time was that?"

"Four-thirty or so."

"What time did the accident happen?"

"Between nine-thirty and ten."

"So what was he doing driving up the Ortega Highway at that hour?"

"That's one thing we can't figure out."

"Nobody has any idea?"

She hesitated, then said, "We have only one clue, and we don't even know if it's really a clue at all."

"What is it?"

She started to answer, but was interrupted by the waitress with our drinks.

When the waitress left, Sharon said, "A note that was left by the phone on his desk. Hugh's secretary found it there the next morning when she came in." She picked up her purse, opened it, and extracted a small piece of paper. The residue of red plastic at the top told me it had been ripped from a pad. Written diagonally in a scrawled longhand was: "Alicia, Alicia, you great big beautiful doll. I love you."

"Who's Alicia?"

"I have no idea."

"You think that's who he was driving to meet?"

"I don't know. But if he was, why did he tell me he would be home at seven-thirty?"

I thought about that. "You're sure he called you from the office?"

She nodded. "He was still working when Ray went home at five."

9

"Who's Ray?"

"I'm sorry. Ray Baumgartner. Hugh's law partner."

"And he doesn't know who this Alicia could be?"

"No. He even checked Hugh's case files to see if she might have been one of Hugh's clients."

I paused before asking, "You think your husband was having an affair?"

She shook her head and a sad sort of bewilderment seemed to cloud her eyes for a moment. "I don't know, Jake. I honestly don't."

"Was your marriage in trouble?"

"Not—no."

"What were you going to say?"

She looked down at the table. "It's just that you're sure of something; then something happens, a note on the desk—and you're not so sure anymore. I was going to say, not that I know of, but until I find out differently, I'll leave it at no." I handed the paper back to her and she folded it and put it back into her purse.

"You said the insurance company is claiming your husband was despondent about his health," I said. "What was wrong with him?"

She frowned. "According to the autopsy report, Hugh had aplastic anemia. It's a blood disease. Really serious, I understand."

"How long had he had it?"

She leaned forward. "That's just it. I don't know. I'm not even sure that Hugh knew." She read the look on my face that said I was not following her too well, and went on. "He didn't look or act sick and he never complained to me about not feeling well. And he'd had a physical only two months before the accident—including a blood test—and there was absolutely no sign of any anemia then."

"You know that for sure?"

She nodded. "I talked to Felix Wasserman—Hugh's doctor—right after I read the autopsy report. He couldn't understand how Hugh could have picked up the bug that caused it. It's supposed to be really rare. Felix thinks the disease had to be in the incipient stages and that Hugh didn't know he had it because there were no symptoms yet. He says that if there were symptoms, Hugh wouldn't have been able to keep it a secret. He would've had to be hospitalized." She cocked her head to one side. "And if he didn't know he had it, that shoots down Transcontinental's theory, doesn't it? I mean you can't be depressed about something you don't know about, can you?"

I didn't know how her deceased husband had felt, but his problems, real or imagined, were beginning to depress me. I took a big swig from my Bloody Mary, searching for the buzz that had eluded me all morning, but my liver was metabolizing the booze too fast.

When our food arrived, we both ate in silence for a few minutes. Then I said, "It seems to me after everything you've said, Sharon, that the burden of proof is still on the insurance company. They have to prove your husband committed suicide. You don't have to prove he didn't."

"That's why I haven't done anything until now. When I first brought up the idea of hiring an investigator to Ray, he was against it. He said Transcontinental would poke around for a while, but in the end they'd have to pay off anyway, so hiring someone of our own would be an unwarranted expense that I really could not afford. But then they came up with the witness. That changed things. They paid him for that bit of testimony, by the way. One thousand dollars. They put an ad in the paper offering a reward for anyone having any information about the accident, and he popped up. There's no telling what other so-called evidence they'll come up with to support their version. Who knows? Maybe there was something mechanical wrong with the car and they've covered it up—"

"I doubt they'd go that far, Sharon."

"All I know is, I'm not going to take their word for it, not when there's two hundred thousand dollars at stake." Her eyes softened. "I know this might sound mercenary, Jake, but I need the money. When Hugh died, he was getting back on his feet, but he wasn't there yet. He left a lot of creditors and no cash. He'd mortgaged just about everything up to the hilt to pay off his debts. From the way it looks, I'll have to sell everything, including the house, just to pay the taxes. There's only the insurance policy. That's all I've got."

I thought about it and shook my head. My emotions were telling me to do one thing and my better judgment was telling me to do the other. "If you want my opinion, I'd say that your husband's partner's advice was pretty sound. I'd wait and see what else the insurance company comes up with before you go to any great expense hiring an investigator. That can run into quite a bit of dough."

She saw where I was going and headed me off. "Please, Jake. Look, maybe I'm grasping at straws, but I'm entitled. I'm drowning. And that goddamn insurance company is trying to hold my head under." Desperation surfaced on her face, through the tension and fatigue.

"When can I talk to your husband's partner?"

I don't know why I said it. I had no intention of getting involved. Maybe it was because after what she'd said about my reaction to her abortion, I felt I owed her one. What the hell. I was down here and the day was shot anyway, so I might as well spend the rest of it talking to people.

She let out a sigh of relief. "I'll call him from here," she said, then reached across the table and put her hand on top of mine. "Thank you."

"I'm not saying I'll take the case—"

"I wasn't thanking you for that," she said. "I was thanking you for coming."

I picked up my glass as an excuse to slide my hand from beneath hers and leaned back, staring out at the ocean, wondering why in the hell she couldn't have been fat.

12

2

The offices of Canning and Baumgartner were in Tustin, about twenty freeway minutes from the restaurant. She volunteered to drive, and since the radio reception in her Mercedes 450 SE was better than I could get over the coat-hanger antenna on my '67 Plymouth and since it was her gas, I didn't fight her over the privilege.

On the way over, she sketchily filled in parts of the past five years she'd neglected at lunch, but mostly she talked about her husband.

She had met Hugh Canning shortly after her affair with the pitcher had been rained out. Canning was young, handsome, but most of all aggressively persistent. She repulsed his first advance, but he tracked down her number through some friends of his who worked with her at Air Cal and began calling her. Finally, he wore her down by attrition and she consented to a date and found herself glad she had. He was witty and fun to be with. She found they had a lot of the same loves—lobster, old movies, Tom Robbins, and fires on the beach. There were no champagne baths or stolen chandeliers, but she didn't mind. In fact, it was a relief. Canning had a serious intensity the pitcher had lacked, and she found herself strongly attracted by his strength and self-assurance. When he proposed four months later, she did not hesitate to accept.

The marriage had been idyllic for three years, then had come The Fall. Canning had become involved in a big business deal and had started to unravel. He turned moody and began to drink heavily. He would become abusive and pick fights with her, usually over nothing at all. They discussed a separation and decided that they would give it another four months to see if things got any better. From that point on, Canning began to straighten up his act. He cut back on his drinking, the deep mood swings became less frequent and more shallow, and his sense of humor returned. His obsessive self-pity turned into an obsessive resoluteness, and he began to work himself out of financial crisis. He had been almost completely back to his old self when his car left the road, ending his Big Comeback.

She pulled off the freeway at Seventeenth, then drove two blocks before turning onto a tree-shaded street lined with cool lawns and older houses, most of which had been converted into or replaced by commercial buildings when the neighborhood had been rezoned. The one we parked in front of was a converted one-story stucco job with a shingle roof and a well-tended bed of red zinnias out front. An ornate wooden shingle by the front door said: CANNING AND BAUMGARTNER, ATTORNEYS AT LAW. We went up the concrete walk and entered a small, arched vestibule guarded by a pudgy, dark-haired receptionist who smiled and said that Mr. Baumgartner was expecting us.

Several clients waited on flower-print couches in what had once been a living room, and we went by them and down a narrow hallway. We passed a small office where two women were typing behind paper-stacked desks, and walked to the end of the hall, where Sharon stopped at a closed door. She knocked twice, then pushed it open and entered.

The man who greeted us had gray hair but probably was no more than thirty-eight or -nine. Whatever had turned his hair gray had left his mustache and eyebrows coal-black, and his face was

unlined and still college-handsome. He had a long ski jump of a
nose and intelligent dark-brown eyes. The mouth was a lawyer's
mouth—ready to smile in an instant, but a suggestion of stubbornness in its turned-down corners. There was a suggestion of
stubbornness in the chin, too, which was wide and jutted out a
bit. He wore no coat; the sleeves of his white shirt were rolled up
to the elbows, exposing a mat of black hair covering his forearms
and the backs of his hands. His gray slacks fit him snugly through
the hips and were slightly belled at the bottoms, and his loafers
were gray suede.

He gave Sharon an affectionate peck on the cheek and said,
"Hiya, babe."

"Ray, this is Jake Asch."

"A pleasure," he said, shaking my hand firmly. "I've heard
a lot about you." I muttered something like the usual "Good
things, I hope," and he rallied back with something like "All
good," then he motioned to two chairs in front of the desk and
told us to sit down.

While he got comfortable at his desk, I looked the place over.
The room was not large, but had a light and airy feel about it and
probably had been a very pleasant bedroom once. The carpet,
walls, and furniture were all done in shades of blue, and on the
one wall that wasn't solid with fat volumes of law books, hung
chrome-framed prints from Galerie Maeght, advertising Chagall
and Klee exhibits. Chrome miniblinds covered the large sashed
window behind the desk, which was a large crescent of some
highly polished inlaid wood, perhaps teak, and to the right of the
desk was a three-drawer blue filing cabinet. There was a hanging
spider plant and several potted kentia palms, and all of them
seemed to be thriving. I'd never had any luck with plants and
wondered how other people kept them alive.

"You'll have to excuse the mess," Baumgartner said, waving a
hand at the stack of papers on his desk. "Things have been rather
hectic since Hugh died. There were just the two of us here and
now I'm having to finish up his cases as well as my own."

15

"Looks like business is pretty good," I said.

He sighed. "Too good."

"Do you intend to take anybody else into the firm?"

"As a matter of fact, I've been interviewing people this week," he said, nodding. "I've boiled it down to three. I'll make my decision in a week or two."

"Sharon tells me you handle mostly personal-injury cases."

"About eighty percent." He glanced at Sharon, then back at me. "I understand you two have known each other for quite a long time."

He smiled when he said it, but something in his tone made me wonder just how much she had told him about us, or how much she had told her husband, for that matter.

"About six years."

"She's filled you in on what's been happening?"

"Some of it."

He picked up a pencil from the desk and began doodling on a yellow legal pad. "When the insurance company first started dragging its feet, I didn't think much of it. It's pretty normal with a claim this large for a company to hold things up until their investigators poke around a bit. Even when the aplastic anemia showed up in the autopsy report and they came up with the bit about the tire tracks, I didn't think much of it. I felt Transcontinental would have to pay up anyway and the expense of hiring an investigator at a couple of hundred a day wouldn't be worth it. But then they came up with that witness."

"The one who saw Canning's car," I said. He nodded, then pursed his lips. "Who is he?"

"A skydiving instructor over at Elsinore named Del Herbert. He claims he saw Hugh's car parked on the dirt turnout around five after ten. He says he thought about stopping because he thought the driver might be having some car trouble, but he didn't see anybody, so he kept going. His girl friend backs him up."

"If I remember right, that highway isn't very well traveled."

"You remember right," he said. "Especially at night. There have been a lot of wrecks up there."

16

"What was this Herbert doing up there?"

"He and his girl friend were coming back from Dana Point, where they'd spent the day sailing with friends. That's what he says, anyway. It seems to check out."

I said, "Sharon tells me they only turned up after a reward was offered."

He stopped doodling and tossed the pencil on top of the pad. "A thousand bucks."

"Which could be an inducement to come up with a story."

He nodded. "That thought had crossed my mind."

"You have a copy of the accident report?"

He shuffled through some papers on the desk and picked up a manila folder and handed it to me. Both the California Highway Patrol accident report and the coroner's postmortem report were in it. The accident report was on top; I started with it.

Canning's red Porsche Carrera had been found on September 9, at the bottom of a rocky ravine two hundred feet below the Ortega Highway, 14.2 miles from San Juan Capistrano. It had been found at 7:42 A.M. by CHP officer Gregory Palladin, who had been dispatched to the scene after a call to the Capistrano CHP office by a passing motorist who had spotted the car while driving down the highway. The car was completely demolished, lying on its top; the driver, who had been partially ejected from the vehicle, was crushed between the door and the body of the car. The speedometer needle was stuck at ten miles per hour and a broken bottle of Early Times bourbon was found on the floor of the car. A strong odor of alcohol was detected in the car by Officer Palladin.

From the path of broken vegetation down the side of the canyon, it was determined that the Porsche had left the road at a dirt turnout on the north side of the highway, and subsequent investigation discovered two deep tire gouges on the dirt turnout, approximately ten feet from the edge of the embankment. There were no skid marks found on the road surface. The weather that night had been clear and the road surface dry. The turnout was just a blind turn in the road, and it was Officer Palladin's conclusion that Canning had been coming down the highway and missed the

17

turn, perhaps because of the effects of the alcohol.

I put the report down and said, "It says here that Canning was traveling *down* the highway."

"That's just conjecture," Baumgartner said. "The tire tracks were pointed that way and the canyon is on that side of the road. If he'd been going up the highway, he would have had to cross both lanes of the road."

"Any idea where he might have been coming from?"

"None," he said. "That's the bitch."

"He told Sharon he had an appointment. Any idea with whom?"

The lawyer stuck out his lower lip and shook his head. "His secretary says he had nothing scheduled, and he never saw clients after office hours, anyway. Unless it was an emergency, of course, like having to get a client out of jail or something. And there aren't any jails up the Ortega Highway." He paused. "There's *nothing* up the Ortega Highway."

"When did you see him last that day?"

"When I left the office, around five-thirty. I poked my head in his doorway and remarked that it was kind of late to be working, and he said he was just finishing up some things and that he'd be heading home soon."

"How did he strike you then?"

"Like the cat that had just swallowed the canary."

"What do you mean?"

"He was grinning from ear to ear. I asked him what he was so happy about and he just smiled and said he'd gotten some news that he'd been waiting for for a long time and that he'd tell me all about it later."

"He never mentioned anything about going to meet a client?"

"No, nothing."

"What about this Alicia? You know who she might be?"

He stroked his mustache and glanced uncomfortably at Sharon. "You mean that note. I have no idea. I've never heard Hugh or anyone else mention the name."

18

I let that one ride for the time being, and went on to the coroner's report. The accident, like most of them, had been messy. An external examination of Canning's body found, in addition to multiple lacerations and contusions, that his skull and chest had both been crushed, presumably the result of his being pinned partially outside the car as it rolled down the hill. Internal injuries were massive; any one or combination of them could have killed him. His skull had been fractured, as well as the right tibia and left humerus, and six ribs. Both lungs had been punctured by the broken ribs, his spleen had been ruptured, and there was massive internal bleeding. There was general edema and subdural hemorrhage associated with lacerations of the cerebral cortex. Irwin Choate, the pathologist who had done the autopsy, noted in the initial report that Canning's bone marrow appeared to be extremely yellow in color and hard to cut. A section of it was taken for further tests.

Upon examination, the marrow was found to be devoid of red blood cells, white blood cells, and platelets, indicating that the subject had been suffering from a condition of aplastic anemia. A blood serology was done for viral isolation, but no virus was found. A blood sample was also taken for toxicological analysis and it was found to have an alcohol content of .008 percent.

The conclusion of the coroner was that the death had been caused by multiple injuries and internal bleeding. Under the entry "Conditions contributing to immediate cause of death," the box next to the word "Accident" had been checked.

In the state of California, a driver with a blood alcohol of .01 was considered to be "driving under the influence." Canning had been drinking before the accident, but he was well below the legal definition of drunk. At .008, it was doubtful that his judgment and reflexes would have been impaired enough for him to have driven over a cliff. Of course he could have fallen asleep at the wheel or he could have flat-out missed the turn. But at ten miles an hour? I was beginning to like it less and less. I laid down the report and looked up.

19

"Did you know he was sick?"

Baumgartner pointed a finger at the report. "The first I heard of it was in there. I couldn't believe it when I read it. Hugh sure as hell didn't look or act sick."

"He never mentioned anything to you about seeing a doctor?"

"Nothing."

"You say his mood seemed good that night. What about in general? Was he depressed lately?"

He looked quickly at Sharon, and then his eyes flickered down and away. He hesitated, then said, "Aside from being law partners, Hugh and I were friends. Good friends. We graduated law school together, built this practice together, and we saw a lot of lean times doing it. I'd seen him when he was down—*real* down. He wasn't down lately. Now if all this had happened last year, I wouldn't say that with so much certainty."

"You mean when he lost that money?"

"Yes."

"What happened there?"

Baumgartner picked up the pencil again, this time grasping it in both hands. "Hugh got involved in a construction deal with a couple of sharpies. George Villalobos and Jackson Meriwether. They formed a corporation to put up a tract of homes over by Mission Viejo, and Hugh wound up personally guaranteeing a construction loan for half a million. He also, for reasons I can't fathom, wound up co-guaranteeing loans for Villalobos totaling another two hundred fifty thousand. I told him at the time he was nuts, but he said Villalobos couldn't get the loan himself because he already had too many other loans out for other projects, but there was no problem for him being good for it. Villalobos had taken Hugh into some smaller deals before that had been quite lucrative, so Hugh trusted him. Besides, at the time, we were doing a lot of business with the Villalobos firm."

"What firm is that?"

"Group Associates. Villalobos investigated accident claims for us and provided translation services for our Spanish-speaking clients."

20

"I'm beginning to get the picture. Canning got stuck for the loans, right?"

His lips compressed, at the same time lifting one corner of his mouth, in a kind of wince. "Villalobos had a lot of irons in the fire and most of them were getting too hot for him to handle, although nobody really knew that. Some things had soured for him, but he managed somehow to keep it all quiet and nobody suspected the trouble he was in. I guess he was hoping that the housing project was going to pull him out of the soup, but there were delays in construction and by the time the notes came due, the project wasn't close to complete. Villalobos filed for bankruptcy and the banks came to Hugh for their money—only he didn't have it. That was when Meriwether stepped in and offered to buy out Hugh's stock in the housing project for a quarter of what it was worth."

"He took it?"

He waved the pencil like a baton. "What else could he do? There was no way he could pay off Villalobos's loans without going under himself. As it was, he lost somewhere around three hundred thousand dollars. He always swore he'd get Meriwether for that. He was sure Meriwether had used Villalobos to set him up."

"Why would he think that?"

He shrugged. "Because Meriwether was the one who put the land deal together and he was the one who introduced Hugh to Villalobos in the first place. Also, Meriwether and Villalobos remained very chummy, even after he went bankrupt. Hugh saw conspiracy in all that, and the fact that Meriwether profited by Villalobos going belly-up."

"Who is this Meriwether?"

"That's just it," Sharon said, uncrossing her legs. "Nobody seems to know." I shot her a questioning look. "He's a millionaire from Texas," she went on. "At least he claims to be. He *does* have a lot of money—I know that for a fact—but where it comes from, nobody knows. If you ask him what he does, he'll just smile and say, 'Ah'm into investments,' in that drawl of his. There are all sorts of rumors floating around that he's into gunrunning in Latin America or hooked up with the Mafia in Texas, and he never really comes out and denies any of them. That doesn't seem to hurt his social standing, though. He's been around Newport for a couple of years and he throws huge dinner parties attended by all the right people. Actually, I think a lot of his high-society party guests get off on the Gatsby role he likes to play. And he *does* like to play it. To the hilt."

"How did your husband get to know him?"

"Some mutual friends invited us up to one of his parties," she said. "I warned Hugh about him, but he wouldn't listen. I didn't like the man from the very beginning."

"Why not?"

Her eyebrows raised. "Oh, he's a real charmer on the surface, full of good ol' boy aphorisms and down-home country wisdom, but all the time he'd be talking to me, he'd be staring as if he were undressing me in his mind or something. It gave me the creeps." She rubbed her arms self-consciously. "I just didn't trust him at all. Hell, I hadn't known him two hours before he tried to get me to take my pants off." I stared at her and she nodded confirmation. "We got into a conversation about vitamins. I told him I'd been a little tired lately and he told me to come into the back room and he'd give me a vitamin shot. In the butt, of course. Told me how wonderful it would make me feel. I'm sure it was more for cheap thrills than out of any concern for my health and I told that to Hugh, but he just laughed it off. He said Meriwether proselytized like that all the time, that vitamins were his religion."

"Meriwether claims he had terminal cancer," Baumgartner broke in in a tired voice. "Says all the specialists had given him up, but then he went to some doctor in Texas who started giving him a special vitamin formula and it cured him."

"I will say one thing," Sharon said. "If that's what vitamins do for you, maybe I need a shot. Meriwether's in great shape for his age. He must be fifty, but he looks a hell of a lot younger and he has more energy than any human being I've ever seen. He's always on the go. He runs five miles a day and works out in a fully equipped gymnasium in his house. He claims he only has to sleep four hours a night. If I slept four hours a night, I'd look like the wrath of God, but it doesn't seem to affect him at all."

I asked Baumgartner, "Have you been up to the accident site?"

He nodded. "I went up there with the insurance investigator."

"Think you could find it again? I'd like to take a look."

"When?"

The day was shot, but I didn't want this to run into two. "How about tonight?"

He tugged on his ear thoughtfully and said, "I imagine I could get out of here a little early tonight. You know where the Ortega Highway off-ramp is on the San Diego Freeway?"

I said I did.

"I'll meet you there at the Tiny Naylor's at five-thirty. It should still be light enough then."

"Fine."

"Now about your fee," he said, clearing his throat and glancing at Sharon. "I realize it's not customary, but Sharon and I have discussed it, and taking into account her current financial position, we were wondering if you would be willing to work on a contingency basis."

I should have known. Not that it mattered. I still had no intention of taking the case. I was just killing time and working off an emotional debt.

"My rate is two hundred a day, Mr. Baumgartner."

His lawyer's smile was back. "Ten percent could net you twenty thousand dollars. That's considerably more than you'd end up with by working per diem."

"That's *if* the insurance company came up with the entire two hundred grand. You could wind up settling out of court or you could wind up going to court and losing."

"It's a possibility. I grant you. What you'd essentially be doing is betting on your own abilities. The investigator in this case will either make it or break it. And if you're half as good as Sharon says you are, you should be willing to place that bet."

It was my turn to shake my head. "I don't gamble for a living, Mr. Baumgartner."

Disappointment clouded his features. He started to say something, but I cut him off.

"But we can talk more about that if and when I decide to take the case. Until that time, I wouldn't feel right about charging Sharon anything. From what you've told me, I'm not sure your original assessment wasn't correct. You may not need an investigator at all."

That seemed to set his mind at ease. He looked at Sharon and smiled, but it was not a lawyer's smile this time, just a tired one. She looked back at him as if to say, "I told you so."

I asked, "Is Canning's secretary still working for you? The one who found the note?"

"Sally? Yeah, sure."

"I'd like to talk to her. And I'd like to see Canning's office."

"It's pretty much cleared out—"

"I'd like to see it anyway."

He shrugged in resignation. "Sharon can show you the way. Now if you'll excuse me, I have an appointment. I'll have Sally come in to you."

"One more thing," I said. "Where are the Transcontinental offices and who do I talk to there?"

"Newport Center. Ask for Leo Arcel. He's vice-president in claims. He's been put in charge of the case."

We shook hands and reconfirmed our 5:30 meeting. I went with Sharon down the hall one door and into an office very similar to Baumgartner's, except that it was done in muted beiges. I sat down in the swivel chair behind the desk and tried the drawers. They opened. The desk had pretty much been cleaned out, except for the remnants of the usual office stuff—stationery, paper clips and pencils, several unused ruled legal note pads. Sharon leaned against the doorway with her arms folded and watched me go through the drawers.

"Who went through the stuff in here?" I asked her.

"Ray and I."

"Was this all that was in here?"

"No. There were some papers. Bills and things. There wasn't anything personal, if that's what you mean. No perfumed letters from Alicia or anything like that."

"What happened to the bills?"

"Sally filed them, I guess."

"Where did your husband have the Porsche worked on?"

"Autohaus in Newport."

I jotted it down in my notebook. "When did he last have it worked on?"

"Just before the accident," she said. "He took it in to have it serviced."

"You know the name of the mechanic who worked on it?"

"I imagine it was Hans. He always worked on our cars."

I nodded and went over to the three-drawer filing cabinet. One drawer was marked Personal. I tugged on it, but it was locked. "Have you been through here?"

She nodded.

"What's in it?"

"Personal business stuff, mostly. Ray and I went through it and picked out everything we thought Fred would need for the probate. There were details about Mission Viejo in there, but Fred's got it now."

"Fred?"

"Fred Rosenberg, the attorney who's handling the probate."

I nodded and said, "You got the keys?"

"No, but Ray must."

I was not too anxious to start sifting through Hugh Canning's life in detail at this time, or at any time, really. I was just going through the motions, doing a shallow mimicry of the ritual. "No need to disturb him now. I don't want to interrupt his meeting. We can always get the key later if we need it."

One of the women we'd seen typing appeared in the doorway.

"You wanted to see me, Mrs. Canning?"

"Come in, Sally," Sharon said. "Sally Branscomb, this is

Jacob Asch. He's an investigator helping us with the insurance company."

The woman smiled and said it was nice to meet me. She was thin with stringy brown hair and makeup so thick that her face and neck were two different colors. When she got closer, I could see that it was an unsuccessful attempt to cover up the ruins of a bad case of acne. I showed her the "Alicia" note. "You found this?"

"Yes."

"Where?"

She pointed to a place by the phone. "Right here."

"When was that?"

"About ten-thirty the morning after—" She hesitated and glanced at Sharon uncertainly.

"Of course, we didn't know at that time what had happened. He'd asked me to pull some files for him in the morning, and I did and went to put them on the desk. That's when I saw the note."

"What time did you leave the night before?"

"About five."

"He was still here?"

"Oh, yes." She fidgeted with the hem of her dress.

"Did anything unusual happen that day?"

She cocked her head to one side. "Like what?"

"Anything. Any unusual phone calls? Anything like that?"

Her shoulders moved but the movement was almost lost inside her baggy dress. "No, not that I can think of."

"You never heard him mention the name Alicia before?"

"No, never."

"Okay, thank you, Sally." She nodded and started to leave and I said, "One thing you can do for me, Sally. Who handles the office bills? Electricity, phone, that sort of thing?"

"I do."

"I'd like a copy of the last three phone bills."

"I'd have to check with Mr. Baumgartner."

I smiled. "Sure."

Another five minutes of sorting through drawers did not turn up

26

anything, so I called Transcontinental. I got Leo Arcel after being put on hold for five minutes, and after I explained who I was he said he could see me at three. I said that would be fine.

Sally came in and handed me a stack of Xeroxed telephone bills, and after she'd gone, I said to Sharon, "Well, at least that's one person we can eliminate as the mysterious Alicia. Can you imagine anyone chasing her around an office desk?"

"Sally's very efficient," she said, her back stiffening to the feminist cause.

"I'm sure she is," I said, a little taken aback by the sharpness of her tone.

"You men are so easily taken in by glamorous showgirl types," she said. "Pretty packages with no substance."

"Like you?" I asked. "I went for you."

"I had more in mind that tall, black-haired dancer you were slavering after when I met you. The one with the I.Q. of a grapefruit."

I turned up my palms. "What can I say? I'm a pushover for a well-turned calf. Besides, as a famous sage once remarked, Beauty may only be skin-deep, but ugly goes all the way down."

She gave me a disgusted look, but before she had a chance to pursue the subject any further, I motioned to the door and we closed up the office and went outside.

When we got into the car, she started to put the key into the ignition, then stopped suddenly and turned to me. "You didn't mean what you said to Ray, did you?" she asked urgently. "About not taking the case?"

"I didn't say I wouldn't take the case. I just said I'd see."

She touched my arm and her voice seemed to quiver a little. "I don't know what I'm going to do if you don't help me, Jake. Please say you'll take the case. I wouldn't be able to trust anyone else."

I thought she was overdoing it a bit. I couldn't tell if it was on purpose. "We'll see," I said quietly, and she started the car, knowing it would be useless to try to talk about it anymore.

3

In order to preserve the charm and art-colony image their town possessed, the moneyed residents of Laguna had succeeded in keeping out the ugly strip of high-rise hotels that inevitably comes to occupy the beachfront of all expensive seaside resorts. What they had created was a strip of small motels and restaurants, tourist shops, and art galleries, all done in a contrived, but somehow appropriately quaint conglomeration of Spanish and pseudo-English Tudor architecture.

The motel Sharon had checked me into was neither Spanish nor English Tudor, but a modern, stucco, three-story motel that sat on the ocean side of Pacific Coast Highway. My room was on the second floor, in the back, and although I couldn't see the ocean from my windows, when I opened them, I could get the nice iodine smell of dead kelp drifting in on the breeze. After depositing my heavy gear in the bathroom and hanging up my creasables in the closet, I locked up the room and drove the five miles to Newport Center.

Newport Center was a group of eighteen-story glass-and-steel radiator boxes and low-rise distressed-wood office buildings set on a tree-planted knoll overlooking the ocean. Transcontinental occupied most of the thirteenth floor of one of the radiators, and I was kept waiting for a while in the outer office until I was finally fetched by a matronly-looking secretary. She led me through a large room that had been partitioned off into a maze of one-desk cubbyholes and down a carpeted hallway. She stopped at an open doorway and motioned me inside and I found myself in a roomy office decorated in autumn rusts and browns. There were two men in the room, one seated at a large mahogany desk in front of a wall that was mostly glass, and another slumped on a settee to the right of the desk. The one behind the desk stood up and smiled as I entered. "Mr. Asch, come in."

He had a neat, trim impeccability about him, like the Constable landscapes on the walls. He wore a tan cashmere jacket and dark-brown slacks, a pale-blue dress shirt and coffee-colored tie covered with blue spots. He had pale, straw-colored hair and a round pink face creased with lines of amiability. His eyes and mouth were small and his fingers were long, with manicured nails.

"I'm Leo Arcel," he said, offering me his hand with a precise movement, then motioned to the man on the couch. "This is Pete Marangi. Pete's the investigator who's been working on the Canning case. I took the liberty of asking him to be here, in case you had some questions you wanted to ask him."

Marangi stood up politely, offered a detached sort of hello, then sat down again, as if not really thinking the whole thing had been worth the effort. He was a short and squat man with dark hair and a dour expression. Most of the dour expression came through the dark, watchful eyes, as most of his face was covered with a neatly trimmed beard. He wore a gray herringbone sports jacket with suede patches on the elbows and gray slacks and a black sports shirt open at the throat.

"Can I offer you some coffee?" Arcel asked.

"No, thanks," I said, and took a rust-colored chair in front of the desk. Arcel sat down and folded his hands on the desk. He smiled.

"How long have you been working for Mrs. Canning?"

29

I smiled back. Marangi didn't smile, he just watched.

"At this stage, I'm operating more in the capacity of friend and adviser than on any professional basis."

"I can understand her reluctance to accept our findings, of course," he said. "It's always difficult to accept the suicide of a loved one. There is always a load of guilt that goes with it. All sorts of uncomfortable questions inevitably arise: Could I have prevented it? Was it my fault?"

"And then there's the money," I said.

He smiled as if pleased I understood. "Yes," he said. "There is that."

"There's also the other side of the coin."

He lifted an eyebrow. "What's that?"

"That if there was any technicality that would save your company two hundred thousand dollars, you'd be tickled pink."

He frowned, but only slightly. The frown didn't discomfort me. It was neat, too.

"We're in the insurance business, Mr. Asch. It's our *raison d'être*. If we didn't pay off on our policies, we would have no reason to exist. I can't say I'm displeased about what Pete"— he glanced toward Marangi, just to let him know he could be magnanimous with power—"came up with, but I can also assure you it's not a technicality. The evidence is overwhelming, if circumstantial."

I glanced over at Marangi, who was still watching me. His eyes were nestled comfortably in their soft beds of flesh, but not so comfortably that they missed a thing.

"As I said, Mr. Arcel, I'm here in the capacity of friendly adviser to Mrs. Canning, and if the evidence is as overwhelming as you say, I intend to advise her to cut her losses and forget it. So why don't I just sit here and let you two overwhelm me, and we'll take it from there."

Arcel looked very pleased by that. He nodded and turned to Marangi and said, "Pete?" Marangi went to the desk and picked up a manila folder. He opened it, shuffled through some papers inside, and picked out half a dozen eight-by-ten glossy photographs, which he handed to me.

Half of the pictures were various angles of a dirt turnout on the bend of a road overlooking a canyon. All of those had been taken from the roadway, and in each, two deep parallel ruts were visible in the dirt, near the edge of the precipice. The other three photographs were close-ups of the two ruts, which were obviously tire tracks.

Marangi sat at an angle on the edge of the desk and draped one leg over the front. With the end of a ballpoint pen he pulled from his shirt pocket, he pointed out the two mounds of dirt piled up behind the ruts.

"As you can see, those aren't *skid marks* of a car trying to stop. If that was the case, the dirt would be piled up in the direction of the skid. In those tracks, the dirt was kicked *behind*, which means that the tire spin was forward." He paused, probably because he wanted me to get the full dramatic effect. "The car that made those tracks accelerated suddenly from a complete standstill."

"There were no skid marks on the road surface?"

"No. And that jibes with the speedometer reading. The gauge was jammed at ten. If Canning had been coming around that curve and not made it, he would have been going a hell of a lot faster than that."

"*If* the speedometer was correct," I threw in.

He let me look at the pictures some more, then I handed them back and he sat down.

"We also have a witness who saw Canning's car parked on that shoulder shortly before it went over."

"Your witness took down the license-plate number, of course."

They looked at each other. "No," Arcel said.

"Then how can you be sure it was Canning's car he saw?"

Marangi flipped an irritated hand in the air. "How many red Porsche Carreras do you think parked there between ten-thirty and ten-forty-five?"

"I wouldn't know," I said. "And neither would you. That kind

31

of an identification wouldn't stand up in court and you know it."
Neither of them seemed too perturbed by that. "This witness," I
said, consulting my notes, "Del Herbert. I didn't see his name on
any of the CHP reports."

Arcel inspected one of his manicured nails. "He contacted
us later."

"After you put an ad in the paper offering a reward."

"That's right."

"Why did he wait until there was money in it before he said
anything?"

"Mr. Herbert didn't put two and two together until later, after
he'd read about the accident. He was not a witness to the accident, after all. He only saw the car *before* it went over. There was
no reason for him to have gotten involved."

"But for a grand, he was willing."

"That's why people offer rewards," he said in an unruffled
tone. "As incentives."

I couldn't argue with that one, so I asked, "Why would Canning have stopped the car and parked on that shoulder? Why not
just drive on over the edge? It seems to me that if he was trying to
make it look like an accident, he was taking a hell of a chance of
blowing it by waiting and risking being seen."

Arcel smiled very, very slightly. "Ever seen the arms of a person who has committed suicide by slashing his wrists, Mr. Asch?
There are almost always hesitation marks where the person made
several false starts before getting up the nerve for the deep cut.
Parking was Canning's hesitation mark. My guess is that he sat up
there for a while, drinking and trying to get up his nerve before he
finally did it."

They had the answers ready, I'd give them that. But then, I'd
expected them to.

"I'd like to talk to this Herbert."

Marangi looked questioningly at Arcel, who nodded, then took
a sheet out of the file, gave me Herbert's home address, and told
me he worked at the Elsinore Skydiving School.

I jotted that down, then leaned back. "Your case, as far as the physical evidence goes, is impressive," I said, "but I would hardly call it overwhelming. And it does leave motive."

Arcel sighed, as if he were suddenly finding the whole business tedious. "We have a motive, Mr. Asch. The man was despondent."

"Both his wife and his law partner disagree."

"You know Canning was suffering from a disease that was quite possibly terminal?" Arcel asked in a rhetorical tone.

"I read the autopsy report," I said. "The question is, did *Canning* know it? His own doctor sure didn't. You guys didn't when you gave him the physical for his insurance policy."

"That doesn't mean that he didn't have it diagnosed somewhere else," Marangi said, stroking his beard.

"Did he?"

"I wouldn't know."

"Have you tried to find out?"

"There's no reason to."

"No? If he didn't know he was sick, your despondency motive goes right down the tubes."

"Mr. Canning's physical health is only part of the picture," Arcel said. "Canning did not respond well to stress, and he'd been going through a lot of it lately. He had tendencies toward manic-depression." He paused before continuing. "You know, of course, that Canning tried to do himself in eight months ago."

Marangi was smiling for the first time. They'd done it for effect, of course. "No," I said. "I didn't."

Arcel nodded. "I'm surprised his widow neglected to mention that. She was there when it happened. They were at a party and Canning was drunk. They quarreled because she didn't want him to drive home and he insisted that he was capable. He wouldn't give her the keys to the car, so Mrs. Canning left him there and had somebody else drive her home. Canning stayed and continued to drink and the drunker he got, the more morose he became. Then suddenly, his mood turned playful and he jokingly announced to several people at the party that his wife was convinced he was going to kill himself driving, so he might as well do it. Nobody took him seriously until he took the car out and drove straight into a brick wall at the end of the driveway. The front end of the car was demolished. He was lucky to come out of it with a concussion and minor cuts and bruises."

I felt the blood flush my face. How could she have thought I would be so stupid that I wouldn't find that out? Both of them were watching me and I felt as if I had to say something.

"Eight months ago Canning was going through a financial crisis. Things had been looking up for him lately."

"He wasn't out of the woods by a long shot," Arcel said, putting both hands on the arms of his chair and swiveling away from me. "Everything he owned was mortgaged to the hilt. And he was going through personal problems. His marriage was very shaky. His wife had threatened to leave him." He paused and looked at me keenly, trying to read my expression. "Or didn't she tell you that, either?"

The sly bastard just kept throwing me change-ups and watched me swing. His smugness was starting to get to me and I didn't want to give him the satisfaction, so I said, "She told me. But she says that they had patched things up during the past few months."

He shrugged. "If things were that good between them, why did she tell several of her friends as late as two months ago that she was contemplating divorce?"

I shook my head. "It doesn't fit with your own theory. If Canning and his wife were not getting along, why would he kill himself and try to make it look like an accident so that she'd get the money?"

He stuck out his lower lip. "Perhaps he wanted to make her feel guilty for not loving him anymore. That's why a lot of people kill themselves, you know. It's a way of having a grip on people, even in death. Or maybe he still loved her and figured he would make one last self-sacrificing gesture."

I winced. "Don't you think that's just a touch melodramatic?"

"Suicide is pure melodrama, Mr. Asch."

I shook my head. "It's all just speculation on your part."

"That's all it ever is and all it will ever be," Arcel said, rocking

34

forward in his chair and putting his hands flat on the desk. There was no smile on his face now, or any in his voice. "Did you know, Mr. Asch, that there are twenty-six thousand suicides in the U.S. every year? That's seventy a day. It's the tenth leading cause of death in this country. Since we're in the claims business, and some of those twenty-six thousand are our policyholders, I've done my homework. And you know what conclusions I've come to as the result of all that homework? That *nobody* can tell me what causes a person to commit suicide. Sure, we've got statistics. I can tell you that men are more likely than women to commit suicide about three to one, or that most suicides are elderly, Caucasian or Oriental, divorced or widowed. But pick me two people out of a crowd with all those attributes and put them under the same stress, and I can't tell you why one of them picks up a gun and blows his brains out and the other one doesn't. All I'll be able to tell you is that the one who did couldn't handle life anymore. Some biologists will tell you it has to do with sex hormones, some psychiatrists say it's the sadism of the superego turning on itself. But what it all boils down to, Mr. Asch, is that the person's psychological defenses were inadequate to deal with life. What final straw finally broke Canning's back—money problems, marital problems, the knowledge that he was suffering from a possibly fatal disease—I don't know. All I do know is that he couldn't cut it anymore."

I sat there for a moment, trying to figure out my next move. It turned out to be standing up. "I guess that's it, then. Thanks for your time."

He watched me, interested, as he took my hand. "Do you intend to pursue this further?"

"I don't know. I'll have to give it some thought."

He lowered his head and his tone grew quietly solicitous. "Please do. And if you are truly a friend of Mrs. Canning, I'm sure you'll advise her wisely. But you can tell her that we intend to stand firm. And we intend to stand firm because we know we're right. We don't manufacture evidence to try to deprive beneficiaries out of their settlements. If we did that, we couldn't stay in business. But to collect on that policy, Mrs. Canning is going to have to take Transcontinental to court, and if she does that, she'll lose, all the way around. She'll only wind up with a lot of bills for attorneys and investigators, and she still won't have her settlement. You can also tell her we will soon be refunding the balance that her husband paid on his policy for the rest of the year."

"I'm sure that will make her very happy," I said, and left.

4

I took the Crown Valley Parkway from the Pacific Coast Highway over the Laguna Hills. It had been a couple of years since I had driven it, and in that time, a sprawl of tract homes, condos, and shopping centers had spread over those graceful, rolling, grass-covered hills like an unstoppable fungus. Soon, I was convinced, the entire nation would be one gently rolling shopping center and the ultimate challenge for the daring outdoorsman would be to climb Penney's.

The daylight was dimming and the lighted Tiny Naylor's sign had a fluorescent halo around it as I pulled off the freeway at the Ortega Highway exit. Baumgartner was sipping a cup of coffee at the counter when I came in. He smiled genially and asked if I wanted a cup of coffee or something before we headed up and I said no, we'd better start while there was still some light. He agreed and paid his check. We went out to the parking lot. He asked me whose car I wanted to take and I said I didn't care. Then he saw mine and said we might as well take his. It was a new Mercedes, like Sharon's, but gold. I was beginning to think Mercedes drivers were all snobs.

On the way out of the parking lot, I glanced at his odometer and noted the reading. We crossed over the freeway and started up the narrow, two-lane highway that wound its way through the grass-covered hills. This was the land of the old Spanish dons, and the plasterboard condo projects that dotted the hills here all had red tile roofs and fancy Spanish names. The tops of the hills that were not built on were shaved flat for future construction, but then, a few miles out of town, the signs of human habitation began to thin and the horizon widened into a barren, almost desolate arroyo. Yellow-white rays of dying sunlight streaked the sky behind us; ahead, the horizon was a dark gray at the bottom, as if the heavier elements of the day were washed out of the sky and settling out. "You saw Arcel?" Baumgartner asked, keeping his eyes on the road.

"Yes."

"What do you think?"

"The evidence they have is circumstantial, but some of it is pretty strong. You may have trouble with it."

He nodded, as if I'd just confirmed what he thought. "I don't like it either. I didn't tell Sharon that, because I didn't want to worry her unnecessarily. She's had a tough enough time, God knows."

"I wanted to talk to you about Canning without Sharon around," I said. "What do you think about it, really? And I'm not talking just about the evidence. I'm talking about the possibility of suicide. You knew him as well as anybody."

He paused, sighed heavily, then shook his head. "I don't know. I mean that sincerely and, believe me, I've given it a lot of thought in the past month. I used to think I knew Hugh, but I don't know. He seems to have been hiding a lot from everybody lately."

"You mean the fact that he was sick?"

"That, and other things."

"So you think it's possible the insurance company is right?"

He took one hand off the wheel and waved it in the air. "Look, who the hell knows when it comes down to making a decision like that? I can't say that Hugh dropped any hints he was going to do it, but then the serious ones never do, I guess. They just do it. But like I said, who the hell knows? Hey, look, even *I've* contemplated suicide before. Who hasn't? Life can be a pain in the ass sometimes. Who knows when idle speculation turns into serious intent? You ever read any Camus?"

"Some," I said.

"I started rereading Camus when Hugh died. I don't know, maybe it was the absurdity of the whole situation that got to me, but I got really depressed one day and dug out a book of Camus's essays. In one of them, he said something that really struck me. He said that there are a lot of reasons for suicide, but that the most obvious ones are often not the most powerful. He said that life can undermine people, and that on any street corner, the feeling of absurdity can strike any man in the face."

"Is that what you think happened to Canning? The absurdity got to him?"

He glanced at me, then back at the road. "I don't know that anything got to him. He may have just gotten drunk and missed the turn. That's what we have to find out."

I watched him to see how he could take my next question. "You know he tried it before?"

His head jerked around, and the surprise on his face looked genuine. "No, I didn't. When?" I told him that Arcel had told me about the incident at the party. He watched the road and his expression grew intense. "I remember the incident, but Hugh claimed that he just got wasted and hit the wall by accident." He paused and said, "You have to remember one thing: Hugh was pretty frantic then. Things were coming apart for him and he was really hitting the bottle. It was a time when he wasn't totally responsible for his actions. Hugh would always say crazy things when he got whacked, even under the most normal of times. Maybe he was just sounding off."

"Maybe," I said. "Arcel told me that Sharon told some of her friends very recently that she was thinking of filing for divorce."

"I wouldn't know about that," he said. "I know their marriage was a little shaky during Hugh's crazy period, but I talked to him about it a couple of weeks before he died and he seemed to think that things were much better between them. When I saw them together, they seemed very happy. I can't imagine her telling anyone something like that."

I grunted and watched the road. The grade steepened as the hills swelled into mountains, and Baumgartner slowed for the curves, which were becoming sharper. Life out here had been dished out sparingly. Chaparral covered the treeless, boulder-strewn slopes like the stubble on the chin of a man in need of a shave.

"Are things as bad for her as she says?"

He frowned. "I'm afraid so. Sharon gets everything, but, unfortunately, 'everything' is mostly debts. Hugh borrowed heavily to stay afloat when he got creamed, and she still owes on those notes. Even with the breaks she'll get on the death taxes as a widow, after the feds and state get through with her, she'll have to sell everything. Unless Transcontinental pays off, which now doesn't look like they'll do without a fight."

"How in the hell could he have been so stupid to get wiped out like he did?"

He shrugged and smiled faintly. "It wasn't too bright, I'll admit, but Hugh wasn't the only one to get hurt when Villalobos went under. A lot of people sharper than Hugh got stung, too. The man put up a good front. Drove a Lamborghini. Still does, in fact. Had a thirty-eight-foot yacht in the harbor and had a lot of influential political friends, both in state government and in Mexico. Which was why Hugh brought him into our office in the first place, by the way. Villalobos does a lot of charity work in the Chicano community—he has a volunteer group that used to work at the county hospital and he's real tight with a couple of state senators because of it. He managed to convince Hugh that his political connections could do us a lot of good."

"You don't sound like he convinced you."

"I don't mean to make it sound that way. Although I must admit I had reservations from the beginning. I don't mean that I thought he was a crook or anything like that. In fact, I've always been impressed by his dedication to the cause of his people. But he's real smooth, you know? He's the kind of guy who will be up and down his whole life. You can make a lot of money being around somebody like that, but you can also lose your ass. As a matter of fact, Hugh wanted me to get into a couple of deals he and Villalobos were into—told me I could triple my money in four months—but I turned down the opportunity."

"Why?"

He shrugged. "I had my money tied up in other things. Some CD's and muni bonds. I've always been more conservative with my money than Hugh. He was a gambler, always looking for a high-risk, high-yield investment. I gave up believing in something for nothing a long time ago and I wasn't about to plunk down ten thousand dollars to speculate on some lots in Mexico I'd never seen."

"Mexico?"

He nodded. "Villalobos has a lot of friends in the Mexican consulate and he makes a lot of trips down to Baja. At least he used to. I guess he has—or had—permission from the Mexican government to sell American vacation lots around Mulegé somewhere. He took Hugh in on a couple of the deals. Hugh went down there with him quite a few times."

The road passed through an occasional stand of oak and then the highway was joined by a wide riverbed filled with pale stones that had been rounded as smooth as eggs by rushing water. There was little evidence of water now, however, rushing or otherwise. An anemic trickle ran down the middle of the riverbed, barely noticeable. I watched it and said, "Do you think Meriwether and Villalobos centered him?"

He made a face as if he thought that a tough question. "I really don't know. There's no reason to think so. An opportunity presented itself and Meriwether took advantage of it. The move was rather ruthless, but most successful businessmen are. As Karl Marx said, 'Money cancels all relationships.' "

His voice grew low and somber. "Look, Hugh was the best

41

friend I had in the world, but he had his faults, like all of us. If you want to know the truth, I'd say, yes, he was victimized. But by himself, not by Meriwether or Villalobos."

"How?"

"Hugh had one big flaw: he was overly impressed by people with money. He grew up poor and was never able to forget that. He never got over those initial feelings of social inferiority. That was what drove him, what made him work three jobs to get through law school. And it's what made him ripe for somebody like Meriwether. Hugh wanted to get into Newport society in the worst way, and that's just how he got in. When he met Meriwether, he fell immediately under the man's influence. He saw in Meriwether everything he wanted to be—rich, charming, socially influential, a wheeler-dealer. It was almost like a hero-worship thing to him. That was why, when the shit hit the fan, Hugh was so bitter about it. He was obsessed with revenge. He said he was going to run Meriwether out of town before he was through. As a matter of fact, the two of them had a public confrontation a couple of months ago in the Balboa Bay Club and Hugh told him that to his face."

"How did Meriwether react?"

Baumgartner shrugged and worked the wheel. "I don't know. Not too well, I suppose. Anyway, they asked Hugh to leave the club. Ask Sharon about it, if you're interested. She was there when it happened."

The slopes of the mountains sharpened abruptly as the road cleaved a sheer rock canyon. We wound around a series of hairpin turns, and the highway veered and clung to the right side of the canyon. To our left, the riverbed dropped away until it was out of sight below. Baumgartner swerved several times to avoid rocks, which littered the roadway from minor slides. We crossed over a concrete bridge, and after another mile or so, he said, "This is it."

He slowed and pulled off into the dirt turnout on the opposite side of the road and stopped. Ahead, the highway wrapped around a rocky outcrop and disappeared; I thought I recognized the turn from the pictures, but I could not be sure. There were probably dozens of turns just like it in the next fifteen miles. According to the odometer, we'd gone 8.2 miles from Tiny Naylor's. I took that down, just in case I wanted to find the place again on my own, and stepped out of the car.

A cement truck lumbered up the grade, its motor laboring loudly under the strain. It was the only vehicle we'd seen on the way up. I could understand how Canning's car had not been spotted until morning. The road was bypassed by the freeway and time. I kept my eyes pinned to the ground as we walked slowly to the edge of the embankment. The tire tracks were gone, compressed and filled in by the tires of other cars that had pulled onto the turnout since the accident. We went to the edge and looked down. The slope was steep and rocky, and the swath of broken vegetation was still visible where the Porsche had tumbled 150 feet to the bottom. The thick bushes below hid the river from us, but the sound of the water trickling over the rocks drifted up to us. A steady, cooler-than-cool breeze hissed in the white-trunked sycamores that grew in a clump alongside the river. It was all very peaceful. I was not feeling very peaceful, though.

I looked up the highway and put myself in Canning's car, coming around that turn. My eyes strained, searching through the headlights for the road and finding nothing—a void—and my stomach came into my throat with the sudden sickening weightlessness as the car became airborne and rocketed nose-first down the ravine. Only there were things wrong with the scenario. "If Canning had been going *up* the highway and missed that turn, he would have spun off the road a hundred feet from where he did. Therefore, he had to be coming down, lost control, and went off here. But he'd have to be going faster than ten miles an hour to lose control—"

"The speedometer could have been wrong," Baumgartner said.

"Maybe. But why no skid marks on the road?"

"He'd been drinking. He could have fallen asleep."

I pointed at the curve ahead. "Not after negotiating that curve he couldn't."

"Maybe his car just drifted off to the side of the road and by the time he realized what was happening, it was too late."

"That could be possible," I admitted. "But if that's what happened, how come he accelerated on the shoulder?"

He shrugged and followed me a few steps to the edge of the ravine. "Who knows if he did? That's the insurance company's interpretation of those tracks. We'll get expert testimony to counter that in court. If Hugh had been drinking and was disoriented, he might have thought he was hitting the brake and put his foot on the accelerator instead."

What he was saying made some sense of the evidence, but something about it, something I could not put my finger on, bothered me. "That leaves the witness."

Baumgartner walked two paces away, cupped his chin in his hand, and tapped the corner of his mouth with an index finger. "Let's just say that this witness is telling the truth. According to the coroner's report, there is a leeway of forty minutes or so in the time of death. What if Hugh stopped here for some reason, drove up the highway, and came back down?"

I bent down and ran my fingertips over the dirt shoulder. "The time can be made to fit, but why would he have stopped?"

"There was a bottle in the car. Maybe he wanted a drink. Maybe he just wanted to think. I've done that—pulled off at a turnout and just shut off the motor and sat there. Who knows?"

I picked up a small rock and stood up and flung it out over the ravine. It disappeared in the dusk about halfway down. "It sure would be nice to know what he was doing up here." I started over to the car. "I've seen enough."

He nodded and went to the car and we started back. A mile or so down the road, he said, "What are you going to do?"

"*If* I was going to do anything, I'd see if I couldn't shake the witness's story down. Then I'd see if I couldn't find a reason for

Canning to have driven up here. Which means finding out who the hell Alicia is."

"You still haven't made up your mind about taking the case?"

I shook my head. "I want to see what Sharon has to say about a few things first. She neglected to fill me in on some details—like the incident at the party—and I don't care for that. I don't like being lied to by a client."

"Go easy on her," he said. "Sharon's a great gal and she's been through an emotional wringer. Having you here means a great deal to her."

I looked out the window at the solid black of the trees. "I don't know why."

"She thinks you're the best. She really does." He turned toward me slightly. "I know you two had something going before she met Hugh."

"That was a long time ago."

"Still," he said with concern, "at this time in her life, she needs people around her who care about her."

Which was, perhaps, one of the dangers of sticking around, I thought.

5

Sharon's street twisted from the Coast Highway into the hills above Laguna Beach, like a snake trying to bite itself. As I drove up it, the sagy perfume of the hills struggled with the heavy, almost palpable smell of the sea, trying to defeat it, but the sea was still there, a feeling more than a smell. I was trying to choose one of the kiss-off speeches I'd rehearsed on my way over when my lights hit a white brick post by the curb with the house numbers on it, and I turned into the driveway. The house was not visible from the street.

The driveway dipped down sharply for a short way before dead-ending into the house, which sat like a growth on the side of the hill. It was white and long, with a brown shake roof, but its exact shape was obscured by a thick planting of semitropical plants and magenta bougainvillea. A lighted glass trapezoidal roof rose from the center of the bougainvillea and stood out starkly against the blackness of the sky. I parked behind Sharon's car and went to the door.

Chimes went off inside when I pressed the doorbell. I didn't hear anything, and then a voice called out, "Who is it?"

"Jake."

There was a fumbling of locks and then the door opened. I

never got a chance to pick my speech. As soon as she saw me, her face contorted and her mouth opened into a black hole and she began bawling like a baby. She just stood there, her hands limply at her sides in a totally defeated pose, and I put my hands on her shoulders and said, "What is it? What's the matter?"

She said something that sounded like, "Look what they did," and stepped away and waved a hand toward the interior of the house. I stepped inside and saw immediately what she was crying about.

The place had probably been beautiful when it was in one piece. Right now it looked like it had been hit by a tornado. The cream-colored cushions had been pulled off the wicker couches and chairs and strewn about the parquet floor. Record albums, cassette tapes, and books had been pulled off the shelves and scattered everywhere. The drawers of a bleached-wood chest by the rattan dining room set had been opened and their contents, mostly silverware, emptied on the floor. There was even some dirt on the floor from the potted plants that filled the place.

"I'm sorry," Sharon said, dabbing at her eyes with a worn tissue. "I didn't mean to go to pieces. It's just that this was the last straw. I don't know, maybe I should feel honored. Maybe I'm being picked out for some kind of special test or something, like Job."

"What happened?"

She shook her head violently. "I don't know. I was out shopping—and I got home around four and found this."

"Is the whole place like this?"

She nodded. "Hugh's office is the worst. It's a complete shambles."

"Did you call the police?"

She hugged herself. "They left twenty minutes ago."

I went over to the back door. It was part of a glass wall that flared up into the section of skylight I'd seen outside. It led out onto a plank terrace that was cantilevered out over the canyon. A neat, round hole with about a nine-inch diameter had been cut out of the glass near the door handle.

47

"Don't you have an alarm system?"

She nodded. "But I didn't turn it on. I was only going to be gone for half an hour."

"Somebody must have been watching the house," I said.

"Thanks. That makes me feel much better." Her voice was shaky. She was staring at the hole, shivering.

"Where's your booze?"

She pointed to a rattan-and-mirrored cabinet along the far wall. The doors of the cabinet were open, but the bottles were still on the shelves. I picked out a bottle of Courvoisier and two snifters from the glass shelving on the wall beside the cabinet and led her over to the white marble fireplace. I poured out two stiff shots and handed her one, then replaced the couch cushions from the selection on the floor and told her to sit down, and some color came back to her face. She took a little of the brandy.

"I feel like I've been raped or something."

"That's a common reaction to burglary. What did they get?"

She blinked twice, befuddled. "I don't know. I can't find anything missing."

"Nothing at all?"

She shrugged and took another sip. "I can't be sure until I take a complete inventory, but there doesn't seem to be anything missing. The jewelry box on my dresser wasn't touched, and there are some things in it—a pair of diamond earrings and an emerald ring—that are worth quite a bit." She hesitated and then looked at me intently. "Will you stay here tonight, Jake? Please? I don't think I could stay here by myself."

Her eyes pleaded with me. Those goddamn eyes. I could still drown in them. "If it would make you feel better."

She smiled. "It would. Thanks."

I drained my glass and said, "Let's go get some dinner somewhere. I'm starved and you should get out of this place for a while."

She shook her head and waved a hand at the room. "But I should—"

"I'll help you get the place straightened up when we get back."

Before we left, I taped up the hole in the door and wedged a screwdriver under the back of it so it wouldn't slide. We wound up stopping at a restaurant on the water that had a rusted roof of corrugated tin and was built to look like a fish cannery. On the way in, I wondered who would want to eat in a fish cannery, and when I got inside, I found out not many people. We sat at a table by the window and ordered drinks and watched the multicolored lights from the neon signs across the channel flicker and burn in the black water while we waited for dinner. When it finally came, we both ate ravenously, despite the fact that the fish was mediocre.

Maybe that was what a burglary did to the appetite. She took a bite and said, "I intended to fix you a home-cooked meal tonight. That's what I went shopping for. I remembered your icebox and thought you probably hadn't had one in a while."

"You're right, I haven't."

She smiled and said almost coyly, "I have to admit, though, when I was trying to get up the courage to call you, I did wonder if you'd found somebody by this time and be all settled down."

I washed down some rice with a swallow of vodka and soda and wiped my mouth. "To tell you the truth, Sharon, I've given up on the idea of finding anything permanent. I've come to the conclusion that all my relationships are like those lopsided rolls of toilet paper—I just give them a little tug to get them started, and they keep unraveling on their own, all over the floor."

"Have you ever thought that you're picking the wrong rolls on purpose?"

I shrugged. "I've wondered that sometimes, but I figure if it's true, it's too late to do anything about it now."

"Want to know what I think?" she asked, sipping her drink and looking coy.

I didn't really, but I thought I'd be polite. "What?"

"I think you actually like it."

"Like what?"

"The pattern you're stuck in, playing Solitary Man. I think if you ever got into a relationship where you had to really expose yourself, you'd freak." She hesitated. "I used to get the feeling

49

sometimes when we were together that you were always really alone, that there was some other person inside there that I never really knew and never would. That was part of our problem."

"Gee," I said snidely, "I didn't know we had any."

"There's no need to put up the old sarcastic shield. I'm not attacking, just making an observation."

"And a brilliant observation it is, doctor." The conversation was beginning to annoy me, maybe because at least part of what she was saying, again, was true; and my annoyance of the afternoon returned. Now seemed just as good a time as any to get things said. Better. At least it would change the subject.

"I talked to Arcel at Transcontinental this afternoon. His position is pretty adamant. You're probably going to have to sue to get your money."

"So, we'll sue."

"I'm not sure you'll win."

The drink stopped on the way to her lips. "What do you mean?"

"I mean, they've got a damned good case." I looked out the window. A light fog had moved in from the ocean, making all the lights across the bay look as if they were filtered through gauze. "You didn't tell me your husband tried to commit suicide before."

Her brows bunched over her nose. "What are you talking about?"

"I'm talking about a party about eight months ago where he got soused and announced to everyone that he was going to kill himself and proceeded to plow his car into a brick wall."

"That was an *accident*," she said, tight-lipped.

"That's not what Arcel says."

"I don't *care* what Arcel says. He didn't mean to hit the wall, he was just drunk. I *told* him he shouldn't drive home. I thought he might wind up doing something like that."

"Why did he tell everyone he was going to kill himself?"

She waved a hand in the air, then folded her arms and turned away from me. "Hugh said a lot of jerky things he didn't mean

50

when he got drunk. The next morning, he didn't even remember what he'd said."

"Arcel also got it from a couple of your friends that you were planning to get a divorce."

"That's a lie," she said, turning back to me sharply. "Look, Hugh and I had our bad time, I told you that. I won't deny there were times during that bad period when I seriously considered leaving him. I may have even mentioned it to a couple of women I know over drinks. But I made up my mind that I wasn't going to let it go down the tubes without a fight. I decided to find out if there was anything worth saving and if there was, I was going to make it work. And I did. *We* did. The last few months we had, I was very happy. And I don't give a damn what Leo Arcel says or what some venomous bitch he gets on the witness stand to say different. I loved my husband."

I shrugged and drained my drink. "Well, regardless, my advice to you is settle if you can."

Her head wagged rapidly, back and forth. "No."

Her stubbornness grated on me, but then it always had. "You've got nothing to fight with, Sharon. You've got nothing to refute their evidence and you've got no money to spend to dig up something that would even put a dent in it."

"I told you I'd pay you ten percent of the policy—"

"Ten percent of nothing is nothing."

She turned away from me again.

"I don't work on a contingency basis, Sharon. I can't. I have a big case waiting in L.A. now. I just can't spend a lot of time running around down here, chasing a phantom twenty thousand dollars."

"What case?" she said challengingly.

I balked, trying to think how to word it, and said, "An industrial espionage case. Some secret formulas of the company I'm going to be working for have been getting leaked to the competition. It could put them out of business. The president of the company wants to find out where the leak is and plug it."

"What company is it?"

51

"The Grandma Johnson Pie Company," I muttered, hoping she wouldn't catch it.

"Pie company?" she repeated, as if not sure what she had heard. "Give me a break." She broke into a wide grin and laughed.

"It may be a joke to you," I said, "but believe me, it's no laughing matter to Grandma Johnson. They've found duplicates of her prune-whip pie as far north as Boise, Idaho."

She laughed even harder and I even had to laugh, it sounded so stupid. I wiped my eyes and said, "It may sound dumb, but they have two hundred a day to pay me. And it's good for business. A lot of my work lately is in the industrial-espionage field. There's a ton of that shit going down now—everything from missile secrets to new computer games. It doesn't matter that it's the secret banana Bavarian chocolate mousse pie that's missing, if I can find the leak, the rep will do me good."

Her laughing subsided when she saw I wasn't kidding. "You're serious."

"Yeah, I am."

"Pies?!" Her voice was almost a shriek.

"I'm sorry, Sharon."

Her mouth was hard now. She wouldn't look at me. "Don't be sorry. You were looking for an excuse not to help. Now you've got one. Go help Grandma Johnson. I'll be in the car." She threw her napkin on the table and stalked out.

I watched her go and signaled the waiter for the check. Women. The government was wasting a lot of brain power and money with nuclear deterrents. All they had to do was send a B-52 over Russia and drop a load of estrogen in the water supply and sit back and watch everyone run screaming in the night toward Siberia.

I paid the check and went outside. She was where she said she would be, steaming up the car windows with every breath. I got in and made one last attempt before starting the car. "Look, Sharon—"

"I don't want to talk about it," she said, holding up her hands. Apparently she didn't want to talk about anything else, either, because she didn't say a word for the next ten minutes. That was all right with me. I put on a Mose Allison cassette, running it back until I found, "Your Mind Is on Vacation," and turned it up. She stared out the window as if there was something to see, despite the fact that all the shops were closed up for the night and the only lighted windows were those of a few art galleries full of trite seascapes.

What in the goddamn hell did she want from me? I wasn't the March of Dimes. I didn't care how ridiculous it sounded, but at least nabbing a pie thief could net me some decent bucks, which I could use right now.

It might be hard for her to face—she had a financial and emotional stake in believing otherwise—but I could face it very easily: Her husband drove up the canyon, drank himself brave, then shoved his Porsche into first and hit the gas. Claim denied—suicide. At least it rhymed.

After a while, I made an attempt to break the silence. "Sharon, I can recommend somebody who might take it on contingency—"

"Never mind," she snapped with a finality that killed any desire on my part to pursue it further.

"You still want me to stay over?"

"I don't know," she said coldly. "How much are you going to charge me?"

"Come on, Sharon," I said with a hint of annoyance.

"If you would," she said, easing up a bit.

"I've got to stop by the motel and pick up some things."

We stopped at the motel and she waited in the car while I ran in and got my shaving kit and a change of clothes.

I pulled into her driveway and she got out and opened the front door while I pulled my gear out of the car. Inside, she said, "You can sleep in the guest room," and moved down the hallway to the first door on the left.

The room was small and was in about the same shape as the rest of the house. The covers on the queen-size bed had been pulled apart and the mattress was off the box spring; the drawers of the double bureau gaped open and empty as did those of the two white Formica nightstands; the framed deco print of a black panther slithering through a canebreak had been taken down and leaned against the wall; some clothes, mostly men's, that had been hanging in the closet had been pulled off the hangers and lay in piles on the floor. I wondered if they were her husband's clothes.

"Welcome to the Palace Hotel," Sharon said, waving a hand grandly at the room. "Every room presearched and guaranteed bomb-free. If it looks as if one went off in here, rest assured, it is only due to the desire of our staff to make your stay a pleasant one."

The disgust in her voice made her attempt at humor fall flat.

She started to straighten up the bed but I told her to leave it, that I would take care of it, and she shrugged and went out. After I'd gotten the room into livable condition, I went out into the living room to see what I could do there. Sharon was in the kitchen, talking to someone on the phone. I'd put the cushions back on the couches and chairs, and was in the process of putting the record albums back on the shelves, when she came into the room. She watched me for a moment, then said, "I've got your money. Two hundred a day, wasn't that what you said?"

I put Joe Sample on the shelf, next to Chick Corea and some of his friends. "Where are you getting it?"

"What does it matter? Is that a question that you usually ask your clients?"

"It matters; and no, it's not a question I usually ask my clients; and anyway you're not my client yet."

She exhaled and threw up her hands. "If you really want to know, Ray is advancing it to me. I just talked to him. He owes me from Hugh's unfinished cases. He said you can go to his office tomorrow and pick up a check. All right? Satisfied? Now you can tell Grandma Johnson she can find someone else to track down her prune-whip pies."

I felt trapped and resented the position she had put me in, but there was nothing I could really do about it except flat-out refuse to work for her. Now that the money was there, my reasons for doing that would be pretty feeble, even for myself. Besides, I hadn't really been crazy about taking the other job. There was an element of social pressure there. I mean, it wasn't the kind of exciting and dangerous caper you'd bring up at a cocktail party, not if you didn't want to be laughed out of the room.

Screw it, I thought. If she wanted to flush her money down a toilet, let her. I wasn't too proud to take it. "Okay."

She nodded as if she thought it would be, then waved a hand at the albums and books still on the floor. "Never mind this. I'll get it in the morning. Right now I'm tired and tomorrow I can get a girl in to help me for a hell of a lot less than two hundred a day."

I poured myself a stiff vodka and took it into my room. I got undressed and turned on the tube, switching channels until I got a "Rockford" rerun. I've often wondered whether Rockford bought a new gold Firebird every time he wrecked one, or just fixed up the old one. The things we detectives went through for two hundred a day plus expenses. I took a sip from my drink and wondered if I'd made it clear it was *plus* expenses.

I was teased awake by the smell of bacon frying. I lay there for a while, letting the aroma work on me, and after about five minutes, it succeeded in pulling me out of bed.

The morning was gray and brooding. The fog had moved out from shore to hug the horizon and the sea stretched out like a sheet of gray Formica. I showered and shaved and put on a clean shirt. In the kitchen, Sharon was standing over the stove, pushing bacon around in a pan with a long fork.

"It's been a long time since I've been awakened by that smell," I said.

"How do you want your eggs?" she asked without turning around.

"Scrambled is fine with me."

"Coffee is right here," she said, nodding toward a Mr. Coffee on the tile countertop.

There was a clean cup there, too. Maybe this was a sign that she was coming out of her snit. I kind of hoped she wasn't. Maybe then she'd fire me.

She took the bacon out of the pan with the fork and laid the strips neatly side by side on a paper towel. "Thanks for cleaning up last night. I wasn't in the mood to cope with it."

"I noticed."

"You made me mad."

"I noticed that, too," I said. "Don't worry about it. It's a natural reaction. Being rejected for prune whip is hard to take. Lemon meringue is one thing, but prune whip—"

She smiled a little. Not much, but a little. "Have I told you lately you're an asshole?"

I gave it some thought. "Not lately, no."

"You are, you know."

"Yeah, I know. Did your husband keep an address book?" I asked as I watched her beat the eggs.

"In his study, on the desk. I saw it there this morning when I straightened up. Why? Whose address do you need?"

"I need a phone number. But I don't know whose yet. Where's the study?"

"One door down from your room."

I fetched the copies of Canning's office telephone bills from my room, then went next door.

The study had the same off-white walls and the same polished parquet floor as the rest of the house. A solid-looking desk of dark wood sat in front of a large bay window that provided a panoramic view of the coast. The side wall was bookshelves and if the books were not just for show, Canning had been a good reader. There was mostly fiction—Hemingway, Faulkner, Dreiser—with only a sprinkling of the usual best-seller crap.

I sat behind the desk. Alongside a marble-based pen-and-pencil set was a flip-top telephone index, and standing next to that was a chrome-framed, color, five-by-seven photograph of Sharon and a man. They were in bathing suits, sitting on the deck of a boat with drinks in their hands, and both looked very happy. He was good-looking in an angular sort of way, with black wavy hair and a Kirk Douglas dimple in his chin. His shoulders were wide and muscular and he looked as if he might have been athletic until just a couple of years ago, when his gut had started to loosen up.

I started with the most recent phone bill. I drew a big circle

57

around the toll calls made from Canning's office the day he died. There were eighteen of them, but none of them had been made to anywhere around the Ortega Highway. The last call had been made at 4:36 P.M., to his home, which synced with Sharon's version of events. The call before that had been made to a number in Newport at 4:25. I slid the indicator along the side of the index to "A" and pressed the button to open it. At "B" I matched the number with an entry for the Balboa Bay Club. That would have been Canning's dinner reservation, which also jibed with Sharon's version of events. So far, she was batting one thousand. The call before that had been placed at 3:51, also to a number in Newport. I put the indicator back at "A" and started again. I was through the "L's" when Sharon appeared in the doorway. "Breakfast is ready."

"Be right there." I closed the lid of the index and moved the finder one notch down.

She watched me curiously and asked, "What are you doing?"

"Seeing who your husband talked to the day he died. If he was going to meet somebody, maybe he called him or her first."

"Find anything?"

"I'm only on the second call. Your husband knew a lot of people."

"What if whoever it was called him?"

"Then we're out of luck. But you have to take the cards that are given you. At least at first. If that doesn't work, then you start pulling aces out of your sleeves."

I stopped what I was doing and pointed to the picture. "Was that him?"

She nodded and leaned against the doorway. "That was taken at the beginning of the summer on the boat of a friend of ours."

"He was a good-looking man."

She smiled wistfully. "Yes, he was."

I went back to the index and the "M's." I pressed the button and the lid popped open and the number jumped off the page at me. "Bingo."

"What is it?"

I looked up at her. "I thought your husband and Jackson Meriwether didn't get along."

"They didn't. Hugh hated the man."

"Well, they must have been spitting venom at each other for four minutes, because Canning called his number at three thirty-one and talked that long."

"That's odd," she said, then a thought struck her. "Meriwether always has a lot of girls around the place. You think this Alicia could be one of them?"

I wrote his address and phone number on a piece of paper. "Maybe I'd better ask him. Where is Camino Norte?"

"In Deep Canyon, behind Fashion Island."

"Baumgartner said something about a row your husband and Meriwether had in the Balboa Bay Club a while back. When was that?"

"It must have been three months ago, at least."

"What happened?"

"We were in the club having dinner, and Meriwether came in with a party of about six people. Hugh had been drinking and as soon as he saw Meriwether, he started to work himself into a nasty mood, and, finally, he got up and said he was going over there. I tried to stop him, but he just sloughed me off and went. I don't know exactly what Hugh said, but it must have been pretty bad because Meriwether's little sidekick or bodyguard or whatever he is jumped up, and for a minute I thought he was going to attack Hugh. He's supposedly a kung fu expert or something. But Meriwether told him to cool it and called the maitre d' over and we were asked to leave."

"You know what your husband said?"

"No. He wouldn't tell me. He was in a mood by that time and pretty drunk. He wasn't even making much sense, really. He just kept saying over and over that he was going to bury the sonofabitch."

"You know what he meant by that?"

She shook her head. "No. You're going to talk to Meri-wether?"

"I'm going to try. I also want to talk to your husband's doctor, the one who gave him the physical. Think you could call him and set up an appointment?"

"After breakfast," she said. "Come on. I can't stand cold scrambled eggs."

We ate in the kitchen. Some of the high clouds had burned off and the ocean had turned from gray Formica to blue cellophane. Between mouthfuls of bacon and eggs and English muffin, I said, "You've been through your husband's effects pretty thoroughly?"

"Most everything," she said, softly. "Ray came over one day and we went through them together."

"Baumgartner?"

She nodded. "He was looking for legal stuff that might help with the probate."

"I thought you said he wasn't doing the probate."

"He isn't. Fred Rosenberg is."

"Why didn't your husband have Baumgartner handle it if he was such a close friend?"

"Ray isn't a probate attorney. Fred is a specialist."

I finished eating and carried another cup of coffee back into the study. It took the better part of half an hour, but I identified eleven of the eighteen numbers on the telephone bill and all of them seemed to be work-related. The other seven were probably clients, but I'd have to call them to find out. I could have continued working on that project, but to break up the monotony, I went through the desk.

There was nothing much out of the ordinary in it: stationery, envelopes, some household bills—all paid—a file containing bank statements, another file holding joint income-tax returns for the past five years. A quick check of these found that even Canning's gross income had remained a steady $90,000 over the years, except for the last one—his bad year. In that year, it had jumped to $122,000. Of course, the interest on the loan he had been forced to assume had provided him with a big write-off, so his net income was way down, but the jump interested me.

Sharon appeared in the doorway again and said, "Wasserman says he can see you for a few minutes around ten-thirty."

"Fine." She started to leave, but I said, "A couple of things you can do for me. It'll also save you some money."

She stopped and looked at me curiously. "What?"

"I've identified most of the numbers that were called from your husband's office on the day he died, but some of them I haven't. I want you to phone *all of them*. The ones we haven't identified, find out who they are. The ones we have, find out what was said. Maybe one of those people knows Alicia, or at least who she is. After that, go through the rest of these numbers from the last couple of months and try to match them up with the numbers in the index. It's a hell of a job—there are three months of numbers here—but it'll free me to do other things, things that will put your two hundred a day, plus expenses, to better use."

Her mouth opened a little. "*Plus* expenses?"

"Always, darling. But don't worry, I'll try to keep them down."

"Just come home for meals," she said, poker-faced. "I don't want any bills for escargot and crepes suzette."

"I'm not an escargot devotee," I assured her. "There's something about the texture that gets to me."

"That takes a great load off my mind."

"Hey, don't bitch. You're getting off easy. Usually I charge fifteen cents a mile for the wear and tear on my car."

She folded her arms and glared at me. "You mean you're giving me a rate? How generous of you."

I grinned at her glare. "Yeah, I thought so too."

One side of her mouth lifted into a disdainful smirk. "You must keep your car parked out of sight somewhere when you meet your clients. If they saw that piece of shit, they wouldn't pay you a cent. All the wear and tear has already been worn and torn."

I put my finger to my lips. "Shhh. She's right outside. She might hear you. She's very sensitive."

I tiptoed out the door.

7

Dr. Felix Wasserman's office was on the third floor of a rounded building that sat like a landed flying saucer on top of a shrub-covered plateau overlooking the Pacific Coast Highway.

When I told the receptionist who I was, she summoned a tall, auburn-haired nurse who took my card and disappeared. I sat down next to a sunken-chested old man whose breath sounded as if he were going into Cheyne-Stokes, and waited. When the nurse returned she showed me into a small, paneled study. I spent the next ten minutes in the leather chair in front of the desk, staring at the bookshelves, which were crammed with such runaway best-sellers as *The Pituitary and You* and *Diseases of the Bladder*, and then Wasserman came in.

He was a short, compactly built man with a lot of furrowed forehead and his pale, bald dome was surrounded by a raggedly tonsured fringe of brown hair. The pair of heavy-rimmed, thick-lensed glasses that sat on the end of his narrow, hooked nose gave his eyes an owllike appearance.

He introduced himself without taking his hands out of his white frock, and moved around the desk and sat down. There was a quick officiousness in all his movements. He glanced at his watch and said in a tone that sounded a trifle resentful, "I'm afraid I can't spare you much time. I have a lot of patients waiting."

"I'll try to make this as brief as possible," I promised. "As Sharon Canning told you on the phone, I'm working for her, investigating her husband's death. I'd like to know what you think of the insurance company's contention that Hugh Canning committed suicide."

He took a hand out of his pocket and made a hopeless gesture. It was a small hand, pale and well-scrubbed. "I don't know what to think of it, frankly. Hugh Canning was a patient of mine, but I didn't know much about his private life."

"Have you talked to anybody from Transcontinental?"

"A few weeks ago one of their investigators came by asking all sorts of questions. I can't remember his name. A man with a beard."

"What kinds of questions?"

He pushed the glasses up the bridge of his nose with an index finger. "Mostly about Hugh's health. He wanted to know if Hugh had been complaining about not feeling well, and if I had diagnosed the anemia. I told him that, aside from slightly elevated blood pressure, Hugh seemed to be in perfect health. Then he asked all sorts of questions about his mental state—did he seem depressed when he was here, things like that."

"What did you tell him?"

"It's not my field, but as far as I could tell, Hugh seemed to be in excellent spirits. He joked around with me during the examination. You can't really tell about a man's true emotional state from such superficial observations, but he certainly did not act despondent."

"When was the last time you saw him?"

"A few weeks before the accident."

"And there were no physical symptoms from the anemia showing then?"

He shook his head and one corner of the pucker lifted. "I couldn't believe it when Sharon called me and told me. I even called the coroner's office and talked to the pathologist who did the autopsy. There is no doubt that Hugh was a very sick man, but I knew nothing about it. I'd given Hugh a complete physical only a month before his death and nothing showed up in any of the tests then."

"You did a blood test then?"

"Of course."

"And the anemia would have shown up, if he had had it at the time?"

He looked at me as if I were stupid. "Certainly. It would have been impossible to miss."

"Excuse me if my questions seem a little dumb, doctor. I don't even know what aplastic anemia is."

He took a handkerchief from his front pocket, then removed his glasses and began wiping the lenses. "There are three elements in bone marrow that make up blood—white blood cells, red blood cells, and platelets. If the marrow stops manufacturing any of those, you wind up with any number of diseases—leukemia, for instance, anemia, thrombocytopenia, hemophilia. Aplastic anemia occurs when the marrow stops making all three. Essentially, it is a complete wipeout of the bone marrow."

"What would cause it?"

He shrugged. "Some types of hepatitis, if left untreated, can result in aplastic anemia, but that's rare. Certain tropical diseases transmitted by African flies, like yellow fever, dengue, chickungunya fever. Bolivian hemorrhagic fever—"

I broke in, "I'm not trying to be smart, doctor, but aren't African flies usually found in Africa? Where could Canning have picked up something like that around here?"

One eyebrow formed a troubled arch and he paused just long enough to give his words a significant weight. "That's what I'd like to know."

"Could it have been caused by anything else?"

He held his glasses up to the light and inspected the job he had done on them. Apparently satisfied, he put them back on and slipped the handkerchief back into his pocket. "The ingestion of a solvent, like benzidine. But that would have shown up in the toxicology report. I specifically asked the coroner if they ran a test for benzidine. They did, and it was negative."

"Then you think it was a virus of some kind?"

"I don't know what else it could have been." His look grew troubled again. "Only serologic studies were done on Hugh's blood, just in case whatever he had was infectious, and no virus was isolated."

I shifted in my chair. "Just how bad off was he, doc?"

He turned up one of his small hands. "That is hard to say. It might have been treatable, if we had been able to find out what he'd contracted. If the bone-marrow damage was irreversible, however, there would have been nothing anybody could have done for him."

"You sound as if he might have been terminal."

He steepled his fingers. "It's quite possible. Even if we could have diagnosed it, there are no effective medicines for some of the more exotic diseases."

A thought struck me. "You mentioned hepatitis, doctor. Could Canning have picked up hepatitis from a dirty needle?"

"It's possible, I suppose, but extremely unlikely. By the time the disease reached the aplastic anemia stage, he would have had other physical symptoms that would have been noticeable. A yellow cast to the skin, fever, a feeling of malaise. More than likely, he wouldn't have even been able to get out of bed."

"Then he had no physical symptoms?"

"Not according to his wife."

"Say he contracted one of the other diseases you were talking about, how long would it take between the time he got it and the time he developed symptoms?"

"Again, that would depend on what he had."

I leaned forward, "Is it possible that Canning did not know he was sick?"

He lifted his shoulders a little and pursed his lips. "It's possible, I suppose. If the disease was in the incipient stages, as it appeared to be."

"Could he have been experiencing symptoms and keeping it to himself?"

He shook his head and frowned. "That's not likely."

"What symptoms would he have had?"

He made an irritated gesture. "You keep asking these questions and I have to keep answering that it would depend on what he had. If the platelets went first, he would have been hemorrhaging. If the white cells went, he would have been experiencing violent chills—"

"But he never complained to you about any of those symptoms."

"I told you, no."

I knew I was going to hit a sensitive chord with my next question. "Think he might have gone to another doctor about it?"

His voice bristled at the suggestion. "Why should he?"

"I don't know," I said. "I was just asking."

He turned sideways in his chair and struck a defensive posture. "I find that extremely unlikely. I've been Hugh's doctor for six years. He might have gone to someone I would recommend—a specialist—but he would have come to me first."

"Nothing happened recently between you two, then, that would have shaken his faith in you as a doctor?"

He glared at me. "Of course not."

I nodded and got off that track, before he turned really hostile. "You said Canning had high blood pressure. You had him on medication?"

"Inderal and Enduron. One is a beta-blocker and the other is a diuretic."

"Would either of those drugs cause depression?"

"No."

"How about the aplastic anemia? Would that have caused depression, even if he didn't know he had the disease?"

"Who knows? If he was experiencing a general feeling of being run-down, it's possible, I guess. I really couldn't speculate." He glanced at his watch again. "I'm afraid I can't spare you any more time, Mr. Asch. I do have patients to see."

"Sure." I put my note pad away and stood up. "Thanks for seeing me. You've been very helpful. Can I call you if I have any more questions?"

He did not seem overly pleased by the suggestion, but said, "Of course."

"And I'll call you if I happen to capture any stray African flies."

His expression soured, and he said gravely, "Do that."

Before I spent money on a fly swatter, I wanted to look for a dirty needle, and I thought I knew where to find one.

8

Deep Canyon was a misnomer. It wasn't deep and it wasn't a canyon. It was a golf course and development of expensive homes that sat in a shallow trough that had been scooped out of the gently undulating hills behind Newport Center. The entire development was surrounded by a high, cinder-block wall that meandered over the hills like the Great Wall of China.

The arthritic-looking security guard at the front entrance was another car snob. He gave my Plymouth a disdainful once-over, and looked very dubious when I told him I was there to see Jackson Meriwether. He took my name and went inside his kiosk, then came back out and told me that my name wasn't on the guest list. I gave him a card and told him it was personal business, very important. He went back into the kiosk and kept his eye glued suspiciously on me through the glass window while he called Meriwether's house. I did not really think I would get in that way, but it was worth a shot, and he surprised me by telling me to go ahead. The suspicion doubled in the old guard's eyes when I asked how to get there, but he gave me instructions.

The road circled around the edge of the tree-dotted golf course where a few golfers whizzed over the sun-drenched greens in electric carts or walked, if they really wanted to feel as if they were getting in some exercise. After a few hundred yards, the houses began. They were spaced out evenly enough so that the view of the golf course was never completely obliterated from the road; aside from that, the only other thing they shared was that they were all mansion-sized.

I turned left on Waverly, which was Meriwether's street. Number 10, the house I was looking for, was the second on the left, a two-story, modernistic structure that had clean, squared-off lines and a bright-blue glazed-tile roof. Both sides of the street in front of it were lined with cars, and the ones that were not new and expensive were old and *very* expensive. What the hell. In another ten years, I'd have a classic, too. I parked behind a $75,000 white Clenet and went to the front door of the house. As I rang the bell, a collective cheer erupted from somewhere behind the house, then applause.

When nothing happened, I pushed the button again. The door was yanked open and I was staring at a girl so fine I would've liked to suck her shadow. She stood at least five-ten in her bare feet and right now her feet were bare, as was most of the rest of her. She had high, firm breasts and a flat tanned stomach, and a tiny waist that widened into a graceful flare of hip before tapering into a pair of incredibly long, slim, coltlike legs, all strung together by a bikini so small I couldn't tell what color it was.

She took a sip from the drink in her hand, brushed back a wild wave of black hair and looked me over, with a feral glint in her green eyes. "Yes?" Her voice was deep, husky. Suffering from a temporary case of leg-blindness, I hadn't really noticed her face. The slight Indian hook at the end of her narrow nose and the hardness at the corners of her wide mouth probably made her a little too coarse-looking to be beautiful, but I was not so stubborn that my mind couldn't be changed about that, with a little argument. "Is Mr. Meriwether in?"

She put a hand on her hip and shifted her weight to that leg, striking what I thought was a rather insolent pose. "Your name?"

"Asch. I called from the gate."

"Oh, yeah. I told the guard to let you up. Jackson couldn't

come to the phone. He's been at game-point seventeen times, but Tony keeps bouncing back."

I felt as if I'd just opened a Robert Ludlum novel at page 100.

"Come on in," she said, a little impatiently. "I don't want to miss the end of the game."

She stepped out of the way and I came in past her.

It was your typical, ordinary living room in your typical, ordinary palace. The room was a good twenty-five yards long and, along its length, white cast-iron Roman columns rose out of the gray slate floor to the ceiling, fifteen feet above. The second floor was an open, loftlike mezzanine, bordered by a brass ship's railing. The way up to it was at the far end of the room, a cubistic stairway that stopped first at a carpeted loungelike platform occupied by a black-laminate-and-chrome bar and a cluster of modernistic furniture. Other arrangements of curvilinear chairs done in gray velvet sat around glass coffee tables throughout the room, but they were dwarfed by the size of the palace. The pale gray walls were mostly unadorned, amplifying the feeling of space. The pedestaled pieces of sculpture placed throughout the room imparted a museumlike atmosphere to the place.

"Not too shabby," I said, looking around. "Sort of reminds me of my own place."

She closed the door. "This way," she said and started off through the Great Hall. Her feet padded silently on the slate floor, but my heels clicked on the hard surface and echoed off the walls. "What's your name?"

"Magma."

"That's an unusual name. What is it, Hungarian?"

"No," she said in a serious tone. "Daddy's a geologist." She apparently didn't think that needed any further explanation because she didn't attempt to make one.

We went through a dining area dominated by a huge glass-topped dining table that had two alabaster sphinxes as a base, and through a sliding glass door to a pool area outside. In the middle of the patio, a Ping-Pong table was set up and around it were gathered a dozen or so bikinied beauties and swimming-attired men, all watching with rapt attention the ferocious, high-speed match. The game was obviously the source of cheering I'd heard out front.

One of the players was a tall, lean, fortyish man whose royal blue Sergio Tachini warm-up suit jacket was unzipped to the waist, exposing an expanse of gray chest hair that was dampened by perspiration. His opponent, a younger, shorter, wiry man, sported a black Vandyke beard, and was wearing a red sports shirt and jeans. Both of their sweat-dripping faces were pictures of total concentration as they smashed the ball back and forth across the net to the ooohs and aaahs of the spectators. The man in the warm-up suit straightened up and his thin upper lip curled under a sly smile.

"Fifty-five, fifty-four," he said in a thick Southern drawl. "Game and set point."

I whispered to Magma, "How long have they been playing?"

"At least half an hour."

"Which one is Meriwether?"

"The one in the warm-up suit."

Meriwether put a lot of top spin on the serve, but the bearded man anticipated it and sliced it with some under spin into the corner, which backed Meriwether off the table. He returned a big backhand, moving the bearded man away, which put both of them three feet behind the table. The movements of both men were flawless, and for a moment I thought the game might go on for another half hour, but then the small man hit a backhand and Meriwether did a little body-juke and put a forehand smash into the corner that just caught the edge of the table. The other man lunged for it, but missed, and a collective whoop of delight erupted from the gallery.

Meriwether put his paddle down on the table and beamed. "Hell of a game, Tony."

One of the female spectators, a blonde who rivaled my guide in the body department, brought Meriwether a towel. "Thank you, honey," he said, smiling. He mopped his face with the towel and said to his vanquished foe, "We old folks gotta show you cubs how it's done every once in a while, just to keep you in your place."

"Old, hell," the other said. "You'll bury us all, Jackson."

Meriwether seemed to like that. He beamed.

"I need a drink," the bearded man said, and moved off toward a bamboo bar that was set up near the pool.

"That ain't a half-bad idea," Meriwether said, then turned to the blond woman. "Samantha, honey, would you be a sweet little thing and get me a glass of OJ? The stuff that was just squeezed, please."

As she turned to go, Meriwether patted her on the rump. She giggled and pranced over to the bar. Meriwether saw us and came over. "I don't believe I've had the pleasure," he said to me.

"Jacob Asch."

"Jackson Meriwether," he said, and held out a big bony hand. He had the grip of a Brahman bull rider. "Welcome to my house. Any friend of Magma's is a friend of mine."

"I'm not exactly a friend of Magma's," I said. I handed him a card. "I'm a private investigator. Sharon Canning hired me to look into the death of her husband. I'd like to ask you a couple of questions, if you wouldn't mind."

His smile stiffened, but remained. "I don't mean to sound rude, Mr.—" He glanced at the card. "Asch. But how did you get through the front gate?"

"I told the guard to let him up," Magma said sheepishly. He looked at her sharply and she said, "Well, you told me to get the phone, Jackson, and you were in the middle of the game, so I just thought—"

He patted her gently on the wrist. "That's okay, Magma honey. Never mind."

He turned the smile back on me and his accent became syrupy. "Just what is it you wanted to ask me, Mr. Asch?"

"The insurance company is denying Canning's accident was an accident."

I paused to see how he would take that. However he took it, he didn't let me see. His expression remained politely inquisitive.

"They're claiming Canning committed suicide and tried to make it look like an accident," I went on. "If they make it stick, it leaves his wife in a bad spot financially."

His eyes widened and he shook his head in concern. "Suicide, huh? I hadn't heard that, although in all honesty I can't say that it surprises me too much."

"Really? Why is that?"

"The last couple of times I talked to Hugh, he acted crazier than a pet coon. The boy was coming completely apart at the seams. I sure am sorry to hear that Mrs. Canning is having trouble, though. I always did admire her. She's a fine little lady."

His train of thought was interrupted by the blond woman who came bouncing back with a big glass of orange juice. Meriwether's eyes roamed over her body admiringly as he took the glass from her. "Honey, I'd like to see you in a pair of cowboy boots and a Stetson and nothin' else."

"Oh, Jackson," she said, grinning mischievously.

He winked at me and smiled. "How about you, Mr. Asch? Some juice? Or a drink, maybe?"

"No, thanks."

He took a drink and smacked his lips. "Aaahh, that's good. Did you know that orange juice loses all of its vitamin-C content forty-five minutes after it's squeezed?"

"Really?" I said.

He nodded. "Sure enough. That's why you got to drink it when it's fresh."

"Sharon said you were big on vitamins."

He regarded me intently. There was a hard, bright light in his eyes and the pupils were constricted to tiny black pinpricks. "Vitamin therapy saved my life, son. I had cancer of the liver. All the hotshot cancer specialists in Houston gave me one year at the most. Then somebody told me about this clinic in Juarez that did antioxidant therapy. See, son, cancer cells grow all the time in everybody's body, but your immune system sort of gobbles them

73

up. It's when the immune system breaks down that they start runnin' wild. So Dr. Marcuse put me on a special formula of B, C, E, selenium, and male hormones, and in four months the cancer was gone from my body. The antioxidants get the immune system working again, y'see." He paused and regarded me intently. "Did you know son, that as long ago as 1949, it's been known that selenium added to the diet reduces the incidence of cancer?"

"No, I didn't." Magma and Samantha looked suddenly bored, as if they'd heard all this about six thousand times before.

"Well, it's a sure enough fact. These doctors don't want cancer cured. You can't make money off a well patient. Keep 'em sick."

Before he had the chance to lay the details of the Great AMA Conspiracy out to me, I said, "You claim Canning was acting crazy the last couple of times you talked to him. How was he acting the day he died?"

His eyes narrowed. "How would I know?"

"Didn't you talk to him?"

"I haven't talked to Hugh in a couple of months."

"That's funny, because on the afternoon of the day he died, about three-thirty, Canning called this number from his office and talked to somebody for about four minutes." A slight tic twitched his left eyelid, but his voice remained a calm, comforting drawl.

"He didn't talk to me."

"It's in his phone records."

He shook his head in bewilderment. "I can't understand that. If I'd talked to the man, I'd surely remember it. I mean, I read about the accident in the papers the day after it happened and I was deeply shocked. A call like that the day before would surely stand out in my mind, don't you think?"

"He talked for four minutes, so it must have been somebody he knew. Who else would he have called here?"

He shook his head again and licked his lips. "I sure enough don't know." He turned to Magma and Samantha. "Why don't you two girls run along and play for a couple of minutes? The man and I have some business to discuss. And tell Tony to come over here."

"Don't be too long," Magma said, in a flirtatious tone as she sauntered away.

"Whatever happened to the innocent, freckle-faced little girls who snapped their gum and smelled like Juicy Fruit?" I asked, wistfully watching her retreating derriere.

"They don't make 'em anymore, son," Meriwether said, seriously. "They never did."

"Tony," Meriwether greeted him, "this is Mr. Asch. Mr. Asch, Tony Halstead."

We shook hands. He was all of five-seven and there was quite a bit of gray in his beard and his hair, which was combed straight back from his forehead, werewolf-style. His green eyes were small and the drooping epicanthic fold on the upper lids gave him an almost Oriental appearance.

"You two are colleagues," Meriwether said casually. "Mr. Asch is a private investigator. He's investigating Hugh Canning's death."

There was an instant animal wariness in Halstead's eyes. His pupils, too, were constricted. "I didn't know there was anything to investigate."

"He was telling me a strange thing," Meriwether went on. "He was telling me that Canning called my number here and talked to somebody the day he died. You know anything about it?"

There was nothing in Halstead's face. "No."

"Who else would he have talked to here?" I asked.

"I sure enough don't know," Meriwether said. "As you can appreciate by the way you got in, we ain't always aware of who picks up the phone around here."

"Would somebody named Alicia have answered it?"

Meriwether's healthy tan turned to the color of mud. I felt Halstead tense beside me. "Alicia?" Meriwether repeated the name. "I don't know any Alicia. Why? Who is she?"

"That's what I'm trying to find out. Canning wrote the name on a piece of paper by his phone the same afternoon he called here."

Meriwether was doing everything he could to appear nonchalant, but the tension was there in the knots of muscles along his

75

jawline. "You ever hear of anyone around here called Alicia, Tony?"

Halstead was on the balls of his feet and his small eyes were glued on me. "No."

Meriwether said, "Why don't we go inside and talk where it's quieter? You don't mind if Tony listens in? He's like my right hand."

"I don't mind."

We went into the house and as we walked through the Great Hall, I said to Halstead: "So you're an investigator, too?"

"Tony's the best electronics man in the business," Meriwether said proudly. "He used to work for Consolidated Security, but now he just works for me. Sweeps this place for bugs once a week, just to make sure everything is nice and tidy."

My eyes roamed over the room, looking for where you would plant a microphone in a place this large. The statues would be an obvious place. As my eyes jumped from pedestal to pedestal, I noticed that although the pieces ranged in style from classical realism to deco cubist, they were all studies of female nudes. "Why would somebody want to bug you?"

He shrugged. "In my kind of work, son, you can never be too careful. Moving fast and moving first is sometimes everything. I once lost two hundred thousand dollars in a stock deal because the word got out I was trying to corner the market, and I wound up moving twenty minutes late."

"Is that what your business is primarily? The market?"

"The market, commodities, real estate, a little of this, a little of that. If something looks good to me, I'll be there."

"Some people around here seem to think you're into gunrunning in Latin America."

He chuckled. "Yeah, don't that beat all?"

"Any truth in it?"

He stopped in front of a doorway and turned. His color was back to normal. He put his hands on his chest and grinned broadly. "No, son. Do I look like a gunrunner?"

"I'm not sure I know what one looks like."

76

"Y'know, I'm not sure I do, either. We can be comfortable and talk in here." He gestured toward the doorway with a graceful wave. All his movements were full of practiced grace, but I could feel a pent-up tightness in him.

I stepped into a large den. Like the rest of the house, it was a mixture of styles, but somehow they all blended harmoniously. A large and very old Chinese tapestry hung on one wall, protected by a Plexiglas case. There was a modern glass-topped desk, held up by two marble female nudes and more curvilinear chairs like the ones in the Valhalla outside. Leather-bound books alternated on the shelves with more sculpted nudes of metal and glass. Halstead and I sat in two of the chairs and Meriwether got comfortable in one opposite us.

"Quite a collection of nudes, you have," I commented.

He smiled contentedly. "I'm quite proud of them. It's a hobby of mine. Some people collect Renaissance art, some people Pop art; I collect nudes." He pointed to a bronze in the corner of a woman lying languidly on a rock. "That there is a Rodin."

"It's beautiful," I said.

"There's something mysterious and almost archetypal in it, the serpentine S-curves of the feminine form. But you didn't come here to discuss nudes. Just what is it you wanted to ask me?"

"When was the last time you saw Hugh Canning?"

He thought about it. "Three months back, I reckon. What do you say, Tony, three months? Tony's got a much better memory for these things than I do."

Halstead nodded. "About three months."

"Where?" I asked.

"The Balboa Bay Club."

"Was that when Canning came over to your table and made a scene?"

Meriwether smiled. "My, my, you have been doin' your research, haven't you? That was the time, all right. The boy was all worked up, frothin' at the mouth like a rabid possum."

"What was he worked up about?"

"The same old nonsense he's been worked up about for the past year. The boy seemed to have fixated on me as the cause of all his problems."

"You mean the Mission Viejo deal?"

He nodded. "The fact is, if I hadn't bailed Canning out of his mess, he would've gone down like the *Titanic*. It wasn't me that told him to go guaranteeing no loans to George Villalobos. I told him he'd be a fool if he did it. It's like my pappy used to tell me; he'd say, 'Son, there ain't been a good deed done that ain't gone properly punished.' But Hugh was smarter than everybody else and went and did it anyway."

"So why did he do it?"

He leaned forward and put his hands on his knees. "Hugh Canning was a bright boy in a lot of ways. Maybe too bright. He let his greed get the better of his judgment. Around that time, he was shittin' in high cotton and wipin' it on a tall leaf. The money was comin' in from the law practice and a few deals he and George had gotten in together and he thought he could do no wrong. And I guess he trusted George."

"And you didn't?"

He leaned back and an easy smile spread across his thin lips. "Mr. Asch, my life has always been guided by what, in my modest observations of life and human nature, I've come to see as certain unwavering truths. One of them is, 'Give anyone enough time, and he'll never fail to disappoint you.' Now, I truly hate being disappointed in people. It makes a man bitter. So I've found that the less I trust people, the less I'm disappointed."

"Are you still friendly with Villalobos?"

He fidgeted and squirmed in his chair. " 'Course I'm still friendly with him. There ain't no reason why I shouldn't be."

"That's right. His bankruptcy helped you buy out Canning—cheap."

His mouth twisted into an almost, but not quite, contemptuous sneer. "What would you have done, boy—bought him out for top dollar because he outsmarted himself and got picked barer than a pecan tree in a swarm of locusts? My momma didn't raise no fool, son."

"How did you make out on that deal?"

The sneer relaxed and he shrugged. "About a million to the good, I guess."

"If I wanted to talk to Villalobos, where would I find him?"

"Probably at his restaurant. Cielo Lindo. It's on MacArthur, near the airport." The tic on his eyelid grew more prominent. It throbbed like a worm trying to break out of the skin. "But tell me, son, what does all this have to do with Hugh Canning's death? I mean, maybe I'm just dense or something, but I can't see where you're trying to go with it."

"I'm not trying to go anywhere with it, Mr. Meriwether. I'm just trying to gather some background information. The physical evidence that the insurance company has is pretty hard. To punch holes in their case, I have to attack it another way. I have to cast some doubt on their claim that Canning had both motive and opportunity for suicide."

Meriwether sat back and pinched his lower lip. "And where does this Alicia Whoever fit into things?" Halstead put his hands on his knees and leaned forward slightly. He began bouncing his right leg.

"I don't know that she does. Right now, we have no reason Canning would have driven up that highway. If he was meeting someone, he might have had a reason."

Meriwether looked at me slyly. "And you're thinking that he was going to meet this Alicia?"

"I don't know, but I'd like to find her and ask her. You think she might have come here as a date with one of your friends and you weren't introduced?"

"It's possible, I guess. I'll certainly ask around, if you think it would help."

"I'd appreciate that."

"And you have no idea at all who she might be?"

He seemed to be fishing for something. I didn't want to take the bait until I had a better idea of what. "Not yet, but I will."

He stood up, saying he had to get back to his guests. I looked him up and down with undisguised admiration.

79

"May I ask you a personal question?"

"Go ahead."

"How old are you?"

"Forty-seven," he said proudly.

I shook my head. "That's unbelievable. You look ten years younger, at least. And all that's because of vitamins?"

He put his hand on my shoulder as we walked through the Great Hall. "Megavitamins, son. There's a difference. Megavitamins, exercise, and fresh air."

"Did Canning ever take one of your vitamin shots?"

His hand dropped from my shoulder. "No. Why do you ask that?"

"He probably should have. The autopsy showed that he had a rare blood disease when he died. He might have been terminal."

"That's a downright shame. I had no idea."

"Nobody did, including his wife or doctor." I could feel Halstead behind me, watching like a cat. "Who is your local doctor, Mr. Meriwether?"

"I don't have one."

We went up the slate steps to the front door. "You mean you fly to Juarez every time you need to see a doctor?"

"I never get sick, so there ain't no need to see a doctor. Preventive medicine, that's the key." He winked at me.

"Who renews your vitamin supply when you run out?"

Halstead was on the balls of his feet now, looking me over as if he would love using me as a pile of bricks in a karate demonstration.

"I fly back to Texas once a month on business," Meriwether said. "I stock up then."

"Well, say I was feeling real rundown and I wanted to get some of your formula and I couldn't afford the airfare to Juarez. Who would I go to locally to get it?"

I could see in his eyes that he knew that I knew. Or at least suspected. "I wouldn't know," he said, and opened the door. He stood back and smiled like a man with rictus, but his eyes were not smiling. They were taking me apart piece by piece and committing the pieces to memory. "My regards to Mrs. Canning. I sure hope you can do something to help her out of her, uh, situation."

"Yeah, thanks," I said, stepping past him.

"A piece of advice, son," he said when I was on the front step. I turned. "If you really want to help the little lady, don't get side-tracked. That was one thing my daddy always made sure I did when we'd go hunting. Stay on the main path, he'd say, and it was sound advice, too. Tall grass can hide all sorts of dangerous things—moccasins, 'gators, quicksand."

"I didn't know they had 'gators in Texas," I said, returning his smile.

"You'd be surprised where 'gators turn up. I hear people in Florida are walking out their front doors and tripping over 'em."

His voice was silky, but only on the outside. Silk wrapped around galvanized pipe. I left them and went down the walkway to the car.

Cielo Lindo squatted obtrusively in the middle of a financial complex, surrounded by ten-story office buildings. It was designed to look like an old California mission, complete with clay-tiled roof and bell tower and patches of brick showing through the carefully created cracks in its whitewashed plaster walls. Although it was not a small building—quite large, in fact—its size was dwarfed by the height of the buildings around it.

I let the attendant take my car and passed through a small brick-inlaid courtyard with a fountain in the middle, to the ornate wood-barred doors, and was immediately hit by the blare of mariachi trumpets and the smell that filled all Mexican restaurants: frying lard, tortillas, and refried beans.

The dining room was crowded, and in its center was a glassed-in skylighted courtyard filled with a forest of kentia palms.

The blond hair and the blue eyes of the girl at the front desk made her look a little too Nordic for the shoulderless Mexican peasant dress she was wearing, but I liked the gardenia behind her ear. She told me Mr. Villalobos was in, but that he was busy at the moment. I told her that whenever he wasn't, I would be at the bar, and gave her my card.

The bar was in a room off the courtyard and it was crowded

with people waiting for tables. The walls were hung with colorful serapes and sombreros and piñatas and old sepia-toned photographs of people I guessed to be Mexican historical figures. At the bar I ordered a Dos Equis, just to get into an ethnic mood.

The bartender put the beer in front of me and I pointed to the big frilly horse-shaped piñata that hung over the back bar. "You know, I've always wanted to give a party and fill one of those with guacamole."

He had a great sense of humor. He glanced over his shoulder at it, looked back at me as if I were wearing a beanie with a propeller on it, and said, "One seventy-five." I gave him two bucks and he went away. I was halfway through my second beer when I saw the woman from the desk step into the room and point me out to a short, dark-haired man. He nodded at her and she went back out and he came over to see me.

"I'm George Villalobos," he said. "You want to see me about something?"

He had a pleasant, round moon of a face the color of heavily creamed coffee and the dimples that creased the cheeks gave him an ingenuous, boyish look. That impression was helped out by the mouth, which was full-lipped and turned up slightly at the corners, making him appear to smile when he wasn't. His black hair was curly and cut fairly short, and his eyes were black, with invisible pupils. His beige suit had wide lapels and had to be custommade to fit him as well as it did. He wore a maroon shirt, a wide tan-and-maroon striped tie, and brown loafers buffed to a mirrorlike shine.

"Jacob Asch," I said, offering my hand. He took it. I looked around. "Real nice place you have here."

"Thank you," he said, unsmiling. His voice was high and devoid of any kind of Latin accent. "Just what is it I can do for you?"

"I'm investigating the death of Hugh Canning. I thought you might be able to help me."

His eyes clouded a little. "What help could I possibly be?"

"The insurance company is claiming Canning committed suicide. I'm trying to gather some background information on Canning, to determine intent. I don't have to tell you how it goes, Mr. Villalobos. We're in the same business."

He shook his head. "I don't see that I could be of any help to you. I haven't had any contact with Hugh Canning in a year. . . ."

"I'd like to get some of your impressions of Canning while you were working together. I just came from talking to Jackson Meriwether. He said some things that I found very interesting. Maybe you could confirm them for me."

That pushed him over the edge. "Okay." He waved to the bartender and said, "If you see Alex, I'm in the office."

We went back through the lobby, where people were now stacked five deep, waiting for tables, and around the palm-filled courtyard to a short, narrow, arched hallway. Villalobos stopped at the door at the end and unlocked it.

The office was small and meagerly furnished. There was a steel desk, some filing cabinets, two leather-and-wood chairs like the ones at the tables outside, and a big Diebold safe in one corner. The walls were solid with framed eight-by-ten glossies of Villalobos in the company of different people. I didn't have to look closely to know that they would all be celebrities. I sat in one of the chairs and Villalobos sat behind the desk, brushed his coat back, and folded his brown hands across his stomach. He smiled slightly and waited for me to begin.

"When did you last talk to Canning?"

He shrugged. "At least four or five months ago."

"Was the conversation friendly?"

"Not particularly."

"I understand there was no love lost between you two."

He smiled strangely, then pushed out his lower lip. "The man was wacko."

"Why do you say that?"

"Because it's true. He cracked up. Everybody knew it who had any contact with him."

"That was after you defaulted on the Mission Viejo loans and

84

he had to pick them up." He just shrugged. "Why did he guarantee those loans for you, anyway?"

He began tapping the letter opener in his open palm. "Because he liked me and I asked him to."

"That seems to have been a mistake on his part."

"Hey, that's the way things go in business sometimes. You win some, you lose some."

"Why couldn't you get the loan without a guarantor?" I waved a hand at the door. "It seems like you've got enough collateral."

He smiled. "I don't own this place, my wife does. I just work here."

I nodded. "Your wife owns your Lamborghini, too? And your boat?"

He was still smiling. "My wife does have a Lamborghini and my father owns a boat. I use them sometimes."

"Where were you the night Canning died?"

He put the opener down and folded his hands across his stomach again. "Right here."

There would be a lot of witnesses to that, so I didn't bother asking about them. "Ever hear of anyone named Alicia?"

He turned the name over in his mind. "Alicia. Not that I remember. Why?"

"I think maybe Canning was on his way to meet her when he got into the accident."

"The name is not familiar to me."

I could not tell if he was lying or not. "Are you still doing investigative work?"

He lifted one shoulder. "Every once in a while. Strictly on my own, though. I dissolved Group Associates when I declared bankruptcy."

"What exactly did Group Associates do for Canning?"

"We would check out questions of liability, photograph accident scenes, and provide translation services when they were needed."

"How many people did you have working for you?"

"Six, besides myself."

"You did work for other law firms besides Canning's?"

"Sure. Four or five others."

"What kind of case load were you handling?"

"Five to six hundred a month."

"That's a big case load," I said. "Did you provide legal referrals, too?"

His nostrils flared. "What do you mean?"

"I mean, did you bring in clients to the firms you worked for?"

His eyes seemed to grow darker. "I do a lot of charity work in the barrio, Mr. Asch, and I run across a lot of Mexican-Americans who need help and don't know where to go to get it. If you're poor and don't speak English and don't know your rights, you make an easy victim for the system, even when nobody in particular is trying to make you one."

"You didn't answer my question," I said.

He parried the thrust with a flip of his wrist. "The answer is yes. If I find someone who needs legal help, I'll help him or her get it."

I nodded. "Did—do you get a fee from the attorney for your referrals?"

The question did not seem to offend him. He smiled easily and answered, "Of course not. That would be capping. My fees are based strictly on an hours-worked basis." He paused, bit his lip, and shifted in his chair. "What are you trying to imply?"

I lifted an eyebrow and smiled. "Like I said, I'm just trying to gather some background information."

"Just what does it have to do with Hugh Canning?"

"I don't know. Maybe nothing."

"I brought Canning some clients, if that's what you're trying to get at, just like I've brought clients to other attorneys I've worked for, but only when I've run across somebody who needed help. I've always felt that some system of referrals should be set up in the county. I tried to do that at the County Medical Center, and in such a way that there wouldn't be any repercussions from the State Bar, but all I got was resistance. I saw firsthand how Mexican-American patients were being mistreated in the facility. I saw patients who had been hurt and crippled discharged without being told that they could get compensation, if only they had an attorney. It was criminal. I told that to Liston Barclay, the Director of Health Services for the county, and gave him a workable plan for patient referrals. He said he'd take up the request with the County Counsel, but he never did. Instead, politics went to work and Amigos got the boot."

"Amigos is your charity group?"

"That's right," he said proudly. "It's always been my dream to do something for the poor Chicanos who came to the country with nothing. I started that way, although I didn't come from Mexico, and I'm sympathetic to their plight. I set up Amigos six years ago as a nonprofit corporation to do that, to help people find help when they don't know how. Then, I was asked to bring a volunteer group into the County Med Center, to help out with the Chicano patients there." He recited it like an acceptance speech at an awards dinner.

"So you were asked to leave because you were helping out too much?"

"Amigos was asked to leave," he said sharply, "because the bitch Director of Volunteer Services, Diane McClurg, didn't like it when I tried to do something about what was going on around there. She was jealous, worried sick I was going to undermine her position with her superiors. She did everything she possibly could to make my people look bad."

"Like what?"

"I don't even want to get into it," he said, waving a hand at me. "All I'll say is that I haven't given up the fight. I won't let my people down. The struggle will continue and we will win."

"So what is Amigos doing now?"

"We still help people get legal and medical aid. We do a lot of clothes drives in the barrio. We even do toy and furniture drives for poor Chicanos across the border."

"I hear you and Canning had some business dealings together in Mexico."

87

He leaned sideways and put two fingers to his temple. "That's right."

"What kind of dealings?"

"Some vacation lots around Mulegé," he said. "I have friends down there who steered me onto a couple of deals. I took Canning in."

In more ways than one, I thought. There was a knock at the door and Villalobos said, "Come in," and the room immediately looked like a Japanese set in a Godzilla movie. The man who filled the door was at least six-five and must have weighed three hundred. He had a meaty, dark-skinned face topped by a greasy wave of black hair and he walked very carefully, as if trying not to pop the buttons on his gray suit.

"Mr. Asch, Alex Cardozo," Villalobos said. "Alex is the president of Amigos."

I stood up and Cardozo held out a hand that looked like a prime rib with fingers. My hand disappeared into it.

"I was just hearing about your great work," I said.

"Nice to meet you," Cardozo said and sort of smiled.

"Mr. Asch is a private investigator," Villalobos said. "He's looking into Hugh Canning's tragic accident."

Cardozo grunted, then leaned against the wall by the door and folded his arms. I tried to picture him on a clothes drive, but somehow couldn't. I turned back to Villalobos. "Did you and Jackson Meriwether ever have any deals together in Mexico?"

Villalobos leaned forward, slowly. "No. Why did you ask that?"

"Just curious," I said. "I just got through talking to the man. He's the kind of person who inspires curiosity. How he makes his money, for instance. He's pretty vague about it."

Villalobos tossed away the question with a curt wave of his hand. "Jackson makes his money wherever an opportunity arises. He doesn't much care where that is."

"There are rumors around that he's into running guns."

"Really? I hadn't heard."

"Some friends of mine in ATF tell me that there is some heavy-duty arms traffic going on across the border right now. I hear a forty-five automatic is worth its weight in gold in Mexico right now."

"I wouldn't know," he said.

"Think there could be any truth to it?"

He smiled as if he thought the suggestion amusing. "Jackson Meriwether, a gunrunner? Yeah. And I'm the head of organized crime."

I watched his face carefully. "His vitamin doctor doesn't seem to think the idea is so farfetched."

One of his eyebrows jumped. "Cassarene? What did he have to say?"

I gave him a perplexed look. "I was talking about the doctor in Juarez. Who is this Cassarene? Is he local?"

He knew he had been had. His lips tightened, and he said, "I don't think I like your style, Mr. Asch. In fact, I don't think I like you. First you come in here dropping hints that my bankruptcy was somehow phony and that I'm some sort of ambulance chaser, and then you cast aspersions on the character of a friend of mine by implying he's into gun trafficking." He looked past me, at Cardozo. "Alex, show Mr. Asch out."

Cardozo moved away from the wall and hovered over me, with his fists doubled and an expectant smile on his face and as if I was Tokyo and he was thinking where he was going to start first. I waited for his greasy black hair to light up and a halitosis heat-ray to come out of his mouth, but he just growled, "Move."

I didn't particularly like his tone, but being a firm believer that the bigger they are, the harder they hit, I moved.

There was only one Cassarene listed under the Physicians in the Yellow Pages: Dr. Milton Cassarene, Orthopedist, 4315 S. Main, Santa Ana. I wrote it in my notebook and drove over to Tustin.

There were three people in Baumgartner's waiting room when I got there, but the receptionist told me that Mr. Baumgartner wanted to see me as soon as I arrived, and showed me into his office.

The room looked even more chaotic than before. One of the women from the other office, a strawberry blonde, was picking up case files from the floor, and Baumgartner sat at his desk, looking harassed.

"Finish that later, Maureen," he said, then told me to sit down. He waited for her to leave, then said, "I keep asking you to excuse the mess, but this time I have a legitimate excuse. Somebody broke in here last night and vandalized the place. We've spent the entire morning trying to get things straightened up."

"Canning's house and here in the same night. That's a hell of a coincidence."

"Isn't it, though? I tried to call you this morning to tell

you about it, but you'd already gone. Sharon told me about the house."

"Was anything taken?"

He looked around, as if taking an instant inventory. "Not that I can determine. They broke into the filing cabinets, and tossed everything on the floor, busted a liquor cabinet in the other room, and jimmied open my desk, but nothing is missing that I can see."

I raked my teeth over my lower lip. The same as at the house.

He leaned forward. "You think it could have something to do with Hugh's death?"

"The house and the office have one thing in common, and that's Canning."

He ran a hand over the side of his head and fell back into his chair. "What the hell could Hugh have had that somebody would do a B and E for?"

"Did Canning ever take any of his cases home?"

"Every once in a while. Every lawyer does."

"Did he take anything lately?"

"I don't know. Sharon would know better than I would."

"How are your cases arranged? Do you have duplicate files?"

"Certainly."

"Are they tagged so that you can tell Canning's cases from your own without opening?"

"Everything in the master file is tagged."

"Have you checked Canning's cases in the master file against the duplicate files, to see if anything is missing?"

"All the file cabinets were broken into. If they took the duplicates, too, it'll be a bitch trying to figure out what's gone, but I see where you're headed. I'll have Maureen get on it right away."

"What was Canning working on lately?" I asked. "Anything special?"

He touched his mustache. "Not that I know of. Just a couple of aggravated-injury cases."

"When you get things sorted out, I'd like to go through them,

91

and whatever else he was working on at the time of his death."

"Why?"

"To see if there is anything in them that might give us an idea what's going on here."

He rubbed the side of his nose with an index finger and shook his head slowly. "I'm sorry, but I can't allow that. I'm sure you understand. My first duty is to my clients. The information in their files is confidential. I'd be breaking a trust by letting you have access to them." He paused. "But I'll tell you what—I'll go through them myself. What would I be looking for?"

"I have no idea."

He smiled mirthlessly. "This is great. The blind leading the blind."

"Something like that," I said. "By the way, do you happen to know of a doctor by the name of Cassarene?"

His dark eyebrows raised. "Milton Cassarene?"

"Maybe. I'm not sure. Is he Jackson Meriwether's doctor?"

"I don't know if he's Meriwether's doctor, but I do know they know each other. Cassarene has been to a couple of his parties."

"Did Canning know him?"

He stuck out his lower lip. "Sure. Cassarene is an orthopedist. Some of his patients are our clients."

"You think Canning might have gone to him for a diagnosis if he felt sick?"

"I shouldn't think so. Cassarene isn't an internist. He's a bone man." His eyes were darkly curious. "Why all the questions about Cassarene?"

"His name just came up, that's all."

"What about the witness who saw Hugh's car parked? Have you talked to him yet?"

I shook my head. "Tomorrow. I got sidetracked by a Ping-Pong game."

He stared at me uncomprehendingly.

"A private joke," I told him, and cleared my throat. "Sharon said something about a check."

"Oh, yes." He opened his desk drawer and brought out a

92

check. He looked at it for a moment with what seemed to be a regretful expression before handing it to me. "Five hundred dollars. If you want to submit your expenses to me—itemized, of course—I'll pay them at the end of the week."

"Sharon said this is money that you're going to owe her from her husband's unfinished cases."

He picked up a pen from the desk and began clicking the retractor with his thumb. "That's correct."

"How much does she have coming?"

He winced. "Not very much, I'm afraid. Half of whatever the fixtures and books in the office comes to, plus twenty-five percent of whatever settlements I realize from the cases Hugh left. Unfortunately, it doesn't look like any of those settlements are going to be very large."

"Twenty-five?" I asked. "What was your split with Canning when he was alive?"

"Sixty-forty, depending on who was taking the case to court."

"What about those cases you yourself were working on at the time of Canning's death?"

"I don't pay the estate anything." I hadn't seen the lawyer smile in a while, but there it was again. He stood up. "I'll go through those files and see what I can find. If you need anything else, just call. And let me know if you turn up anything." I promised him I would on all counts, and left, feeling a little more secure with the check in my pocket. At least I was two and a half days ahead of the game. I figured it would take about another two and a half before I started feeling like a *schmuck* again.

Urban renewal had not gotten around to downtown Santa Ana yet. Instead of going to all that trouble, the county had simply moved all of its offices a few blocks away to spare its employees the view of the blight and left the core intact, a collection of four- and five-story dirty brown brick buildings that housed thrift shops, discount department stores, and shops selling candles and statues of the Blessed Virgin, the names on at least half of which were in Spanish. It was ironic that on Sunday mornings most of the restaurants in what had once been thought of as the center of Wasp-white Orange County conservatism had signs in their windows advertising *menudo*—tripe soup, the traditional Mexican cure for Saturday night.

A block past Cassarene's address, I spotted a parking space and pulled in. As I locked up the car, a blue '64 Chevy covered with spots of gray primer cruised slowly by. The blond passenger in the front seat was busy picking his nose and I wondered what it was about being in a car that made people want to pick their noses. Maybe it was the feeling of being in a self-contained envelope of space that made them think they were invisible to the outside world. Or maybe they didn't give a good goddamn who saw them because the fact that they were moving made it unlikely that they would ever see those witnesses again.

I started up the street. Halfway up the block, Mexican music splashed onto the sidewalk through the open door of a record store and a cluster of Chicano kids with greasy pompadours and dark smooth faces stood outside, bouncing to the rhythm. The Latin beat was infectious, and I found myself snapping my fingers as I walked back to the corner.

Cassarene's building was the kind of nondescript, four-story smooth stone structure that the WPA had put up a lot of in the 1930s. The lobby had polished green marble walls and a green-and-white-checked linoleum floor that was long past cleaning. I stepped into the elevator and punched the button for the third floor.

The door opened into a dim, tired-looking hallway that smelled of dust. I found Cassarene's name on a frosted glass door at the end of it, spread out in gilt letters.

A bell bonged when I opened the door. The waiting room was small and inexpensively furnished with green Naugahyde chairs that didn't quite match the green carpet and some blond Formica tables covered with magazines. All the chairs were occupied, and I counted two neck braces, one arm cast, one set of crutches, and a cane.

The frosted-glass window in the middle of the Venetian canal scene on the wall slid open and a dark-haired woman wearing a white nurse's cap stuck her face out. "Can I help you?"

She was middle-aged and big-boned, and her face was large but pleasant. I handed her a card. "I'd like to talk to Dr. Cassarene."

She inspected the card, then asked the inevitable question. "Do you have an appointment?"

I smiled as warmly as I could. "It's not a medical problem. At least not mine."

"What is it concerning?"

"A death," I said.

"A death? Of one of Dr. Cassarene's patients?"

"That's what I'm trying to find out," I said. "It'll only take five minutes."

"Just a moment, please," she said uncertainly, and slid the glass window shut.

I looked around the room and smiled at the dark, saturnine faces that stared at me. Nobody smiled back, but then none of them looked as if they had much to smile about. Out of the six people in the room, four were Mexican, and all of those were dressed in khaki work clothes or shabby thrift-shop dresses.

After a couple of moments more of being stared at, I saw the door to the right of the painting of the Venetian gondolier open, and the nurse poked her head out. "Mr. Asch, would you come in, please?" I went through the door and found myself in a small vestibule with more gondoliers and a small desk on which sat a telephone, a Selectric typewriter, and a stack of bills being prepared for mailing. The nurse told me to wait there and disappeared into the back; she returned momentarily, trailing a tall, thin man wearing a doctor's white coat. My card was in his hand and he looked from it to me questioningly. "Now, what's all this about a death?"

He had an angular, pale, humorless face with tight, unlined skin and a clean jawline. The nose was high-bridged, with slightly flared nostrils, and he had a full mouth with a prominent lower lip. His eyes were somewhere between brown and gray, surrounded by long, almost feminine lashes, and his hair, too, was brown-gray, and wiry. He tilted his head slightly upward and sighted me down his nose as if he were being confronted by a peasant with a petition.

"I'm investigating the death of Hugh Canning," I said.

He looked at the card again. His fingers were long and thin. They reminded me of pale hairless spiders. "I'm afraid I can't be of any help to you. I don't know anything about it."

"You were friendly with Canning, weren't you?"

He put both the hands into the pockets of his smock, leaving the long thumbs on the outside. "Some of my patients were clients of his," he said noncommittally.

"When did you last speak to him?"

"It's hard to remember exactly. Months ago, anyway."

"On the phone, or in person?"

"On the phone."

The nurse had sat down at her desk and was sorting through the bills she had typed. Cassarene had his back to her so he did not see her look up suddenly and open her mouth, as if to interject something. She apparently changed her mind, however, because she shook her head almost imperceptibly and went back to her work.

"What was the conversation regarding, do you remember?"

"A patient of mine," he said quickly. "I don't remember which one."

"Did Canning ever consult you as a patient himself?"

Without hesitation, he said, "No, never."

"He never asked your professional advice about any physical complaint he might have had?"

"No. Why do you ask?"

"The autopsy on Canning showed that at the time of his death, Canning was suffering from aplastic anemia. I wondered if he'd come to you complaining about any physical symptoms."

The nurse's head snapped up again and she said: "Doctor, that's—"

Cassarene whirled around abruptly and said: "I'll handle this, Irene."

I looked down at her. "What's what?"

Her eyes were still locked on Cassarene's. "Nothing," she said, dropping her gaze back to her bills.

Cassarene turned back to me and the corners of his mouth lifted into what might have been a smile or a wince. "It's an uncommon condition, and very serious. That's what Irene was reacting to. Isn't that right, Irene?"

She looked up briefly and smiled uncomfortably. "Yes. That was it."

"Where did Canning pick it up?" Cassarene asked, his spidery hands dancing with one another.

I kept looking at the nurse, but she wouldn't look up now. "That's what I'm trying to find out."

"I'm afraid I can't help you," Cassarene said. "Canning never came to me for any diagnosis. I wasn't even aware he was ill. So if that's all you wanted to know, you'll have to excuse me—"

I wasn't going to let him go yet. "You did have some contact with Canning socially, didn't you? Through Jackson Meriwether?"

He shifted his weight uncomfortably from one foot to the other. "I believe I saw him once or twice at Jackson's house. At parties. But we never went out socially other than that."

"Isn't that how you first met Canning? Through Meriwether?"

His eyebrows knitted irritably. "It may have been. I don't remember. It was a long time ago."

"Are you good friends with Meriwether?"

He bit the inside of his cheek and held it. "I wouldn't say good friends. I've been to his house several times, as I said."

"For parties."

"Yes, that's right."

I poked a hitchhiking thumb back at the anteroom. "No offense, doc, but your clientele out there doesn't exactly look like it stepped out of the *Bluebook*. Not exactly the kind to put you in contact with the *haut monde*, like Meriwether. Where did you meet him?"

"I really don't see that my social life is any of your business," he snapped, his voice honed to a sharp edge.

I glanced down at the nurse's desk for a name plate, but there was none there. "I'm sorry if I seem nosy, doc, but I'm just trying to get some background—"

"What possible bearing could that kind of information have on Hugh Canning's death?"

"I'm just curious."

"Well, I'm much too busy to stand around here and satisfy your curiosity, Mr. Asch, so if you'll excuse me—"

"Did you first meet him when he became your patient?"

He had been reaching for the handle of the waiting-room door. He cocked his head up to me. "Jackson Meriwether is not my patient."

"That's not what he says. He gives you and your vitamins full credit for saving his life."

He put his hand back into his smock pocket, stared me straight in the eye, and said, "Jackson never told you that."

I smiled easily. "Sure he did. How else would I have gotten the idea? What's in that formula, anyway, doc?"

His eyes brightened, but he was doing everything he could to make his face calm. "I wouldn't know where you picked up the idea, but it is erroneous. I do not supply Jackson Meriwether's vitamins, and I don't know what's in them. I myself think the therapeutic effects of megavitamins are minimal and I certainly think the claims Jackson makes for them are grossly exaggerated. The effects are in his mind."

I shook my head skeptically. "I don't know, doc. I saw him this morning. That's a lot of energy for it to be just in his mind. There was a doctor in New York who used to deal in vitamin shots. Max Jacobson. Ever hear of him?"

"No," he said, but he was lying. His face was like a plaster mark.

"They called him Dr. Feelgood because he put zip into his patients' days. Made them feel almost as good as Meriwether. Of course, he cheated a little. He used to slip a little speed in with the vitamins, just for that extra bit of firepower."

His face turned pink and his mouth twisted slightly at one corner. "Are you trying to insinuate that Jackson Meriwether takes drugs or that I am supplying them?"

"Me?" I put a hand on my chest, trying to sound shocked. "I'd never imply anything like that. Why should I?"

"Then what are you getting at?" He was barely in control now.

"Not a thing, doc. Just making conversation."

"Well, I'm afraid I'm too busy to make conversation. I have patients to see." He reached past me and opened the door. "Don't bother coming back."

"It's been real, doc," I said, then looked down at the nurse. "Good-bye, Miss—"

"Lyle," she said, her eyes darting up at me, the doctor, then back down to her papers.

I started out, then wheeled around abruptly. "One more thing, doc. Know anyone around named Alicia?"

"No," he said quickly. "Miss Lyle, call the next patient."

He shut the door and the glass window slid open and Miss Lyle called, "Mr. Gonzales."

One of the patients with a neck brace got up and went stiffly past me. His expression lightened as he neared the door and he finally looked as if he were almost smiling. Why not? He was going to get an audience with the mayor of Whiplash City.

The door shut behind me and I stood in the hallway, listening to the dust settle on the floor. I wanted to talk to that nurse again, without the benefit of the good doctor's baleful stares, which meant I had a good hour and a half to kill.

I went down to the car and drove a few blocks until I spotted a pay phone outside a 7-Eleven store. I pulled in there and dialed Sharon's number, but got no answer, so I went inside and bought a Coke and drank it in the car.

My mind was cluttered with disparate pieces of the dialogue from the day, and none of the pieces was very dramatic. The people hadn't been very convincing in their parts, either. Everybody in the play was just a little off. Whether that had anything to do with Hugh Canning's death, I didn't know, but it was an incestuous little group of players, that was for sure. Villalobos had business dealings with Canning and Meriwether and had worked out of Canning's office for a time. He also knew Cassarene, because he was the one who came up with the name. Cassarene perhaps was supplying Meriwether with vitamins, and also took care of some of Canning's clients. And the shin bone's connected to the knee bone and here's the word of the Lord.

By the time I'd finished my Coke, I'd taken the connections

apart half a dozen times and reconnected them without coming up with a clear picture of anything.

I tossed the empty can on the floor and started the car. I looked over my shoulder and began backing out slowly, when a car materialized behind me like an apparition. I knew it was not an apparition when my backward motion was halted with a jolting bang and the sound of breaking glass. My gut was filled with a sickening weighty feeling as the knowledge sank in that I'd been hit, and I pulled forward and killed my engine. I'd barely been rolling and the sound had probably been worse than the actual impact, but that was little consolation right now. I cursed all the fates that had put me in this particular time and looked in the rearview mirror. That was when I knew that I was in more trouble than my insurance company could fix.

The blond nosepicker I had noticed earlier was still sitting shotgun in the blue primer Chevy. It was his side I'd backed into. The driver was already out of the car, surveying the damage. He was short and thickly built, and his long black hair was pulled back and tied in a ponytail. He was wearing a black T-shirt with a Harley-Davidson emblem on it and a pair of grease-stained jeans. I locked my door and rolled down the window about six inches without trying to be too obvious.

The driver straightened up slowly from his inspection of the dented door and sauntered over with a rolling gait. He stuck his face in the window and smiled through a droopy black mustache. His breath was bad and I turned my head slightly away to avoid its full bouquet.

"You don't watch where you're goin' too good, do you, man?"

"Sorry," I said, as apologetically as possible. "I didn't see you. You pulled up so fast—"

He put a black-knuckled hand on his chest and reared back indignantly. "*I* pulled up so fast? You tryin' to say this is my fault, man?"

I forced myself to turn and get a good look at him, just in case things didn't work out and I had to I.D. him later from a photograph. He had a wide, flat nose, dark piggish little eyes under

101

pencil-thin brows, and a thick-lipped mouth, all set into an incongruously baby-fat-round face.

"I'm not trying to say it's anybody's fault," I said, more to stall for time than anything else. "I'm just saying I didn't see you." I glanced in the rearview mirror. The impact of the collision must have jammed the passenger door of the Chevy shut and the others were having to get out on the driver's side. That was taking them a little time.

The driver bent down again and rested one of his hairless forearms on the chrome strip outside my window. I took in his two tattoos: a dagger through a heart, and a smiling skull with the words DEATH RIDER beneath it.

"Look, I'm sorry for any inconvenience I've caused you. I'm sure my insurance will take care of it."

His dark pig's eyes wandered over the seat next to me, and he broke into a wide grin when he saw nothing there. The grin reminded me of the skull on his arm, but maybe that was just the mood I was working into.

"Sure," he said. "We'll get it all settled. Why don't you step out of the car?"

I smiled back. "Why don't we call in some law?"

The smile evaporated and he tried the door. The frown got deeper when he found it locked. "Come on out of the car, man. Let's compare driver's licenses."

The butterflies were starting as the adrenaline began to pump, getting my body primed. I could see the nosepicker in the rearview mirror. He was out of the car now, moving toward the back of mine. He was a foot taller than Death Rider and built along the same general lines, except for the beer belly that hung over the top of his jeans. He was holding one hand behind him as if he didn't want me to see what was in it. I thought I'd better get things rolling before his two buddies joined him and he felt secure enough to show me. I looked up at Death Rider and said, "Tell me, shit-breath, are your greaser friends as stupid as you are, or are you just an example of what happens when the fetus doesn't get enough oxygen?"

102

Anger flashed in the dark eyes, and suddenly the pig was a wild boar. "You're dead meat, motherfucker—"

He reached through the window for the doorlock, but I'd been preparing for that move from the time I saw him getting out of the car. I grabbed his wrist with both hands and slammed it down across the window, forcing it downward with all the weight I could get into it. There was a loud, sickening snap as his forearm broke somewhere between the elbow and the wrist. He screamed and collapsed on the pavement below the window.

I rolled up the window, started the car, and looked into my rear-view mirror all at the same time. The scream had temporarily halted the other three, but they were running for the car now, and they were no longer bothering to hide what they had in their hands—big, heavy metal things that did not look compatible with my skull.

I got the window all the way up just as they came up on both sides of the car. I put one hand over my eyes and turned away from the window, as pieces of splintering glass hit me on the cheek.

My tires exhaled smoke and the rear end of my car smashed into the side of theirs and pushed it back about two feet. They shouted and ran after me, their rain of destruction continuing indiscriminately on my car hood, side mirror, anything they could hit. There still wasn't room to get out, the impact had not moved their car far enough, so I put it into drive and pulled forward again to the curb. Then I shoved it into reverse again and floored it. My neck snapped back as my car smashed into theirs again, but I still did not have enough clearance.

The nosepicker ran around behind me and began to go to work on the back window. That was the last window I had any visibility out of at all and if I didn't want to navigate by Braille, I knew I'd better make it out on this shot.

My tires screamed as I pulled up to the curb and I nearly ripped out my transmission jerking it into reverse. I turned the wheel so that I would hit the rear of their car where it was angled, and kept my foot to the floor. Smoke from my burning tires billowed up outside the windows and the shrieking, nails-on-blackboard sound of metal scraping against metal mingled with their shouts as my car smashed into and slid along the side of theirs. I couldn't see a damned thing through my windows, but suddenly the resistance was no longer there and I was accelerating backward. I hit the brakes, put it into drive, and took off in the direction I thought the driveway to be. The front end of my car bucked as I hit the street. There was a loud blaring of an angry horn as a car swerved to miss me, and I yanked on the steering wheel to get over. I could hear the driver shouting as he went by. Everybody seemed to be mad at me today.

They had punched out a tiny hole in the windshield, just under the curve of the steering wheel, and I drove, looking through that until I could roll down what was left of the driver's window and stick my head out to see if they were following. They didn't seem to be. I made a right at the next block, then a left, then another right, and found myself driving down a narrow residential street lined with slat-sided houses painted in pastel colors.

I felt like a dog, driving with my head out the window, but the wind felt lovely and cool on my sweat-covered face. I drove for a while, making random lefts and rights, then pulled up in front of a peeling green stucco house with a large century plant out front. Two small raggedy Mexican kids were playing with sticks on the front porch. They stopped what they were doing and stared at me strangely.

My clothes were soaked with perspiration and I was still shaky. I leaned my head against the back of the seat and closed my eyes and took deep, even breaths, breathing consciously from the diaphragm. After a few minutes of that, I'd unwound enough to survey the damage.

Most of the window on the driver's side was in pieces inside the door and there was a generous and attractive assortment of deep dents over my hood and doors.

Those boys had had mayhem on their minds, there was no doubt about it, and it had not been any spur-of-the-moment whim on their part. They'd followed me, and set me up. The question was why? And by whom?

I debated about whether or not to go to the cops. It wasn't much of a debate, really. They were probably already looking for me anyway. There should have been enough eyewitnesses inside the store to back up my side of it. Besides, I was not about to eat the tab for the car and I sincerely doubted that Sharon would, which meant I was going to have to file a police report on it for the insurance company, and if I didn't do it then—and tell the truth— I was going to have to do it later and make up a phony vandalism story, which wouldn't stand up for fifty-seven seconds if the cops did have my plate.

The two kids on the porch laughed when they saw me pull away from the curb with my head out the window, so I barked for them as I drove off.

The Santa Ana PD was in a new glass building in the civic center and its clean and glossy modernism succeeded only in looking uneasy and contrived against the seedy backdrop of the downtown area. After telling the cop at the desk that I wanted to report an accident, I was turned over to a middle-aged, uniformed sergeant from Traffic named Neely whose beefy, red-nosed face carried in it the tired resignation that making out reports of traffic violations was the best he could expect to get from life. He took me back to a desk in a large, brightly lighted room filled with desks and began asking me questions in an expressionless monotone and punching out my answers on a typewriter with two-fingered disinterest.

After he had finished, he yawned, then picked up a porcelain mug with the name BUZZ on it in gilt letters, excused himself, and left the room. When he came back five minutes later, the mug was full of black coffee and there was more interest on his face. "We had a call about this about twenty minutes ago. The manager of the Seven-Eleven called in your plates."

I leaned forward. "Did he get the plates of the other car?"

"Yeah."

I waited. He waited, too. Apparently, he came to the conclusion that I was going to wait longer than he, because he said, "What kind of a car did you say it was?"

" 'Sixty-four Chevy. Blue with primer spots."

He nodded. "That fits the description called in by the manager of the Seven-Eleven, but that's about all that fits."

"What do you mean?"

He rubbed the back of his neck and made a face as if he'd gotten a sudden pain there. "The plate number the manager took down was from a 1959 Ford Fairlane. Only that car isn't on the road anymore. It was in an accident and scrapped four years ago."

I mulled that one over. "Switched plates?"

He shrugged. "Maybe. Maybe the witness screwed up writing down the number. It happens. Just in case, though, I'm running a description of the car through the computer to see if we can come up with any stolens that match." He paused. "You say these guys followed you?"

"I'm pretty sure of it."

"What makes you so sure of it?" he asked skeptically.

"I told you, I saw them earlier—"

"Low riders like to cruise. It's more likely you just both happened to be in the same place at the same time."

"Let's just say it's a feeling I have."

"A feeling," he said skeptically.

"I *am* a detective," I reminded him. "As a cop, you probably rely on those feelings often in your work."

He shrugged nonchalantly and said: "And you think they followed you in order to work you over?"

"That'd be my guess."

"Why?"

"I don't know."

"You down here on business or pleasure?"

I saw no reason to go into it with him. He didn't want to hear it anyway. "Visiting a friend."

He asked for the name and address, and I gave them to him.

He sighed heavily and asked, "If we find them, you want to file criminal charges? You might make a vandalism charge stick. Maybe. But from what you told me, I doubt an assault rap would get very far. There seems to be a question about who assaulted who. Sounds like you did more damage to them than they did to you."

"I don't want to file charges. I just wanted to get my version into the records in case *they* file assault charges against *me*. Or in case they try it again."

He nodded and gave me a small approving smile, to tell me I'd made the right decision. No more typing.

"Personally, I think you're off base there, Mr. Asch. I personally think you were in the same place by coincidence, weren't looking where you were going, and they got pissed when you backed into them. But if they do turn up, or if the car comes up stolen, I'll let you know."

I used the pay phone out front to call the local Farmer's Insurance office and explained my situation to an agent there. She gave me the address and name of a body shop and told me to have the car taken there, that an adjuster would be out in the morning to inspect the damage. The address was not far from the police station, but too far to risk driving the car in that condition. My eyeballs were getting windburned.

It took the AAA half an hour to get there and hook up my car. I rode with the driver over to Sampson's Body and Glass, where a redheaded man in dirty overalls gave me a repair estimate of $827.

When I told him not to count the radio antenna in the estimate, that I wanted it left alone, he looked at me as if I were the worst trained-bird act he had ever seen, muttered something unintelligible, and told me to knock twenty bucks off the tab. I gave him Sharon's number, told him an insurance adjuster would be by in the morning to look things over, and took a cab over to the closest Avis office. The cheapest thing they had was a year-old white Nova. I took it and drove around looking for a bar. I needed a drink and I needed a telephone, so I figured I might as well combine the two. I wound up in a place called The Hair of the Dog, whose interior design and clientele matched its name. I ordered a vodka-tonic. The bartender, an amiable and immensely fat man who moved surprisingly lithely, told me that the phone was in the back. I paid him for my drink and went to look for it. I found it and a copy of the phone book equidistant between two restroom doors marked SETTERS and POINTERS, and looked up hospitals in the yellow pages. Since the County Medical Center was the closest to where I'd broken Death Rider's arm, I started with it.

After getting Emergency, I identified myself as Sergeant Neely of the Santa Ana PD and said there had been a report of an accident an hour ago in which an unidentified Caucasian male, mid-twenties, long black hair, five-nine, one-eighty, with a skull tattoo on the right forearm, had possibly broken his arm. The woman told me that there had been nobody admitted with a broken arm for the past six hours. Twenty minutes later, I'd called fourteen hospitals and gotten two broken arms—a thirteen-year-old girl who'd fallen off her bike and a seventy-year-old man who had broken his wrist tripping over a sprinkler. Maybe I hadn't broken Death Rider's arm after all. Or maybe he hadn't gone to a hospital.

I called Cassarene's office, but got no answer. It was after six and everybody had probably gone home. There was no Irene Lyle listed in the phone book, but there was an I. J. Lyle listed in Santa Ana. I dialed the number, but got no answer there, either. She may not have made it home yet—if I. J. Lyle and Irene Lyle were the same person.

I went back to the bar and finished my drink. She could wait until tomorrow. You could buy just so much for two hundred a day plus expenses.

108

12

Sharon opened the front door holding a barbecuing fork in her hand. I held up both of mine. "I'm unarmed. You wouldn't fork a man in cold blood, would you?"

She smiled coyly. "I think I'd try to heat it up a little first."

I walked in past her and went directly to the couch and collapsed. She shut the door and said, "You're late."

I felt the day catching up with me and closed my eyes. "Yeah. I ran into a little trouble."

"What kind of trouble?"

When I opened my eyes, she was standing over me. "What kind of trouble?"

I proceeded to tell her about playing bumper cars with Kool and the Gang. She listened with rapt attention, then said, wide-eyed, "You mean you think those men were sent to beat you up?"

"I don't have any proof of it. It's just an educated guess on my part."

She sat down on the edge of the couch. "But . . . why?"

"Want another educated guess? To get me out of the way. Somebody obviously doesn't like the questions I've been asking. Whoever it is probably figured I wouldn't ask too many with my jaws wired shut."

"You mean about Hugh?"

"I need a drink," I said petulantly. "Get me one, and I'll tell you all about it."

She stood up. "I've made a pitcher of vodka gimlets."

"Sold."

She went into the kitchen and came back a moment later with a gimlet over ice. I sipped it and smacked my lips. There was just the right amount of lime juice in it, just enough to take the edge off the vodka, but not enough to overwhelm it.

"Perfect."

"Are you hungry?"

I thought about it and realized I hadn't eaten all day. "Famished."

"The coals are about ready, so come outside and tell me about it while I put on the steaks."

In the kitchen, she picked up a platter with two beautifully marbled New Yorks, and we went outside on the wood-planked terrace. The lights of the city below were like a thousand flickering fires along the beach. She put on the steaks while I stretched out on a chaise with my drink and told her about my day. When I got to Cassarene, she turned and said, "I met him once. At one of Jackson Meriwether's parties." She looked at me keenly. Her eyes were colorless in the washed-out light coming from the house. "Where do you think he fits in?"

"I'm not sure he does. But I know one thing: Meriwether was flying when I saw him this morning and it wasn't on selenium and B. And I got a definite rise out of Cassarene when I mentioned Max Jacobson's name."

"Who's Max Jacobson?"

"He was a prominent physician in New York who used to specialize in vitamin injections. They called him Dr. Feelgood because his shots would make his patients feel terrific. And he had some celebrities as patients. His particular formula was a mixture of B-vitamins, methamphetamines, male hormones, and the phosphorescences of certain minerals given off under ultraviolet

110

light. It was the meth that made them feel good, of course. The rest of it was snake oil. They called the stuff 'redline' because whoever took it was taching pretty high. Cassarene looked like he was going to throw a breaker when I mentioned his name."

"Is that what you think Cassarene is doing?"

"I don't know. I don't even know for sure that he's supplying Meriwether with anything. But if he is, it would explain why both of them would be reluctant to admit it. Dr. Feelgood got his license yanked for dispensing his elixir."

The steaks sizzled loudly as she turned them over. "But what does any of that have to do with Hugh?"

"Whoever broke in here and your husband's office was looking for something. Something they thought he had. If they knew he had it before he died, it would create a whole other dimension to this thing."

"What dimension?"

"Murder."

She turned to me wide-eyed. "My God. You're telling me Hugh was murdered?"

"I'm not telling you anything at this stage, except that your husband had somebody very nervous about something."

She waved the fork in the air and said in a tense whine, "But what? Who would have wanted to kill Hugh?"

"If we find a why, then we can talk about a who. I've worked a lot of cases, but none with more goddamn connections than this one. We've got a mystery-man millionaire who runs around like he's jockeying for pole position all the time and who is rumored to be running guns to Latin America and who your late husband publicly threatened. We have an accident-investigator–restaurateur whom your husband also hated and who has his hands into everything and anything that will net him some bucks and who has political ties in Mexico, where guns are worth more than diamonds. We have a doctor who knew all three of them and who may or may not be supplying vitamins or speed or both to Meriwether—"

111

"You think one of them did it?" she asked anxiously. "You think Hugh had proof that Meriwether was running guns and they killed him because of it?"

She was getting ahead of me. "Whoa. I'm not saying anything yet. I'm just saying we've suddenly got another possibility."

She shivered and her eyes drifted away. "Murder. The thought of it is horrible."

"Not from one standpoint. If he was murdered, the insurance company has to pay off."

Her eyes snapped back to me and she said crossly, "Do you think it would make me happy that Hugh was murdered, just so I could collect the insurance money?"

"Don't be silly. I was just stating a fact."

She pointed the fork at me. "If Hugh was murdered, I want whoever did it brought to justice, but not because of the insurance money. I want it for Hugh. I don't want them to be able to get away with it, Jake."

I stood up and went to her and put my arm around her shoulder. "I know. And don't worry. *If* something like that went down, we'll find out about it. Right now, though, it's just a possibility, and a dim one at that. It could all turn out to be smoke in the end." I pointed at the barbecue. "Speaking of smoke, the steaks are done, I believe, and I'm starved."

She took them off the grill and went inside. I got the potatoes out of the oven while she tossed the salad. I popped the cork from a bottle of Cabernet and she lit the candles on the dining-room table. We ate in front of the windows, framed by Laguna lights. She ate pensively, her eyes troubled, and did not say half a dozen words through the meal. After we took the dishes into the kitchen, we sat on the floor in front of the crackling fire, sipping Colombian coffee and snifters of Grand Marnier. She still was not talking and she wouldn't look at me. She seemed to be trying to work something out. Finally, she turned to me and said: "Maybe we should forget the whole thing, Jake."

"What whole thing?"

"The investigation."

I pulled my head back and looked at her.

"All through dinner, I've been thinking. The money isn't worth it. If what you said is true, if Hugh really was murdered, it could be dangerous for you—"

"Don't worry about that."

"I can't help it," she said, her face contorting. "If anything happened to you, I'd never forgive myself."

"Nothing is going to happen to me."

She looked up. "But if it did—if those men had hurt you today—I couldn't take that. Not now. When I asked you into this, I didn't know it would be dangerous."

"I'll be okay," I assured her. "Occasionally in this business you run into a risk factor. Not often, but occasionally. It comes with the territory. Actually, it makes things a little more interesting. It's whetted my curiosity."

"I can remember a few times when your curiosity almost got you killed."

"Almost doesn't count. Anyway, it's better than tracking down stolen pie recipes in Boise."

She touched my hand, lightly. "I'm not saying all this for altruistic reasons. It's for my sake I'm saying it. I couldn't stand to lose two men I love this close together. I really don't think I could handle it."

"What do you mean, 'two men you love'?"

Her eyes probed mine. "You know I love you. I always have."

I kept staring into her eyes, trying to see the lie there. "Bullshit."

"It's true."

"You just got through telling me how much you loved your husband."

"I did. But that doesn't mean that I stopped loving you."

I turned away. Those were the words I'd been waiting five years for. This was going to be my big Bogart walkout scene where I would display cool indifference to her teary groveling. Only I

113

wasn't feeling much like Bogie at the moment. More like Fred MacMurray facing Barbara Stanwyck in *Double Indemnity*. Christ, how did I get myself into this?

I got up and moved to the window. I needed some distance, fast. I stood there, looking out at the lights, thankful she did not follow me.

She was vulnerable and confused and probably even believed what she was saying. But I was not confused or vulnerable and I was not about to get caught up in that shredder again, even though I didn't blame her totally anymore. After what she had told me, I guessed I had done my own share of shredding five years ago.

I turned back to her. She was watching me. I needed to change the subject.

"So you never really did tell me what happened between you and the ball player."

"You won't let that one go, will you?" she asked, with some amusement in her voice.

"You know me," I said, grinning. "Mr. Detective. Never could stand an unsolved mystery."

She sipped her drink. "For one thing, Sparky was married."

"Jesus. This gets better and better."

"Oh, that didn't matter, really. He kept promising he was going to leave his wife and marry me, but it was really a game we both played. We both knew he never would, but that wasn't important then. It was one party after another, which was what I needed after us, I guess. Now that I think about it, I guess I was kind of using Sparky to get over you."

"So what happened?"

She shrugged. "I woke up in a hotel room in Cincinnati one morning and realized I was thinking beyond the next day's game. I was thinking beyond the end of the season. Ball players never grow up, Jake. They don't have to, not while it lasts. They go from high school to college right into the pros, and they never have to think past the end of the season. So I told Sparky I was leaving, and I left."

"Didn't he try to stop you?"

114

"Sure he did. He cried. He swore he'd file for divorce the next day if I wanted, but I knew it would always be the next day for him. I didn't want him to, anyway. It wasn't him I'd been in love with, it was the whole scene, the franticness of it. Once that didn't hold any more magic for me, there was no way it was going to work."

I came back over and sat down on the floor next to her. "Tell me something."

She leaned close. "What?"

"If I'd stolen a chandelier for you, would you have stayed?"

"I don't know."

"I was never the chandelier-stealing type."

"I know," she said, smiling gently. "I wouldn't have you any other way."

She leaned over and stroked my cheek with the back of her hand, then pulled my mouth toward hers. Her lips parted and her tongue hotly searched for mine; then she pulled back suddenly, and we stared at each other. She might have found panic in my eyes if she looked hard enough.

She ran a hand slowly down my chest and farther down, stopping to trace the outline of the bulge in my pants. I reached over and slid my hand into her blouse and cupped her breast. She moaned softly and shivered as the nipple hardened between my fingers. I unbuttoned her blouse all the way and pulled her breasts to my mouth and she dropped her head back and opened her mouth, wide, but no sound came out. Her grip on my crotch tightened and she fumbled with the zipper. She pulled my pants off almost angrily and began exploring with her tongue. She moaned as her mouth worked until I felt close to coming. Then she stood up suddenly and said urgently, "I want you inside me."

She undressed hurriedly and lay down next to me. I lifted her legs high in the air and plunged deep inside her. She frantically licked inside my ear and whispered my name over and over and I was lost in her. Then she was screaming that she was coming and I exploded inside her. For a long time after that, we just lay there, holding on to each other.

115

"God, I needed that," she sighed after a while.

I didn't say anything.

"You know, for the last eight months we were married, Hugh and I never made love. He'd lost interest in it. He claimed his mind was on too many other things. He swore it wasn't me, but I never believed him." She rolled over and propped herself up on one elbow and ran a hand gently over my chest. "You're still the best."

"Only with you."

She smiled. "I do love you, you know."

I still didn't say anything. What could I say? That I hoped to Christ she was telling the truth because I felt the same way and that I'd known it the moment I'd heard her voice on the phone? That what I'd felt for her five years before had never left me? That all the rest of it, even my agreeing to work for her had just been a diversionary tactic to salve a wounded ego? To tell her any of that represented a somehow irrevocable step and the fact was, I didn't yet trust her enough to make it. And I didn't trust myself. I'd been telling her the truth when I said that lately I'd begun to doubt my own ability to sustain a relationship with anyone.

I leaned over and kissed her tenderly and we made love again, more slowly this time, more intimately, and she cried when she came. Maybe it was an illusion, but I felt as if I'd reached inside her and touched something I'd never touched before.

She slept after that and I lay awake for a long time, listening to her breathing. There were a lot of things to think about. It was sometime after one when I finally managed to drift off, without coming up with any solutions.

13

The log in the fireplace was as gray as the dawn outside the windows when I woke up. I sat up, and Sharon came out of the hallway, belting a red silk kimono. She bent down and kissed me on the forehead. "Good morning," she said cheerily and continued out to the kitchen.

"What time is it?" I called to her.

"Ten to seven."

My head was a little fuzzy from the Grand Marnier and my body was telling me it could use another hour or so of sleep. In the kitchen, a pot clanged and I knew I wasn't going to get it. I pulled on my pants and went in. "Why, may I ask, are we getting up at ten to seven?"

She poured out two cups of coffee and handed me one. "You've got a lot to do today."

"Really? What?" The coffee was strong, the way I liked it. I sat down at the breakfast table and she sat across from me.

"That's just what I was going to ask you."

"Remind me never to move in with a client again."

"Never move in with a client again."

"Thanks." I took another sip. I took too much and it scalded my tongue. I muttered an obscenity, softly.

She hunched over the table and said, "I've been thinking about some of the things you said last night."

I panicked and thought back, trying to remember if I'd told her I loved her. She defused my fears by saying, "If Hugh had something on somebody and they didn't find it, they might come back looking for it again."

"I doubt it. They tore this place apart pretty good. At least good enough to be convinced whatever it was isn't here. Anyway, I wouldn't worry too much about them coming back here. You have a gun in the house?"

"A gun?" She seemed surprised by the question. "No."

"I've got one in the trunk of the car. I'll give it to you if it'll make you feel safer."

She shook her head. "It wouldn't. I wouldn't have the nerve to use it if something happened, anyway."

I looked at the clock on the wall, then pointed to the phone on the counter behind her. "Hand me the phone, will you?"

She did, and I dialed Jim Gordon's home number in Playa Del Rey. Jim was an L.A. County Assistant D.A. and longtime friend who was built like a little bear and who had the same temperament in court; whatever attorney he was up against had better bag him with the first shot; otherwise, the man was bound to get mauled. He answered the phone with a crisp "Hello?"

"Jim, this is Jake."

"Jake. What's happening?"

"Same old stuff. What's new with you?"

"I'm in the middle of a trial right now."

"Something juicy?"

"Just a routine little murder case. A fag cut up his ex-lover and the ex-lover's roommate with a band saw, arranged the pieces on the lover's bed, and set fire to the house. The fireman who went in had quite a surprise when he grabbed an arm to pull the guy out."

"Sounds charming," I said.

"It's the 1980s version of *An American Tragedy*."

"Listen, Jim," I said, before he tried to relate the entire novel,

118

"I'm calling because I need a favor. I need a couple of names run for priors."

"No sweat. Let me get a pencil." He was gone momentarily, then was back. "Go ahead."

"Jackson Meriwether." I spelled it for him. "George Villalobos. Tony Halstead. Alex Cardozo. Milton Cassarene."

"A couple means two."

"I was speaking figuratively."

"Apparently."

"When do you think you can have it?"

"I'll have one of the investigators run them when I get to the office, but I'll be in court all day, so I won't be able to get back to you until tonight. Where are you going to be?"

"I'll call you at home. Say, around seven?"

"Yeah, that's good."

Sharon looked at me curiously as I hung up.

"Who is that Cardozo you mentioned?"

"One of Villalobos's henchmen. I met him yesterday."

"You really think any of them have any criminal records?"

"We'll know by tonight," I said. "At least it might give us a better idea of who we're dealing with."

She got up and poured herself another cup of coffee. "You want some breakfast?"

"No, thanks. I'll grab a bite on the way."

"On your way to where?"

"I thought I'd take a little drive over to Elsinore and talk to Transcontinental's prize witnesses. After that, I don't know."

She gave me a sidelong glance. "Seems like a rather haphazard way of conducting business."

I nodded. "I always got Unsatisfactory in school for sloppy work habits. But don't worry. You'll get your money's worth."

I took a fresh cup of coffee into the bathroom. After getting shaved, showered, and dressed in a navy-blue short-sleeved shirt and gray slacks, I called the Elsinore Skydiving School, just to make sure Del Herbert was going to be in that day. The man who

119

answered the phone said Del would be in around 8:30.

I kissed Sharon good-bye and told her I would be back at seven at the latest. At the front door, she said, "Please be careful, Jake."

"I've got to be. I couldn't stand to listen to you howl about paying for hospitalization on top of the car rental." She pinched the back of my arm hard, above the elbow. It hurt, but I didn't let her know it. I just grinned like the iron man that I was and went out to the rara Avis in the driveway.

A light morning fog clung to the tops of the mountains above the pass as I drove up the Ortega Highway. When I got to the spot where Canning had gone over, I pulled off and killed my engine. I sat there thinking and listening to the water hiss over the rocks below. After ten minutes, I started up the car and took off. The fog had burned off by the time I reached the top of the mountain range and Lake Elsinore glistened below me in the sun like some incongruous blue waterhole set into an arid, brown land. I made the steep, winding descent down the side of the mountain and drove into town.

Despite its name, the ghost of Hamlet's father had never been reported walking the dusty roofs of Elsinore. No ghosts at all, in fact, unless you wanted to get metaphorical and count the ghost of the town itself. What had in the 1920s been a busy resort was now just a sleepy, run-down little town of characterless court-type motels and old wood-sided, prairie-style houses, with an occasional decayed Victorian mansion thrown in for gothic flavoring. The old mineral baths where the old and the lame had flocked to cure their ills were still operating, and the lake was still a tourist attraction, but the lake had been steadily drying up for the past ten years, and an aura of decay hung over the old baths, its clientele having deserted it for newer, more chic health spas.

I pulled into a gas station and asked where the skydiving school was; the attendant told me to drive around the lake and keep going for about a mile and I'd see it.

The lake was very blue and looked deceptively deep behind the moth-eaten palms and willowy elms that lined its shore, and then there were no more palms and no more water, just dry grass, and an occasional scrub oak. After a half mile or so, I saw a sign for the school and turned off onto a narrow cement road and pretty soon came onto a group of low, Quonset-hut–type buildings. I parked in front and got my cassette recorder out of the glove compartment and went inside.

A young, short-haired man at the desk inside fit right in with the army-barracks feel of the place. He told me that Herbert was outside with a class and pointed the way out back.

I followed the high wooden fence to a large, fenced-in corral-like area, at one end of which was a wooden platform about eight feet off the ground with steps leading up to it. A small group of men and women was lined up at the foot of the steps; one at a time, to the commands of a man standing at the base of the platform, they would climb the steps and jump off.

The man was tall and lean and was wearing a pair of faded Levis and a khaki-colored T-shirt with an open parachute and the logo of the school on the front. He was in his early twenties and had a square-jawed, handsome face without much intelligence in it. His sun-streaked brown hair was long and unkempt and he had to keep brushing it out of his eyes with quick flicks of his hand.

After a bit, he stopped the group from jumping and told them that they could take a break for ten minutes, and I took the opportunity to approach him.

"Mr. Herbert?"

He turned. "Yeah?"

I offered my hand. "My name is Asch. I'm a private investigator." His handshake, as I expected, was strong. "The people at Transcontinental told me where to find you. I'd like to ask you a couple of questions, if you don't mind."

He squinted at me. "I already gave them a statement of what I saw. How many times do I have to say the same thing before I get my money?"

"I don't work for the insurance company," I said. "I'm working for the widow of the man who died in the accident. Your testimony is an important piece in Transcontinental's claim that her husband committed suicide. The thousand bucks they're paying you for it is costing her two hundred thousand."

"I'm sorry about that," he said defensively, "but I can't help it. What I saw is what I saw. What they want to make of it, however they want to interpret it, is up to them."

"I realize that," I said. "I would like to ask you a few questions, though, just to make sure in my own mind what you really did see. Okay?"

I asked him if he would mind if I taped our conversation and he said he wouldn't, so I suggested we talk away from the class so we wouldn't pick up their voices. We walked down a few yards and I set the recorder on the fence and turned it on.

Herbert told me the same story I'd read in his deposition. On the evening of September 9, he and his girl friend were returning home from Dana Point when they saw a red Porsche parked alongside the highway. The time had been ten-thirty or a little after, he was sure about that, because they had stopped for some dinner at a restaurant in Capistrano and had left there at ten-fifteen. The spot where they had seen the Porsche was no more than fifteen or twenty minutes up the highway. He said he slowed down when he saw the car because he thought at first that the driver might be having mechanical problems, but he didn't stop. He and his girl friend were anxious to get home and Herbert figured that if the driver of the Porsche was in trouble, he would have flashed his emergency roadside lights or gotten out of the car to wave Herbert down.

He got touchy when I noted that he had only stepped forward after a reward was offered, but I really didn't think there was much that could be done with that. The one thing he said that I found extremely interesting that the good people at Transcontinental had not apprised me of was the position of the person Herbert had seen in the Porsche. According to him, the solitary figure in the car had been sitting in the *passenger's* seat. At first I thought he had made a mistake, that he'd meant to say driver's seat, but he insisted he had only seen one person's head through the back window and that it had been on the passenger side of the car. He did not get a good look at the figure, however, and could not state positively whether it was a man or a woman, although his feeling was it was a man. The position of the Porsche's passenger was another reason Herbert had not stopped. The thought had struck him that there might have been another person in the car, out of sight, and that he or she might have been engaged in some kind of extracurricular oral activity and did not want to be disturbed. I was going to castigate him for having a dirty mind, but then thought of a few incidents in my own salacious past and kept my mouth shut.

Herbert's girl friend worked in a drugstore in Elsinore, and her boss let her stop selling Tylenol long enough for her to give me a statement. She was a buzzy little blonde, who answered all my questions with a vibrant alacrity and most of the answers matched Herbert's. There were some differences, but the kind that would be due to differences in perception. She had seen somebody sitting in the car, too, on the passenger's side, but her identification of the gender of the person was even more vague than Herbert's.

It was almost noon by the time I pulled out of town, but my mind was only half on the curves and cutbacks of the highway. I kept going over Herbert's story, searching for weak points, but could not come up with many. If that pair got tripped up, it wouldn't be because they were lying, which meant we had to fit their testimony into the fatal scenario. Except how the hell did it fit? Was Canning alone, and if so, why had he been in the passenger's seat? Had someone else been driving? The mysterious Alicia? Maybe Herbert's dirty mind was not that far off the mark. Maybe both he and his girl friend were mistaken about the person in the car. Maybe one of them was mistaken and the other was extremely suggestible. Maybe, maybe, maybe.

I was rudely shaken out of my ruminations as I rounded a blind curve and nearly ran up the exhaust pipe of a semi pulling a flatbed loaded with lengths of steel pipe. I hit my brakes and fell in behind. The chrome smokestack of the truck belched out a black cloud of diesel and the huge engine roared beleagueredly as

123

the driver downshifted and I looked at my speedometer. The needle pointed to ten.

The line in the middle of the road was double yellow, and I edged the nose of the rental as close to it as I could get, just to see if there was someplace ahead where I could pass safely, if illegally; but I couldn't see around the corner of the flatbed. There probably was not, anyway—we were going through a series of blind curves—and the prospect of being stuck behind this turtle for the next ten miles began to irritate me. Then I took a deep breath, thought, to hell with it, and tried to relax. There was nothing I could do about it anyway. I went back to thinking about the case and waited for a passing lane.

The lake below was small, a piece of blue plastic inserted into the land, and I was looking down at it when I heard the noise over the song of my radio. The hollow sound of metal sliding against metal. My eyes jerked up to see the top piece of pipe sliding backward off the top of the stack of the truck bed. I instinctively jerked the wheel to the right; the cliff side of the highway loomed up before me, and I whipped the wheel the other way as hard as I could, just as the piece of pipe left the truck bed. The huge pipe seemed to be suspended in air, poised above the car. I slammed on the brakes and threw myself sideways across the seat, as the front windshield shattered, showering me with glass, and the steel tube rammed over my head, through the car like a giant skewer.

The car hit something, stopped, then stalled, then started moving again—backward. As I lay across the front seat, a thousand thoughts jammed my adrenaline-filled mind, but one of them crowded the others out—the thought of that 1,500-foot drop a short distance to my right. I sat up and hit my head, hard, on the pipe, screamed an obscenity, ducked under it, and jerked on the handbrake.

I looked around. My car was stopped diagonally across the oncoming lane of the highway, on a blind curve, its nose about ten feet from the rock face of the mountain. That was when I thought about head-ons.

I shoved it into park and scrambled out of the passenger side and ran up to the bend in the road. There were no other cars coming or going. The truck was nowhere in sight, but I could hear its engine laboring up the grade. I looked back at the rental. The pipe had entered through the right side of the windshield and crossed the car diagonally, exiting the side window in the backseat. An Avis shish kebab.

I heard a car motor and looked up the highway to see an old Pontiac coming down the road. I ran into the middle of the highway, frantically waving my hands, and it slowed. A grizzled old man eyed me suspiciously as I came up to his window, but his look softened a bit when I told him there was an accident up ahead and that I'd appreciate it if he'd tell the CHP's when he got down to Elsinore.

He promised he would, and I stayed and slowed down the cars coming down the highway. I figured it was the least I could do after causing all the trouble.

14

It took the CHP's half an hour to get to the scene and another hour to get the car towed away and a report made. I wasn't much help to them. I hadn't noticed the color, make, or license number of the truck, or much else about it, for that matter. By the time those things were of any interest to me, I had had other matters on my mind.

I called Sharon from the Highway Patrol station in Elsinore. I told her I'd had a little mishap and asked if she could pick me up. She wanted to hear all about it, of course, but aside from telling her that the car was wrecked and I was okay, I didn't tell her much. I just told her that I would give her all the details when she got here.

It was nearly four by the time Sharon came walking through the doors of the Highway Patrol station. She stopped and put her hands on her hips and shook her head. "If this is your idea of being careful, I'd hate to be around when you're living dangerously. What happened?"

"I almost got made into a corndog, that's what happened. Asch on a stick."

"What in God's name are you talking about?"

126

I put my hand around her waist and began steering her toward the door. "I'll tell you all about it in the car."

The CHP station sat right on the lake, and the late-afternoon sun silvered its surface. We got into the Mercedes and she said, "Okay, out with it. What happened?"

"I ducked."

"Be serious."

"I *am* being serious," I protested. "I ducked, therefore I am. Pull in anywhere that you see a sign that says 'liquor.' I need a drink." As she drove, I filled her in on a few details.

"And the driver of the truck didn't stop to see if you were all right?"

"No, and I'm glad he didn't. He might have come back and finished the job."

"You think it was on purpose?" She wasn't asking.

"I think I'm getting tired of accidents waiting for me to happen to them. I haven't been in an accident in eight years and suddenly I'm in two in two days."

"You think it's because of Hugh?"

"Good old Hugh is the only reason I'm here."

I was beginning to resent Hugh. He had succeeded in unnecessarily complicating my life and now he was trying to get me killed. Just by dying. She picked it up and said, "You sound mad."

"I always get mad when I have no idea what's going on and somebody tries to kill me for it."

"You could quit."

"Believe me, I'm giving it serious consideration."

We passed a row of eucalyptus trees and the sunlight reflecting off the lake made a strobelike effect through them.

"What did Herbert say?" she asked after a bit.

"Both he and his girl friend seem pretty straight." I told her about the person Herbert and his girl friend had seen being in the passenger seat.

"Passenger seat? Why would Hugh have been in the passenger seat?"

127

"I have no idea."

"Well, it's got to mean something."

"Maybe it does, maybe not. It's curious, anyway."

She fell into a pouty silence. I spotted a small market by the lake where the highway turned and went up the mountain, and told her to stop. I went inside and bought a half-pint of 114-proof Old Granddad and managed to kill a good portion of it before we reached Sharon's house, but my liver must have been working overtime because I was no drunker than I'd been when we left Elsinore.

Sharon made herself a drink while I called Jim, and she watched as I scribbled notes. When I hung up, she picked up the paper and looked at it. "What do all these letters mean?"

"That your husband was friendly with an interesting group of guys."

"What's B and E?"

"Breaking and entering."

"Halstead was arrested for that?"

"Arrested, but the charges were knocked down to illegal trespass. He was also arrested and convicted for illegal wiretap in '74, for which he had his private-dick license yanked."

She poked at the paper with a forefinger. "What's ATF?"

"Alcohol, Tobacco, and Firearms. It's a federal agency. They arrested Meriwether in '77 for possession of illegal firearms and possession of a blue box."

"A what?"

"A device that allows you to make long distance phone calls for free. That bust was thrown out of court for illegal search and seizure, though."

She said excitedly, "Then it looks like the rumors about him being a gunrunner are true . . ."

"Not necessarily. That bust may be how the rumors got started."

She didn't seem to be listening to me. "Maybe Hugh found out Meriwether was running guns and they killed him—"

"Hold on," I said, waving my hands at her. "We don't know that anybody killed him—"

"They tried to kill you."

"We don't know that for sure, either. Somebody tried to get me out of the way for a while, but a couple of months in traction would have done that nicely."

She made a face and looked at the paper again. "God, these people are gangsters. Cardozo was arrested for assault and possession of cocaine, Villalobos was convicted of forgery and what's this? 'Capping?' "

"That's right."

"What's capping?"

"Ambulance chasing," I said, and watched her to see how she would take it. "The illegal solicitation of clients for attorneys."

She stiffened. "Are you saying that's what Villalobos was doing for Hugh?"

"I don't think I said that."

She frowned. "But that's what you're thinking. That Hugh was some kind of a shyster attorney who ran behind ambulances like some hyena loping behind a rhinoceros, waiting for the shit to drop. You'd *like* him to have been that—"

"Believe it or not, I'm not jealous of your late husband." I tried to cut her off before this got completely out of hand. "*I* didn't program the C.I.I. computer in Sacramento to print out that Villalobos was a capper, and I'm not attacking any memory you might have of Hugh Canning. I'm just a confused little man whose job it is to gather facts and try to make some sense of them. One of those facts is that somebody is willing to cancel my show to keep me from doing that, and I'd like to find out why before they succeed. So retract your claws, lady."

She got that pouty look again and I ignored her while I called information for I. J. Lyle's number. I dialed it and a woman answered.

"Hello?"

"Ilona?"

"Pardon me?"

"Isn't this Ilona Lyle's residence?"

"I'm afraid you have the wrong number."

"I got this number out of the book. I. J. Lyle—"

"This is Irene Lyle. There is no Ilona here."

"I'm terribly sorry," I said and hung up.

I held out my hand to Sharon. "I'm going to need your car for an hour or two."

She folded her arms again and struck an obstinate pose. "No way. I've seen what you do to cars."

"Come on. You want to get your two hundred dollars' worth, don't you? I've only worked half a day today."

"I thought you were going to quit."

"I was thinking about it, but I haven't wrecked my quota of cars yet."

"Well, mine's not going to be next."

"Come on, Sharon," I said impatiently. "The girl might leave." I looked at my watch.

"What girl? Where are you going?"

"Santa Ana."

"Who's in Santa Ana?"

"Cassarene's nurse."

"Okay," she said, then put her drink down and stood up. "Let's go. I'll drive."

I shook my hands at her. "Oh, no—"

"Why not? What's the big deal?"

I looked at her skeptically. The thought of being chauffeured did not particularly bother me, but her being present while I was questioning Irene Lyle was out. "You'd just wind up sitting in the car while I talk to the woman."

She shrugged. "So? I'll sit in the car." She knew she had won before she got a response. She picked up her purse from the table and started for the door. When she got there, she stopped and turned around. "Are you coming?"

"Well, maybe just for the ride," I said, and followed.

Irene Lyle lived on a palm-tree-lined street not far from Cassarene's office. Sharon let me off in front of a group of inexpensive town houses whose sharply jagged roofs and mud-colored walls reminded me of termite hills washed in pastel floodlight. I told her to give me at least fifteen minutes.

The numbered sequence of the units jumped around without apparent order, and it took me a while to find 901. The button for the doorbell was lighted; I pressed it. I could hear the television voices inside, but no live ones.

The door opened and Irene Lyle's eyes widened in surprise when they saw who it was. "You."

"Me," I agreed.

It did not look as if she intended to go out. She was dressed in a loose-fitting, long-sleeved plaid shirt, the sleeves of which were rolled up to the elbows, a pair of white shorts, and navy-blue espadrilles. Without the starched uniform, her body looked more lush than bulky.

"What do you want? How did you know where I live?"

I smiled reassuringly. "I'm a detective, remember? I looked you up in the phone book."

"What do you want?" she asked again.

"May I come in?"

"What for?" The surprise in her eyes was now being crowded by suspicion.

"I'd like to ask you a couple of questions."

"What kind of questions?"

"Questions I didn't get a chance to ask Dr. Cassarene yesterday before getting the bum's rush."

"What could I possibly tell you about Hugh Canning? I only met the man a couple of times when he came to the office."

"That's one thing I'd like to talk to you about—"

She shook her head. The suspicion was now being jostled by anxiety. "I don't think so."

"It could be important."

Her eyes darted past me, as if to see if there was anyone out-

131

side, watching. "I'm sorry, but I don't think that would be such a good idea. I already got chewed out once for even announcing your presence in the office."

"By Dr. Cassarene?"

She nodded. "After you left, he launched into a real tirade. He said that if you ever came around the office again, he didn't want to see you and that I shouldn't talk to you. . . ."

"Did he tell you why?"

"No, and I wasn't about to ask."

The resentment in her voice and the curiosity in her eyes told me she really wanted to ask me. I cut her a little slack. "Look, Miss Lyle, I don't want to get you into trouble with your boss, but Hugh Canning's widow could wind up in the street if I don't get some questions answered pretty soon. And Dr. Cassarene isn't around. . . ."

She flung her hands out from her body. "But I don't know anything about Hugh Canning. What questions could I possibly answer?"

I turned on my most persuasive smile. "Why don't you let me ask them and we'll find out? What can it hurt? You'll have lost five minutes of watching the news, that's all. The news is probably bad anyway."

She balked and I said: "I swear to you, whatever you tell me will be kept in the strictest confidence. Dr. Cassarene will never know you talked to me."

"Well . . . all right."

The living room was small, furnished in inexpensive Mediterranean and decorated with framed Aaron Brothers prints and frothy green plants hanging in macrame hammocks. Delicious tomato and meat smells wafted from the kitchen, and the genuine wood-grain Formica table in the dining alcove was set for one. It looked as if I'd been right about her not going out.

"Smells terrific," I commented.

"It's just some leftover lasagna I made last night," she said, closing the door.

"Actually, I think lasagna is better the second day. Gives all the flavors time to settle."

She smiled. Her initial tension seemed to be easing a bit. She went to the dining table and picked up a long-stemmed glass half-full of white wine. "Would you like a glass of wine?"

"Sure," I said, trying to ease the tension even more.

She went into the kitchen and I plopped down on a tweedy couch across from Dan Rather, who was looking particularly stiff-faced. He was saying something about the fact that because of recent budget cuts, the IRS would no longer be able to help people fill out their tax forms. With only four exceptions—the mentally handicapped, the physically handicapped, illiterates, and members of Congress.

She came out and handed me a glass of wine and took a chair opposite me. She leaned forward and balanced her freshly filled glass on her knees with both hands. I took a sip of mine and lied that it was good. She smiled and I asked, "How long have you worked for Dr. Cassarene?"

"Almost three years."

"A long time."

She raised an eyebrow. "I'm beginning to think *too* long."

"You sound as if he's a hard man to work for."

She looked into her glass. "Sometimes."

"Like yesterday?"

She exhaled through her nose and smiled. "Like yesterday. Dr. Cassarene shares a trait with most other doctors I've worked with. Every once in a while, he gets taken by these moods when he thinks he's God."

She was loosening up and I didn't want her to stop.

"You've worked for other doctors, then?"

She sat back and waved a hand in the air, the one without the wineglass in it. "Oh, yes. I'm an RN. I was just playing receptionist yesterday because the other girl was sick. I used to work at the County Medical Center. In the orthopedic ward. That's where I met Dr. Cassarene. I took care of some of his patients, and he

133

offered me a job in his office at a substantial increase in pay." She paused and made a face. "That was the last substantial raise in pay I've had in the past three years. Mention raise to Dr. Cassarene and he suddenly develops a hearing problem." She raised her wineglass in a toast. "Here's to money. The name of the game."

Her glass was almost empty. I drained mine quickly, and handed it to her, hoping she would fill both of them at the same time. "May I have another glass?"

"Sure," she said affably, and went into the kitchen. When she came back, both glasses were full. She handed me mine and sat back down and tucked a leg underneath her in the chair. I sipped my wine and said nonchalantly, "So what was the good doctor afraid you were going to tell me that he had to jump all over your case about it?"

"He wasn't *afraid*," she said, waving a disparaging hand. "He's just real touchy about his wife, that's all."

"His wife?" I asked. "What does she have to do with it?"

"He doesn't like to think about her. The memory is painful to him. I guess he loved her a lot." She read my look of confusion and said, "She died just before I came to work for him. He's always told me never to mention her around him. He said he buried a good part of himself with her and he didn't want to have her dug up again."

"I didn't know I had," I said. "What, do I look like her or something?"

"No, no," she said, dead serious. "It was when you mentioned the aplastic anemia." She looked at me and blinked. "That was what she died of—indeterminate aplastic anemia."

Bells and buzzers were going off in my head. Three years. I wondered what the life expectancy of tropical flies was. Maybe Canning had been bitten by the same fly that had bitten Dr. Cassarene's wife. Or maybe by its offspring.

"I'm not a medical expert, but that's not too common a disease, is it?"

"No. That's why it struck me when you said Mr. Canning had had it."

"You said it was 'indeterminate.' They never found out what caused it, then?"

She shook her head. "They could never isolate anything. I was working at the hospital at the time. The doctors were going crazy trying to figure out what she had." She stared into her wine, as if looking at an image there, a memory, perhaps. "The two weeks she was there, Cassie was at her side almost twenty-four hours a day. We talked quite a bit about it. He needed a shoulder to cry on and he used mine. That was when he asked me to work for him. I really felt sorry for him. He really loved her."

"What was her name?"

"Deirdre," she said, then paused. "Her death sort of soured him, I think. He changed after that. He used to be a really good doctor. That's why I went to work for him when he asked. He used to really care about his patients."

"He doesn't anymore?"

"It's the bucks now," she said bitterly, then leaned forward. "You know how hard it is to—" She stopped, smiled strangely, then shook her head and leaned back. "Never mind."

"What?"

"No, never mind. I've already said too much. Maybe Cassie's right. Maybe I do talk too much." Her eyebrows knitted. "Jesus, why am I telling you all this? I don't even know you."

"Maybe that's why you're telling me."

The smile broadened. It was a nice smile. "Maybe."

"You said you met Hugh Canning a couple of times."

She took another sip and said, "I talked to him quite a bit on the phone. He would call the office pretty often to discuss his clients' injuries with Cassie. But I only met him a few times."

"Was he in the office the last couple of months?"

She thought about it and shook her head. "Not that I can remember."

"Were a lot of Canning's clients patients of Dr. Cassarene?"

"Quite a few," she said. "We handle a lot of insurance cases, as you can imagine."

"Did Canning refer his clients to Cassarene or did the referrals go the other way for the most part?"

"Mostly the referrals came from Canning's office. At least until six months ago."

"What happened six months ago?"

"I don't know. We just stopped getting patients from him. We still get a lot of cases sent over from his office, but they're all Mr. Baumgartner's clients."

"How about Jackson Meriwether? Does he ever come around?"

Her expression turned serious. "I can't discuss any of Dr. Cassarene's patients."

"I'll take that to mean that Meriwether is one of his patients," I said.

"I didn't say that."

"Does Dr. Cassarene ever make house calls?"

"*Nobody* makes house calls anymore," she said, then studied me thoughtfully. "You really upset him with that crack about Max Jacobson."

I nodded. "I wanted to see how he would react."

Her eyebrows shot up. "He reacted, all right. Christ, I thought he was going to have an aneurysm after you left. Ranted and raved about how dare you cast aspersions on his professional integrity." Her face tightened into an intense knot and she asked, "Do you know something for sure or were you just fishing? If that's what's going on, I'd like to know."

"I was just fishing," I said.

"Well, you really hit a nerve."

I said over the rim of my glass, "You think Cassarene could be pushing speed?"

She shook her head vehemently. "No. There wouldn't be any reason for him to. He's got a lot of money. He has a good practice. I know. I see what comes in there. He wouldn't jeopardize his license to do anything like that."

I shrugged. "He wouldn't have to be doing it strictly for the money."

"I sincerely doubt it." Her tone turned suddenly businesslike and she said, "Look, this discussion is getting a little . . . inappropriate. I don't think I should talk about Dr. Cassarene anymore. You said you wanted to know about Hugh Canning."

"All right. What do you know about Hugh Canning?"

"Nothing," she said. "I told you that."

"I believe you."

"Then why did you come here in the first place?" She lifted one eyebrow. "You didn't really want to ask me about Hugh Canning at all," she observed. "You wanted to pump me about Dr. Cassarene."

"Only partially true. I'm only interested in Cassarene as to how he relates to Canning's case. And I was curious about your reaction when I mentioned aplastic anemia."

"You're the one who called and pretended to have the wrong number."

"I had to be sure you were the same I. J. Lyle."

One corner of her mouth lifted into a sort of amused crooked leer. "Do you always operate in such a sneaky manner?"

"Only when I can." I stood up and finished my wine. "What do I do with this?" I held up the glass.

"I'll take it," she said, and carried it into the kitchen. When she returned, she seemed to be looking at me in a completely different way. "Would you like to stay for some lasagna? I've got plenty."

"I'd love to, but I've got a lot of other sneaky things to do tonight. I'll take a rain check, though."

She nodded and then her eyes clouded with concern. "You won't let Dr. Cassarene know—"

"I sneak silently," I said, patting her hand. "Thanks again for the wine."

As I came down the walkway, a pair of headlights flashed on up the street and a car pulled out from the curb. I stopped in my tracks, seized momentarily by uncertainty, but relaxed when I saw it was the Mercedes. I got into the car, and Sharon said, "You were in there longer than fifteen minutes."

"Yeah, well, that's because I had to get her drunk to get her to talk. It took a little time."

"Did you find out anything interesting?"

"Yep."

"What?"

I told her what Irene Lyle had told me about Cassarene's wife.

"My God, don't you think that's kind of strange, I mean, both his wife and Hugh having the same disease?"

"It's an interesting coincidence, let's put it that way. I'm going to have to do some research tomorrow to find out if it could be more than that."

She said in an excited voice, "Remember that doctor down in Texas—the one they wrote the book about—who raised bacteria in petri dishes and injected them into his wife's éclairs? You think Cassarene could have done something like that?"

"What? Raised cultures of African flies and sicced them on his wife?"

Her face fell. "It does sound dumb, doesn't it?"

"No dumber than the rest of this case. It's like trying to put a jigsaw puzzle together from pieces from four different ones. Pretty soon, you get so pissed, you start trimming the pieces to make them fit."

"You know what?" Sharon asked after a while.

"What?"

"This is kind of fun."

"What?"

"Doing this together."

I decided to play dumb. "Doing what together?"

"You know. Working on the case together. I feel like Myrna Loy in *The Thin Man*."

"And I'm William Powell?"

"Yeah."

"What about Asta?"

138

Her head bobbed up and down. "That was that cute little terrier they had, right?"

"Right. To do this up right, maybe we should go buy one."

She thought for a moment, then said seriously, "I know someone who has one of those dogs. Maybe she'd loan it to me."

"Christ," I said, and put my hand over my eyes.

15

The morning was as overcast as my thoughts. I was sitting at the breakfast table trying to get more than two brain cells to fire at the same time and dispel some of the fog, when Sharon rolled up her bathrobe sleeves and said, "Well? Where are we going today?"

I put my coffee cup down. "What do you mean, 'we'?"

She shrugged as if the meaning were clear. "You don't expect me to sit here doing needlepoint while you wander around town all day in my car, do you?"

"No. I thought you'd drive me to a rental agency other than Avis, where I am now persona non grata, and I could rent one."

She picked up her cup with two hands and watched me over the rim. "After you get a car, where do you intend to go?"

"The County Medical Center."

"What's at the County Medical Center?"

"Diane McClurg."

"Who is Diane McClurg?"

"The head of Volunteer Services at the hospital."

She put her cup down and said in an annoyed tone, "I swear to God, you're like a tire with a slow leak. You can tell me what

140

you're doing, you know. I mean, I *am* your client. I am paying you, remember?"

"Yeah, and after last night, the rates should go up, just for the wear and tear on my body. You should see the goddamn scratch marks on my back."

"I didn't hear you complaining last night."

"I didn't want to say anything. I thought you were trying out for a part in *The Howling*."

She smiled. "I'm sorry. I guess I did get carried away. But I can't help it. You have that effect on me." She reached over and grabbed my hand and we sat there for a moment before she said tenderly, "So why are we going to see this Diane McClurg?"

"*I'm* going to see her because Villalobos blames her for giving Amigos the boot at the hospital. I want to know why."

She nodded as if that satisfied her, and stood up. "Okay. I'll be ready in twenty minutes."

I shook my head. "It's just going to be boring routine—"

"No more boring than sitting here would be."

"If whoever tried to kill me makes another attempt—"

"They wouldn't try again so soon. It'd be too obvious."

There was logic in that, but I thought I'd try again, "It was obvious after the first time, too. If they *do* try again—"

"Then it *really* won't be boring," she said, and left the room.

I sighed in frustration, knowing that any further attempts to deter her would be spitting into the wind. Maybe it was the best thing. If she got bored enough—and I would try to make sure she did—maybe she would get the compulsion to play Mr. and Mrs. North out of her system.

Actually, I wasn't totally averse to the idea of her coming along; to be honest, I was beginning to enjoy having her with me. I'd realized it that morning when I rolled over and saw her sleeping and had not had the overwhelming compulsion to slip out of bed and start a stealthy search for my clothes. I'd slept so long alone or with women I couldn't wait to get rid of in the morning—or before, if possible—that I'd forgotten that that was not

141

necessarily the natural state of affairs. It was like waking up after sleeping in one position too long—I was getting the feeling
back in parts that had been numb for so long, I'd forgotten they
were there.

While she dressed, I called Sergeant Neely at the Santa Ana
PD and told him about the "accident" the day before. He didn't
sound particularly impressed, but then I had not expected him
to; I just wanted it on record in case there was another attempt.
Maybe after I'd amassed enough incidents—if I wasn't dead by
that time—somebody somewhere might get curious enough to investigate. He asked me a few perfunctory questions about the
accident, then told me that he'd run the Chevy through the computer and hadn't come up with any recent stolens matching its description. He said he doubted that the two accidents were related,
but that he would check into it and get back to me.

Sharon came out as I finished the call, looking beautiful in a
blue-and-white striped sweater and a navy-blue skirt. "Ready?"
she asked, snatching her purse from the table.

The County Medical Center was a dingy, rambling complex of
blocky stone buildings that might have once been white, but were
now just a dirty yellow-gray. Sharon parked in the public lot and
I told her that I would meet her by the front entrance in half
an hour.

"I have a better idea," she said. "I'll go with you."

"Oh, no," I said, shaking my head. "I told you before; I
work alone."

"You will be working alone. I'll remain unobtrusively in the
background. You won't even know I'm there."

"Uh-uh."

"I know shorthand, you know. I can take notes." She pulled
a pad of lined paper out of her purse. "See, I even brought a
notebook."

I shook my head adamantly.

"You can introduce me as your assistant. I won't say a word, I
promise. I'll just sit there and listen." Her voice turned wheed-

ling. "Please, Jake. I don't want to sit here in this ugly parking lot for an hour—"

"Half an hour."

"That's what you said last night. Come on. I'm not going to screw anything up for you."

If my hunch was correct, she was not going to like what Diane McClurg was going to say, but she was eventually going to have to hear it from someone. I figured it might as well be from Diane McClurg as from me.

"All right," I said. "But not a peep out of you. No matter what's said, not a word. And just follow my leads."

She squirmed like a delighted child and piled out of the car. We went inside and, after wandering around a maze of antiseptic-smelling corridors for what seemed like half an hour and asking directions from half a dozen people, we finally managed to locate Volunteer Services.

I gave Diane McClurg's secretary my card. After making us wait five minutes, she ushered us into a small, neat, gray office. Diane McClurg rose to greet us as we entered. She was in her mid-thirties, with short black hair and a small, triangular face that might have been called borderline cute, if you were going to call it anything at all. A pair of oversized, rectangular glasses sat on a tiny bump that was her nose, and she wore a green dress and a blue silk scarf knotted at her throat.

"Mr. Asch," she said, offering her hand primly.

I took it and motioned toward Sharon. "This is Ms. Loy. She is one of my operatives."

Sharon threw me a dirty glance over Diane McClurg's shoulder, then smiled at the woman and said, "It's a standard joke around the office."

Diane McClurg smiled at her strangely as if she could not think what the joke could be.

She clasped her hands on the top of the desk and asked, "How can I help you, Mr. Asch?"

Sharon got out her note pad and a pen, and poised them for action.

143

"Ms. Loy and I are down here working on a case with Trans-continental Life, Ms. McClurg. An automobile accident. A man died in it, and there is a lot of insurance money involved. In the course of our investigation, quite a few peculiarities have arisen. Insurance companies are very wary of peculiarities when large sums are at stake, as you are probably aware. I'm trying to iron some of them out, and I'm hoping you might be able to help me."

"How?"

"Every time I turn around, George Villalobos's name keeps popping up. I want to know why."

Her small mouth contorted into a wry smile. "I'm sure if you investigated the cases of half the accident victims in this country, Villalobos's name would pop up."

"Why is that?"

Instead of answering my question, she asked, "Is—was—the man who died in the accident a patient at this hospital?"

"No."

She seemed to relax a little at that and leaned back in her chair. "Why would you come to see me about George Villalobos?"

"I understand he has a volunteer group—Amigos—that worked here."

"Not anymore."

"I know. That's why I'm here. To find out why."

"Let's just say that Mr. Villalobos and I had a mutual agreement that his group's services were no longer required."

"He doesn't say it was so mutual. He says he got the boot unfairly. By you."

"I can't give the boot to anyone," she said. "If I could, Amigos would have been out of here a lot sooner than they were. The head of Health Services, Mr. Barclay, is the only one with the authority to expel a group from the hospital."

"And he did."

"Yes."

"At your recommendation," I said, and glanced at Sharon, who seemed to be taking it all down.

"Yes."

144

Just to get her going, I said, "Villalobos claims you had him thrown out of here because you were jealous of his influence and because you were afraid of his exposing mistreatment of Chicanos at the Medical Center."

Her face suffused with a warm flush and her lips tightened. "That's a laugh. You know what people in the barrio call Villalobos and his kind, Mr. Asch? 'Coyotes.' They're scavengers, feeding off the lame and the weak." She leaned back in her chair and said, "Just how is Villalobos involved in the accident you're investigating?"

"That's what I'm trying to pin down. He's mixed up with the people trying to collect the settlement, although it's not clear in what capacity. I tried to talk to him about it, but he was not very cooperative. He had me escorted out of the restaurant by an associate of his who looked like Rodan."

"Alex Cardozo," she said with undisguised contempt.

"That's him. Villalobos said he was the president of Amigos." She nodded stiffly. "On paper."

"Villalobos doesn't seem to like to put his name on things."

The wry smile returned. "He's what you would call an elusive man."

I leaned forward and said in a sincere voice: "Frankly, Miss McClurg, this is not our first go-round with Villalobos. He seems to pop up with regularity when there is a big settlement involved. There is usually nothing we can do about it, but this accident occurred under some very strange circumstances." I paused for effect, and looked at her knowingly. "*Very* strange."

She nodded as if she knew exactly what I meant. I thought she was ready for a repeat of my earlier question: "Why did you recommend Amigos' expulsion from the hospital?"

She took off her glasses and laid them on the desk. She was one of those weak-eyed women who looked better with glasses than without.

"About six months ago," she began, "a patient worker, Sylvia Rhodes, came to see me and said she'd noticed lately that a lot of accident patients on the third-floor orthopedic ward had been re-

145

fusing to sign accident lien forms. That's a form we use if a patient has been in an accident and has expressed intent to sue. What it is, basically, is an agreement that the county will keep the hospital bill in abeyance until a settlement is made. The county collects later from the settlement."

"Go on," I said, smiling.

"Miss Rhodes noticed that most of the patients refusing to sign the forms had Spanish surnames and she thought that peculiar, so she started doing some checking with the patients in the ward and found out that Amigos volunteers had been handing out attorneys' business cards and advising the patients not to sign anything the hospital gave them or divulge any information about their accidents to anyone. I decided to look into the matter and started following the Amigos people around."

"How many volunteers did Amigos have working here?"

"Three," she said. "Alex Cardozo, Angel Martinez, and a woman named Tina Berndale." I nodded and Sharon took down the names.

"I followed them around for a couple of weeks and nothing happened," the woman continued. "Then, one day, I came into the ward and caught Cardozo standing over an elderly woman patient. The woman had been admitted only a few hours before and she was still half-dazed from the drugs they'd given her and in a lot of pain from a collarbone fracture, and Cardozo had hold of her arm and was trying to get her to put her thumbprint on a piece of paper. I came up behind him and snatched the paper out of his hand and saw it was a contract for the woman to hire a certain attorney. She was a Mexican national and didn't know how to write—that was why he needed her thumbprint."

"What happened?"

"I told Cardozo to get out of the ward, that I didn't want to see him around the patients anymore, but he just grabbed the paper back and started getting loud. He said I didn't have the authority to tell him to get out of anywhere. But he did leave."

"And that was it?"

She looked at me as if I were a little off. "The workings of a

146

bureaucracy are never quite that simple, I'm afraid. Actually, Cardozo was right. I didn't have the authority to throw him out of the ward. I made out a report and submitted it to my unit administrator, recommending that Amigos be barred from the hospital grounds, which he, in turn, submitted to Mr. Barclay. Mr. Barclay pulled me into his office and wanted to know exactly what was going on. He was very concerned, especially since he'd been the one who'd brought Villalobos into the hospital in the first place. I gave him everything, including a list of all the attorneys Villalobos's people had been referring patients to. He felt as if he'd been used in a most vile manner."

"How was that?"

She put her glasses back on and went back to being cute. "Mr. Barclay and Villalobos knew each other socially. It was at a party, in fact, that Villalobos approached Mr. Barclay about putting his volunteer group into the hospital."

"Don't tell me," I said. "The party was given by a man named Jackson Meriwether."

She looked at me strangely. "I think that's what he said the man's name was. How did you know?"

I winked. "Just a hunch."

She shrugged, apparently willing to let it go at that. "Well, after he was satisfied that what I'd been telling him was the truth, Mr. Barclay got quite upset. He said that for the past four months, Villalobos had been urging him to set up some kind of referral system at the hospital and he wanted office space for Amigos here so that he could supervise the program. And that wasn't all. He said that Villalobos had approached him with a proposal to set up a program to aid the widows and orphans of patients who died at the Medical Center and he wanted to be supplied with death lists. He was especially interested in aliens, illegal or not. He had said he had influential friends in Mexico and wanted to aid those relatives in Mexico of aliens who had died up here. Since Amigos does charity work in Mexico, of course it would be the perfect vehicle for funneling that aid."

"You think he wanted to set up some kind of scam operation?"

147

"I didn't say that." She turned away, then looked back at me out of the corner of her eye. "But I wouldn't put it past him. Villalobos is a very resourceful man. And one without many scruples. While the whole thing was going on here at the hospital, he tried everything to get me off his case. First he tried to get me fired by telling Mr. Barclay that I'd trumped up the charges against him out of jealousy, that I felt he was trying to infringe upon my territory. When that didn't work, he tried to get me to recant my testimony—first by cajoling me, then by threats, and finally by trying to bribe me."

"He offered you money?"

She nodded, and a stiff line appeared below her mouth. "Five thousand dollars. Unfortunately, it was done on the phone and there were no witnesses. I don't even know if it would have made a difference if there had been witnesses, it was done in such an ambiguous way. But the meaning was clear to me. It made me so mad that I went to the District Attorney, to see what could be done about Villalobos's little operation."

"What did he say?"

"He wasn't interested," she said. "The prosecutor I talked to told me it would be a waste of his time to try to run down every ambulance chaser in the country. Besides, the way the law reads, although it's a misdemeanor for a capper to solicit clients for an attorney, it's only unethical—not illegal—for an attorney to hire a capper. What it all adds up to is that the D.A. won't bother to prosecute unless there's clear-cut evidence of insurance fraud or grand theft. And if the D.A. won't prosecute, the police won't waste their manpower tracking it down."

I nodded sympathetically. "How many clients would you say Villalobos was pulling out of here a month?"

"From what we can estimate, between seventy-five and one hundred," she said without batting an eye.

I did some rapid calculating in my head. The going rate a capper got from an attorney nowadays was around $300 per accident victim delivered. That meant Villalobos was knocking down

$30,000 a month, just through his "charity" work at the hospital. With whatever else he was scavenging from his other connections, he was probably making more than the lawyers he was working for. A hell of a lot more.

"I even went to the State Bar," she said. "They said they were aware of the problem, that this sort of thing was rampant in the business, but there was little they could do about it unless I had proof. They only had a few investigators, the man told me, and they couldn't stop to investigate every capping complaint that came into the office. He said he would look into it, but I got his meaning."

"You say you have a list of the attorneys the Amigos people were soliciting for?"

"Yes."

"May I see it?" Before she could answer, I said, "As you can well understand, Miss McClurg, Transcontinental is very interested in curtailing the activities of operators like Villalobos and the attorneys who pay him. They cost not only the company, but the public—you, me, everybody—billions of dollars every year. As you've found out, attorneys are very reluctant to move on their own people unless they have to. If the names on that list are who I think they are, put together with the information I have, they might have to."

She tapped an unpolished nail on her chin and measured me through her glasses. "I don't have to get the list. There were only four names on it."

I glanced over at Sharon, who was waiting, pen ready, for the recital.

"Barry Reid. Canning and Baumgartner. Oliveres and Jordan. Conrad, Conrad, and Fitzgerald."

I was filled with that tingly, excited feeling I got when my suspicions were confirmed.

"Canning and Baumgartner?" Sharon blurted out.

Diane McClurg looked at her. "Yes, why?"

"It's another name that's cropped up in our case," I inserted

149

quickly, and threw a shut-up glance at Sharon. Her eyes sparked defiantly. I asked, "What percentage of Villalobos's referrals were going to Canning and Baumgartner?"

"The bulk of them."

I was beginning to make out the shape of the something that was lumbering slowly out of the fog. "What about recently?"

"I'm talking about recently," she said. "At least up to the time that Amigos was expelled from the Medical Center. In fact, that old woman I was telling you about, the one with the broken collarbone? It was a contract from their office that Cardozo was trying to get a thumbprint on."

The shape of the something had suddenly changed on me. I looked at Sharon. She had stopped writing and was staring at a spot on the floor. She looked up and her mouth opened but before she could say anything, I jumped in. "That's strange. I was told that Villalobos was thrown out of Canning and Baumgartner's law firm last year."

"All I know is that most of the patient referrals the Amigos people were making were to them."

"Were most of the patients being referred to Canning or to Baumgartner?"

"I don't know about that."

"Did you give Canning's name to the State Bar?"

"Yes, but I don't think they ever did anything about it."

"Do you remember the name of the person you talked to there?"

She thought for a second. "Keyes, I believe. He was a prosecutor there."

"Did you ever hear back from him?"

"No."

"Did you ever follow it up yourself?"

A bit of tongue protruded from her mouth and moistened her lower lip. "I must confess, I didn't. Getting Amigos out of here was my main concern. When that happened, I sort of lost interest, I'm ashamed to say. I'd done all I could do about it and I had a myriad of other problems to attend to at that time."

"I understand."

She said almost guiltily: "Frankly, I thought to continue would just be beating my head against a wall. My attitude about the efficacy of bodies like the State Bar and the Board of Medical Examiners has grown rather cynical in the past few years, I'm afraid. I thought the most the Bar would do would be slap everyone on the wrist and send them on their way."

"I doubt anyone is going to be slapping Canning's wrist," I said. "You are aware, I assume, that he's dead."

Her hand went up to her throat and she shook her head. "No. I hadn't heard."

I nodded. "He was in an automobile accident a month ago."

"I'm sorry to hear that. I certainly didn't wish that kind of harm on him." She paused and said dreamily, "Strange."

"What?"

"That a man like that, who lived off accidents, should die in one."

I glanced quickly at Sharon. She was glaring at Diane McClurg, and a red flush was creeping up her neck. I knew I'd better get her out of there before she said something I would regret. I thanked Diane McClurg for her time and hustled Sharon out into the hallway.

When we got out of earshot of the office, I said, "Now you know why I didn't want to take you along."

Her head jerked around, and she said sharply, "What are you talking about?"

"You were ready to blow it in there."

"I was under control."

"Barely."

"That woman is off base," she said as we walked. I didn't comment. After a few paces, she asked crossly, "You don't believe all that stuff about Villalobos capping for Hugh and Ray, do you? Hugh couldn't stand to hear Villalobos's name mentioned, never mind having him around the office. It's stupid."

"You want to prove her wrong?"

"How?"

151

"You still have your husband's keys to the office?"

"At the house."

"We'll have to go back and get them."

She turned her head slightly to one side. "What for?"

"It saves breaking and entering. We're going to do a little research tonight."

"Tonight?"

"Baumgartner was real touchy about me looking through your husband's case files. Diane McClurg might have just told us why." I took her elbow and started moving down the hall. "In the meantime, we've got some stops to make."

"Where?"

"First, the County Clerk's office. After that, UC Irvine Medical School."

"What's there?"

"MEDLAR."

She pulled her elbow from my grip and kept walking. "And what, may I ask, is MEDLAR?"

"Medical Literature Analysis and Retrieval System. It's a computerized bibliographical system run by the National Library of Medicine. It has stored references to every article printed in almost four hundred medical journals all over the world."

We wended our way through cars, then I spotted the Mercedes and headed for it.

"What are we going to look up?"

"Anemia. Of the aplastic variety. I want to see if there might have been some non-African flies in the ointment."

The County Clerk's Fictitious Names Statements Division was in Room D-100 on the ground floor of the courthouse. Before going in, I used the pay phone in the corridor to call the State Bar.

Diane McClurg had been right about the name of the man she had talked to. She had also been right about what the State Bar had done about Villalobos and Company—very little. Keyes was a very curt man with a suspicious voice. He remembered the case, but he did not care to discuss it with me, except to say that after looking into the matter, he had not found enough solid evidence to justify a full-fledged investigation. From what I could pick up from his Hemingwayesque sentences, his "looking into" the matter had consisted of a phone conversation with Hugh Canning, who had vehemently denied having any kind of business dealings with Villalobos after Villalobos had been thrown out of the office the previous year for unethical conduct. Canning had concurred with Diane McClurg's estimation of Villalobos, but insisted that all of the work Group Associates had done for his office had been taken over by another firm. Keyes would not give me the name of the firm. He very grudgingly did give me the date that the phone conversation with Canning had taken place—September 3. Six days before he had careened into oblivion.

After that, I saved a trip by calling the reference library at UC Irvine Medical School. The clerk I talked to said it would cost me nine dollars to run something through MEDLAR, but that I couldn't do it until tomorrow, because the line was booked all day. I gave her my name and told her I would be in tomorrow with my nine bucks.

If you are doing business under a fictitious name or as a corporation in almost any county in California, you are required to file papers with the county telling the function of the business and its principal owners. If the business is a corporation, a copy of the incorporation papers filed with the Secretary of State's office in Sacramento is usually included in the file. A quick check of the index showed that the business license granted to Cielo Lindo had been taken out by a firm called Felicidad, Inc. Group Associates and was owned by a corporation called Azteca, Inc. I had the clerk pull both those files, but Amigos did not have a file, probably because it was allegedly a nonprofit corporation, which meant I would have to check its credentials through Sacramento.

Felicidad, Inc., had been formed in September 1978, in Santa Ana, and, according to the file, Cielo Lindo was its only business concern. Its principal officers were Salvador Villalobos, president; Edward Covar, vice-president; and Sandra Villalobos, secretary-treasurer. Sharon recognized Sandra Villalobos as being Villalobos's wife, but she did not recognize the other name.

The functions of Azteca, Inc., seemed to be more diverse. Not only was it a landholding company, owning the property that Cielo Lindo occupied, and another piece of property at 1134 Fourteenth Street, Santa Ana, but it had also purchased Group Associates, a firm performing "investigational and translation services," in 1979. The person from whom they had purchased the operation was George Villalobos, who had apparently been its sole owner. The principal officers were predictable: Salvador Villalobos, president; Sandra Villalobos, vice-president; Edward Covar, secretary-treasurer.

I went back outside to the pay phone and called the State Board of Equalization in L.A. and asked for Wayne Herlihy. Wayne was an auditor there who owed me a couple of favors dating back a few years. Although I'd stretched that couple into a dozen or so, he hadn't griped about it too much. He sounded harassed when he answered the phone, but agreed, albeit in a slightly irritated tone, to get me the information on Amigos by that night.

"Where to now?" Sharon asked as I hung up.

I glanced at her, then away. "Back to your place. There's nothing much else we can do for the rest of the afternoon; at least it's comfortable there."

When we got to the car, she grabbed my arm and stopped me. Her voice was tentative and fumbling like a little girl unsure of herself. "I'm sorry, Jake."

"For what?" I was going to milk the scene, make her work.

"For taking it out on you. It's not your fault, I know that." Her hands began to make tight, tense little motions in the air. "It's just, you have a picture of someone, of how things are, a picture you're sure of, and then suddenly that picture changes and you begin to doubt yourself, to wonder if you really know who anybody is."

"People are like prisms," I said. "They look different from different angles. That doesn't make any of the sides less real."

"You look real to me from all sides."

"I didn't always," I reminded her.

154

"What I saw then is still there." She paused and tilted her head up to stare straight into my eyes. "You're the only solid thing in my life right now, did you know that? So if I yell and throw a tantrum, it's only because I know you'll be there tomorrow. You understand?"

"Yeah," I said and smiled. "I do."

16

The street was quiet and dark. Not a car had gone by us in either direction for the three or four minutes we had been parked, and the only noises that could be heard were the crickets in the bushes and the soft whooshings of traffic a few blocks up.

"Why did we have to park this far down the block?" Sharon asked in a petulant tone.

"In case Baumgartner comes back for some reason, I don't want him to see your car parked out front, that's why."

The orange tip of her cigarette glowed as she took a deep drag. "It—I don't know—it just all seems so underhanded and sneaky. Ray's been a good friend all these years. I feel as if I'm betraying his trust."

I didn't say anything.

"Just what do you expect to find in there?" she asked.

"I don't know."

"Don't lie to me, Jake. You must have some idea."

"Not really."

"Then why are we going in at all?" The tip of the cigarette made orange trails in the air as she gestured with her right hand. "Look, if Hugh was into something crooked, I don't want to know about it."

"You said you wanted to know the truth."

"I want my money," she said. "I don't care about the truth if it's ugly. I've gone through enough of that lately."

I grabbed the door handle. "Come on. Ready?"

She sighed heavily, mashed out her cigarette in the ashtray, and opened the door. We were halfway up the block when the darkness was splintered by the glare of headlights turning onto the street from Seventeenth. She started to freeze in the light like a cornered rabbit, but I gave her a tug and she kept walking. An old pickup rattled up slowly, then hung a left at the next corner. I could feel her release the breath she had been holding. "Relax, will you? We're not trying to take the guns of Navarone here. There's nothing dangerous or illegal about it. That's why you're here. You've got the keys and you're letting me in."

"That's exactly why I'm nervous," she said, quickening her step. "I feel like a condemned person here. If we get caught doing this, my relationship with Ray will be permanently changed. He'll never look on me as a friend again. If we don't get caught and find something, I'll never look on him as a friend again. If we go in there and find nothing, I'll still feel dirty every time I talk to him."

"You know something?" She looked at me. Her face was pale in the darkness. "With that attitude, you're going to make a lousy detective."

She smiled. "Yeah, I guess I probably will."

"Try and get over it; otherwise the agency is going to have to let you go."

We turned up the walkway that led to the front door of the law offices and stopped as Sharon fumbled with the keys. I checked out the street. No more cars had passed since the truck, and the sidewalks were empty. Sharon opened the deadlock with one key, then used another on the door handle. She went in first and reached for the light switch, but I stopped her hand. "No lights in here," I said, closing the door. "Only in back."

The room was very dark. I let her lead. When we got into the hallway, I asked, "You know where the master file is?"

157

"I think in here," she whispered, indicating the door to the room where the secretaries were working the other day. The hallway was darker than the anteroom, and I could only vaguely make out her shape. "I have a question," I whispered back.

"What?"

"Why are we whispering?"

"I don't know," she said, speaking in a normal voice. "It just seems like we should be."

The door was shut, but not locked. We went in and closed it again and she hit the lights. Against the wall facing the shelves of law books were four three-drawer filing cabinets. I passed between the two steel desks to reach them.

The drawers were all marked by year and went back to 1976, except the top drawer of the one on the right, which was labeled "Active." They were all locked, as I had expected. I asked Sharon for the keys and looked through the ring until I found one that seemed right and tried it on the "Active" drawer, but it didn't work. It took less than a minute to pop the pushbutton with my picks. All of the files in the drawer were filed alphabetically according to the client's last name; all were clearly tagged with either Canning's or Baumgartner's name, just as Baumgartner had said. Quite a few of Canning's files were also tagged with little red flags with a "B" on them. Those would be the cases that Canning was still working on when he died, that Baumgartner was finishing up. I pulled out all the files in the drawer and took the stack over to one of the desks, then began sorting out all of those tagged with Canning's name. After that, I went through the stack again, taking out all those cases dating from the three months before Canning's death, June through August.

Sharon watched me with anxious curiosity. "What are you doing?"

"Getting a reference point," I said. "There's too much here to go through in a week, never mind a couple of hours."

"Hours?" she exclaimed. "We're going to be here for *hours*?"

"That depends on how long it takes us to find what we are looking for."

158

"What are we looking for?"

I looked at her as blankly as I could. "I don't know."

"Sounds like a good plan," she said, nodding. "Did you happen to lead the raid into Iran to get the hostages back?"

"How did you know?" I snapped, scowling. "Only Haig and I were supposed to know that."

There was a sudden scratching at the window. Sharon's head jerked and she jumped about a foot.

"Jesus Christ, relax," I said. "It's just the wind blowing a branch against the window."

"I can't help it," she said, hugging herself.

"Remind me never to pull a heist with you."

I counted the folders in front of me. Two hundred seventy-one. That was a lot of cases for one attorney to handle in three months, even a p.i. attorney. I opened the desk drawer and found a yellow legal pad and wrote, "Canning—June thru Aug. '82—271," then went through the stack again and pulled out all the cases of clients with Spanish-sounding surnames. I counted those. One hundred sixty-seven. Baumgartner had not been lying about having a large Spanish-speaking clientele.

Sharon was standing in front of the desk, watching me with her arms folded. I divided up the stack of folders into two piles, and put the smaller pile in front of her. "Idle hands make the devil's workshop."

One corner of her mouth frowned. "And what am I supposed to do with these?"

"The same thing I'm going to do with these. Skim them."

"And what am I supposed to be looking for?" She held up both palms like a crosswalk guard trying to stop traffic. "Don't tell me: You don't know."

"For starters, you can look for any mention of Villalobos or Group Associates, or for the name of the outfit that's been handling the work they used to do. You don't have to go through all of them. Just pick out fifteen or so at random."

It took me about fifteen minutes to skim twenty cases. In seventeen of the twenty, Canning had paid for either investigative or

159

translation services, and in fifteen of those, the firm he had employed was an outfit called Nadir Industries, Inc. Copies of the billing statements from Nadir were also in the files, all but two of them for the amount of $350. There were also typewritten memos in the files dictated by Canning, relating the substance of telephone conversations held with the various involved insurance companies, and from what I could see, it looked as if almost all of the cases were going to be settled out of court. One other thing did jump out at me from the pages: in nine of the cases in which Nadir had been employed, the physician who had filled out the medical reports was Dr. Milton Cassarene.

I put down the file I'd been reading and asked Sharon, "What are you coming up with?"

"Nadir Industries?"

"Right. You get an address?"

"Just a P.O. box in Santa Ana."

"Yeah, that's all I've got."

"Cassarene's name pops up an awful lot, too."

"Yeah."

"What do you think it means?"

"Probably that he takes the Hippocratic oath with a grain of salt."

I went to the 1981 drawer and went through the same procedure, separating out June through August. A year ago, in the same three-month period, Canning had handled 242 cases, 120 of which had Latino surnames. That was not what I had expected to find. "When did Villalobos start working for your husband?"

"God," she said, touching her temple with her fingertips, "I don't remember exactly. It must have been two years ago, at least. It must have been that because he was in the office for almost a year and it was around Christmastime when he went bankrupt."

I put those cases to one side and pulled Baumgartner's cases for the same three months from both the "Active" and 1981 files. I counted them and jotted down the results on the pad next to the figures for Canning: Active—231, 154 Sp.; 1981—227, 149 Sp.

"That shoots the shit out of that theory," I said, leaning back and tossing the pen on the pad.

"What theory?"

"I thought your good friend Baumgartner might have retagged some of your husband's cases to make it look like they were his own to avoid paying you your twenty-five percent. But Baumgartner's case load a year ago was just as heavy as this year. Almost no change, in fact. And your husband's case load was actually heavier than the year before."

"I told you Ray wasn't that way," she said defensively.

"Maybe. But there's something about the man that doesn't sit right with me. I don't know what it is. I just can't put my finger on it." I picked up the top folder from the pile and opened it. "I'll tell you one thing, they ran a goddamn factory here."

"What do you mean?"

"The only possible way that two men could handle this number of cases is to settle them. They obviously went in for volume, the bulk of which were Latinos. And that percentage didn't drop much after Villalobos split."

I casually glanced over the case of Jesus Conrado, who, on March 14, 1982, had been crossing Windsor Street on foot at the corner when a Mrs. Helen Boswell had made a right hand turn from Eleventh and had hit her brakes too late to avoid hitting Mr. Conrado. He had been taken to the County Hospital with a broken arm and multiple lacerations. He had been released, at which time he had come to the offices of Canning and Baumgartner for legal counsel. By that time, complications had set in with his broken ulna and he had developed "severe back pain," for which he was going to Dr. Milton Cassarene for treatment. Mrs. Boswell's insurance company was Farmers. After four telephone calls by Baumgartner and several threats of a lawsuit, the case had been settled for $10,500, out of which Mr. Conrado had been paid $2,025.

"What's the matter?" Sharon asked, noticing I was staring in a funny way at the open page.

"I'm not sure. It looks like a dental problem."

"A what?"

"A bad case of overbite."

I began riffling through the pages in the folder. Everything seemed in order. There was a photostat of the bank draft issued by the insurance company, endorsed both by Baumgartner and Mr. Conrado; itemized copies of hospital and medical bills, fees for investigative services and expenses, bills for physical therapy and a few miscellaneous expense items that were more vague—one marked "Witness" for $150, and another for "Auto," for $100. I turned a new page over on the legal pad and scribbled down figures, then picked out another file at random and went through it. The story was basically the same there, as it was in the five others I combed through. I slumped back in the chair and looked at them, shaking my head.

"Talk to me," Sharon pleaded. "You've found something?"

I sighed. "Most p.i. attorneys work on a contingency basis, anywhere from thirty to fifty percent of the insurance settlement. The procedure usually followed is that when the attorney agrees to represent a client, he sets up a trust account in the client's name into which goes any settlement money and any money the attorney may advance the client, and from it, the attorney writes checks to cover the client's expenses—medical, investigative, whatever. When the insurance company and the attorney agree to a settlement amount, a bank draft is usually made out jointly in the attorney's and client's names, and both of them have to endorse it before it goes into the account—just so everybody is informed as to what is going on. Then, after all the bills are paid off, the attorney and the client split according to the agreed-upon percentage. Your husband and Baumgartner work on fifty percent." I began tossing folders in front of her. "In this case, Farmers settled for $10,500, out of which the client and Baumgartner each got $2,025. In this case Allstate settled for $9,600; the client and Baumgartner each got $1,950. In this one, Transcontinental, the settlement was $12,900, and the client was given a check for $2,950."

162.

"That doesn't seem like much," she said reasonably. "How much were the expenses?"

"Too much. Everything checks out, though. At least on the surface. The expenses and the net all balance and there are canceled checks and bills for everything."

She lifted her shoulders and held out her palms. "So then, what?"

"There isn't any reason for the expenses to be so high in any of these cases. They never went to court. None of them. They were all settled over the phone in a month or two, and they were all open-and-shut, which was why they were all settled so fast. Yet Nadir's fees and expenses are at least twice as much, and in some cases, triple, what they were in similar cases your husband handled. Cassarene's, too." I pulled one file back and opened it. I found an item and stabbed a finger at it. "Here. Hospital bills for $2,600. The man had a broken arm and was released the next day. *Twenty-six hundred bucks?*"

"A good argument for socialized medicine," she said, deadpan. "But why would the expenses on Ray's cases run so much higher than for Hugh?"

"I think that's something we should look into. Another thing I want to look into is why all the clients in these cases are Chicano and all patients at the county hospital." I took a handful of cases from the top and passed them to her. "Here, pick out ten cases that follow the same pattern—big insurance check, small client check—and get the names and addresses of the clients. The most recent ones. I noticed a couple of cases I looked at were illegal aliens and half of them have probably moved by now to keep a step ahead of the border patrol."

Within a few minutes, she had ten names and addresses and I had fifteen. We put all the files back and locked the cabinets. I looked at my watch: 9:40. We'd been there for almost two hours.

We straightened everything up, then turned out the lights and went out into the hallway. When I turned right instead of left, she said in an urgent whisper, "It's this way. Where are you going?"

"You're whispering again," I told her and kept feeling my way

163

along the hallway. I went into Baumgartner's office and turned on the lights. There was nothing out of the ordinary in the desk and all the files seemed to be tagged the same way as in the master file. Sharon helped me straighten up and we went down one door to Canning's old office.

The room looked about the same as the other day. I popped the lock on the filing cabinet without any trouble and pulled open the "Personal" drawer. The manila folders in the drawer were tagged with different-colored plastic tags on top into which labels had been inserted—"Taxes," "House," "Contracts," "Insurance," etc. The folders were loose between the metal separators that held them up, as if quite a few of them had been extracted. As if to make sure I wouldn't make any mystery of that, Sharon said, "Fred took a lot of the files he thought might be pertinent to the settling of the estate."

Most of the papers in the folders must have been two or three years old; Fred must have taken a lot of the new papers, along with the other folders. I pulled out one labeled "Misc. Expenses" and started rummaging through it.

There were loose receipts inside for gasoline-credit-card purchases, hardware-store receipts for paint, one to a carpet-cleaning company for steam-cleaning a carpet, a couple of bills to Autohaus for work on the Mercedes. One receipt caught my eye, and I pulled it out. It was a bill from the Bank of Newport for the rental of a safe-deposit box, number 722. It was made out to a Harold Cavanaugh, P.O. Box 7891, Laguna, and in pen across the front was written: "Paid, 8/2/82, Chk. #1512."

"Where do you do your banking?" I asked Sharon.

"Barclay's."

"You ever heard of Harold Cavanaugh?"

She paused and thought for a moment. "No. Why? What is that?"

I handed it to her. "That look like your husband's handwriting?"

She stared at it and nodded, very slowly. "Yes . . . it does."

"Can you think of any reason your husband would pay for Harold Cavanaugh's safe-deposit box?"

She handed it back to me. Her eyes blinked rapidly. "No."

"But you're sure it's his handwriting?"

"Let me see that again," she said, taking the slip back. She pursed her lips and scowled. "It looks like it—Wait. . . ."

"What?"

She looked at me and said excitedly, "When I was cleaning up the mess after the burglar or whatever got in, I picked up a key with that number, 722, stamped on it. It was on the floor by the desk and I thought it was strange because it looked like a safe-deposit key and I knew that wasn't our box number."

"What'd you do with it?"

"Put it back on the desk."

I put the slip in my pocket and put the file back in the drawer.

"Why would Hugh keep a safe-deposit box under an alias?" she asked in a bewildered voice.

"A lot of men do it," I said, trying to make light of it. "A lot of men don't like their wives to know exactly what they have, just in case it comes down to divorce settlement."

She shook her head. "This is getting weirder and weirder."

We turned out the lights and made an uneventful exit from the building. When we got into the car, she said, "I need a drink."

"You want me to stop somewhere?"

"No," she said in a tired voice. "Let's just go home."

She was silent on the way back to Laguna. It wasn't an angry silence but a heavy, thoughtful one. She unlocked the front door and went directly to the liquor cabinet and made herself a stiff Dewar's and water, then disappeared down the hallway. I looked up Nadir in the phone book in the kitchen. There was a telephone number but no address. I went into the living room and sat down with the phone. Wayne was still up when I called.

"I was wondering when you were going to call," he said through a yawn. "I was about to give up on you."

"I got hung up. Sorry. You get the skinny?"

"Yeah. Hold a sec." While he was off the line, Sharon walked by and dropped a key in my lap, said she was going to take a shower, and disappeared again. I picked up the key and inspected it. It was shaped like an hourglass at the top and the numbers 722 were stamped clearly into the metal.

There was a rustling on the line. Wayne said, "Okay. Here it is: Amigos was incorporated as a nonprofit organization in 1977. It was granted tax-exempt status in 1979. At the time it was incorporated, George Villalobos was president, but he was replaced last year by Alex Cardozo. Villalobos still retains a majority of stock, however. The other officers are still the same: Paul Covar, vice-president; and Albert Dunne, secretary. Okay?"

"Super, thanks." I paused. "I've got one more for you. . . ."

"Jesus Christ—"

"Nadir Industries," I got out before he could finish.

"—I do have other things to do during the day, you know."

"Do I have to beg?"

He sighed resignedly. "Okay, okay. But this is the last one."

"Absolutely," I promised.

"How do you spell it?"

I told him and he told me to call him at the office by noon. "Righto, buddy. You're a lifesaver. Oh, and Wayne: see if you can get me the address of the corporate headquarters, will you?"

He said he would and I made myself a bourbon and water, then went into Canning's old den. I went through the desk and took out one of the envelopes containing Canning's bank statement and extracted three checks at random. I layered them on the desk, so that the signatures were visible on top of one another. They all matched fairly closely. I selected one, then rummaged through the top drawer until I found a piece of very thin onionskin paper and placed it on top of the check. Luckily for me, Canning had picked a name containing most of the same letters; in fact, the only letters not common in the two names were *i* and *v* and those I would just have to guess at. Starting with the *H*, I moved the tracing paper over the signatures until I'd put together a composite of

166

"Harold Cavanaugh," then put it next to Canning's signature and compared. It looked passable.

Sharon appeared in the doorway in a red kimono and a brown towel wrapped around her wet hair, turban-style. She had a full drink in her hand. "What are you doing?"

"Making a template."

"A what?" she asked, coming in to see.

I showed her the composite. "That's how your husband probably signed 'Harold Cavanaugh.' "

"How could you know that?"

"I don't know for sure. I'm just guessing. He changed his name. There wouldn't have been any reason for him to change his handwriting, just because he changed his name. Renting a safe-deposit box isn't illegal."

"No," she said with what sounded like bitterness, "but who the hell knows what he was doing that for? Maybe he was leading a double life with Alicia and there were a bunch of little Harold Cavanaughs running around somewhere. Maybe he was Harold the Ripper, who stalked the streets of Santa Ana at night, looking for female victims to slash with—"

"I think you're making a little too much out of all this."

"Really?" She gave me a hard look. "How would you like to live with somebody for five years, somebody you trusted and thought you knew, and then roll over one morning and find yourself in bed with a stranger?"

She turned her back to me and sat on the edge of the desk. "Aw, hell, I don't know, Jake. Maybe I am overreacting. Maybe I'm just feeling sorry for myself. But for the first time I'm really beginning to resent the position Hugh left me in. It would've been okay if things had just happened, but it's beginning to look like he was the one who made them happen. And even when they were happening, he didn't tell me a goddamn thing. I'm starting to feel distinctly like a fool."

I got up and went around the desk and put my arm around her, then tilted her chin up with my fingers. "There is no reason to.

167

The man was not a werewolf. I think it's safe to assume he was using Villalobos as a capper, and after that, Nadir, whoever the hell they are. But it's like McClurg said, capping may be unethical, but it's not illegal. Even so, it's not something you come running home to tell your wife about. What did you expect him to say—listen, honey, I want you to know how I'm buying this Mercedes for you; I've got some guys fishing Mexican patients out of the Medical Center third-floor orthopedic ward?"

"I suppose not," she said grudgingly.

"Of course not," I said and pecked her lightly on the lips. "Come on. Let's go in the other room. I need another drink."

We went into the living room and while she fixed two more drinks, I put a log on the fire. I found a jazz FM station on the tuner and we sat on the floor in front of the fire.

After a while, she said, "Thanks for being so sweet through this whole thing, Jake. But no matter how things come out, I want you to know you saved my life. I don't know if I could have held together if you hadn't been here. After what I did to you before, I wouldn't have blamed you if you'd refused to help me."

"You did, though."

"Did what?"

"Blame me."

"I guess I did act like a bitch, but I was desperate."

"And I was scared."

She looked at me curiously. "Are you still scared?"

I thought about it. "Yeah."

"The only reason you're scared is because of before. I wish we didn't have any before. I wish there was just now."

"If we didn't have before, there might not have been a now."

She cocked her head to one side. "Maybe that's true." She touched my face. "It'll be good this time. We understand each other better, I think. You'll see, Jake. I'll make it good."

She unzipped my pants gently and went to work with her mouth, and when I was hard, she unsashed her kimono and lowered herself onto me. She ground her pelvis into me, and her thrusts became more and more violent until she finally screamed

168

and began shivering, and then I let go and she collapsed against my chest.

"I need you, Jake," she said, after a bit. Her voice sounded almost sad. "I really do."

"Right now, you probably do."

"What do you mean by that?"

"Just that there are other issues involved."

Her face turned somberly earnest. "You can't think that that's all you mean to me. You can't think I'm that good an actress."

"No," I said, smiling. "I don't."

I didn't need her, but I sure as hell wanted her.\I wanted to tell her that, but the old fear crept up in my gut again and held me back. I tried to focus in on exactly what I was afraid of. It was ridiculous to equate five years ago with now; we were both different people. The timing had been bad then and timing was everything in life. Maybe, just maybe, the timing was right this time.

And so what if it wasn't? The worst that could happen would be that I would wind up getting reamed again. I'd lived through it before, I'd live through it again.

She brought out a comforter and spread it on the floor in front of the fireplace and we snuggled down in it. I'd tell her, I decided, snuggling against the warm silkiness of her back, as soon as I was convinced of the reality of her feelings and my own. Working on this case, my sense of just what and who was real had probably become a little shaky.

I woke up feeling as if Fred Astaire and Cyd Charisse had done an arrangement of "Dancing in the Dark" on my back. I was getting too old to be sleeping on floors; I wondered why lately I seemed to keep winding up on them.

Sharon was still asleep. I got up without waking her and hobbled into the bathroom. I stepped into a hot shower to loosen up some of the kinks and managed not to scream when the water hit my knees. I looked down and discovered there wasn't much skin left on them. The floor routine would definitely have to go.

By the time I'd shaved and dressed, most of the soreness was gone from my joints, and I was feeling agile enough to tackle the barrio. I found Sharon in the kitchen in her kimono.

"Good morning," she said cheerfully, even though the day was gray again.

She poured two cups of coffee and I said, "You can drink yours while you get dressed. We've got a full schedule today. Got to get moving."

"We?"

"I thought you liked feeling like Myrna Loy."

Her eyes skirted mine. "I just thought, well, that after yesterday, you might not want me around. And I can understand why. I was acting like a jerk."

"True," I agreed. "And today I'm going to give you a chance to redeem yourself. I need your services."

Her eyes darted up. They were in an indigo phase this morning. "*My* services? Doing what?"

"You still fluent in Spanish?"

She nodded.

"Good. I don't think many of those clients whose names we took down last night are going to *habla inglés* too good. You're going to have to ask the questions and translate answers."

She stood up and saluted. "I'll try to make you proud to have me in the agency, sir."

"Asch's Angels," I said, testing the sound of it. "Not bad. You have two girl friends?"

"None I'd trust around you."

While Sharon got ready, I located the addresses we wanted on a map and numbered them according to their proximity to minimize driving time. Three of the addresses on the list were for the same building in Santa Ana, so we went there first.

The address was in south Santa Ana, on a street of peeling slat-wood and stucco houses, across from a weedy patch of grass named Delhi Park. The apartment building would have been a natural in Delhi or even Calcutta. Three stories and battleship-gray, it looked as if it had survived the blitz—barely. Trails of rust ran down its sides from its window screens, and there were big patches of white showing through where the plaster had fallen off. The landlord was probably afraid to paint the place because he would have to cover the *placa*, that ornate, barbed, gang-writing that had been spray-painted on every square foot of available wall space, and to cover or X-out somebody's *placa* was a declaration of war. From what I could see, the place was the turf of either the "King Cobras" or the "Delhis," and a group of what might have been one or the other stood outside in the early-morning shadows watching us sullenly as we pulled up. Whichever they were,

171

their dark, saturnine faces said that whoever's turf this was, it wasn't ours.

Sharon watched them nervously, and said, "You think it'll be all right to leave the car here?"

"They know cops don't drive Mercedeses," I said. "Besides, these cars have funny lug nuts, and unless they have a special wrench, they won't be able to get them off. There's not much they can do, except vandalize the car."

"Thanks," she said. "I feel much better."

We locked the car and went up the cracked walkway to the front entrance. The pack watched us and several of them made lascivious remarks in Spanish as we walked by, and they all laughed. Sharon's neck reddened and her mouth tightened angrily, but she didn't say anything and I didn't ask her to translate.

The hallway we entered was dark and the smell of cooking lard, refried beans, and dried urine hung like a heavy, sodden blanket. Behind closed doors and paper-thin walls, Spanish voices sold cars and washing machines and babies wailed.

We found apartment 12 and knocked. There were quick, furtive footsteps behind the door and it opened a crack, revealing a dark eye and part of a woman's face. The woman became immediately nervous when she saw two Anglos standing at her door, and Sharon tried to calm her by declaring the speech we had rehearsed, that we did not represent any federal, state, city, county, or collection agency, that we were from the insurance company and we were looking into the claim of Mr. Angel Cruz. It looked as if a mistake had been made on the payment of his accident settlement, and if that were the case, we owed Mr. Cruz money. A great deal of money. That did not seem to allay the woman's nervousness much, however, and she told us in a shaky voice that she had moved into this apartment two months ago and that she did not know any Angel Cruz. We thanked her and went down the dim hallway, looking for apartment 21.

"You believe her?" Sharon asked.

"Who knows? These people all live in deadly fear of *inmigración*. We can't do much about it if she is lying. It'd be a little difficult to inconspicuously stake out a place like this, waiting for Mr. Cruz to come home."

We got pretty much the same story in apartment 21, except the woman there would not open the door. She talked through it. No José Martinez. Gone. Forwarding address? Sure. General Delivery, Mexico. *Muchísimas gracias.*

The man who answered the door of the next apartment was shirtless and his hair was tousled by sleep, and when Sharon asked if Guillermo Duran was home, the sleepiness in his eyes was replaced by wariness, and he replied that he was Guillermo Duran. The wariness was replaced by joy when we gave him the "error in the settlement" story, and he thanked some saint whose name I couldn't catch and pulled us inside.

The apartment was one tiny, messy room filled with cardboard boxes and a few pieces of soiled, threadbare furniture. From the look and smell of things, Duran did not live alone. The room was divided into two sections by a dirty sheet hanging from the ceiling; a dirty mattress lay in front of it on the floor by the wall and the smell of soured bodies and sheets, cigarette and marijuana smoke had soaked into the pasteboard walls through years of communal living. Duran pulled up chairs for us at the dining-room table, a cardboard card table. Sharon looked at the chair with trepidation before sitting down.

Duran was a short, dark pudgy man who could have been thirty or forty-five or anywhere in between. He watched us warily and started to get spooked when I set up my cassette recorder on the table, but Sharon allayed his apprehension by assuring him that the tape would be kept strictly confidential and not played for anyone outside the insurance company. He spoke no English, so Sharon put to him in Spanish the questions I gave her.

Duran was a dishwasher who had come across the border legally from Hermosillo two years earlier. Seven months ago, he had been riding as a passenger in the car of Angel Cruz, when they had been broadsided by a produce truck. He, Cruz, and another passenger all wound up with injuries, and it was while they were in the County Hospital being treated that they had been approached by Alex Cardozo, who had persuaded the three of them to retain Ray Baumgartner as their attorney. Cardozo told the men that Baumgartner was the best claims attorney in the county and would get them the maximum possible settlement.

Duran had never seen or talked to Baumgartner; all his contact with the lawyer's office had been through Cardozo. It had been Cardozo who had kept Duran informed about the developments in the cases and it had been Cardozo who had referred him to Cassarene. Cassarene had seen Duran a total of twice, treating him for a broken wrist and acute neck pain, which had gotten so intense at one point that it had prevented him from working and had cost him his job.

The case had dragged on for four months; whenever Duran tried to question Cardozo about money, he was stalled, being told that litigation of this nature took time. Finally, a month later, Cardozo showed up at Duran's apartment with some papers written in English and told him that the case was close to being settled and that Duran had to sign the papers to secure release of the money. When Duran had asked how much he was to get, Cardozo had told him, "around six thousand dollars." Duran had signed the documents even though he couldn't read them and Cardozo had gone away. He returned a week later, with a check from Baumgartner for $1,200. When Duran asked what had happened to the $6,000 he had been promised, Cardozo had simply shrugged and said that Duran had misunderstood, that the $6,000 was the total amount of Duran's settlement; the rest of the money had gone to pay medical and legal expenses.

Upon checking, Duran found that his friends had received similar settlements. It was a couple of weeks later that he and the others started getting past-due notices from the hospital saying that he still owed a balance of $732.41 on his bill. He had tried to argue that the bill had been paid by his attorney, but the hospital credit people were adamant, saying that the bill had not been paid and that Duran was past due. Duran tried to get in touch with Baumgartner, but was unable to get the attorney on the phone; he

174

was always out or in conference. Luckily for Duran, he had put his $1,200 in the bank. He paid the hospital, leaving him a total of $467.59 for his pain and suffering; but his friends had not been so lucky. They'd spent most of their settlement money already and had returned to Mexico to avoid paying their hospital bills, which had also not been paid.

Duran pleaded with us to try to get him some of the money he had been promised; he had a wife and four children in Hermosillo he had to support and he had been unable to send them any money ever since he had lost his job. We told him in soothing tones that we would see what we could do to get his money, and we left to his grateful repeat chorus of "Muchas gracias."

Por nada, Mr. Duran. Exactly right. For nothing.

The King Cobras were still out front and as we went by, the decision was made for them, and they did their little catcall routine at Sharon. After listening to Duran's story, my mood was running toward mongoose, but I let it slide and went to the car.

After a block or so, Sharon said, "I felt terrible lying to the man like that and getting his hopes up."

"I know, but there wasn't much else we could do. He wouldn't have talked to us any other way."

She shuddered and made a face. "I thought I was going to faint from the smell in there. It's hard to believe that people actually live that way."

"They do," I said. "A lot more of the world than live in houses in the Laguna Hills." I consulted the list, then the map. "We go up here to Lucretia and make a left. It should be about seven or eight blocks."

"How much did the insurance company settle for?" she asked.

"Nine thousand."

"They took seventy-eight hundred dollars from that man and didn't even pay the goddamn hospital bill." She tossed a hand angrily in the air. "How could they do something like that? I mean capping is one thing. It may be unethical, okay. But *that's* immoral."

175

"Not to mention illegal," I said.

"That man has nothing and they squeezed the blood out of him."

"Grand larceny. Which was why Duran was picked. He's a perfect victim."

"Why?"

"Because the chances of him doing anything about it are pretty slim. He can't speak English and has no idea of how the judicial system in this country works or where he could go for recourse. He's scared to make any waves because he's an alien and lives in constant fear of being shipped back to good old Mexico. And he's poor, so even if he wanted to hire another lawyer—which at this stage he would probably be afraid to do anyway—he couldn't, after being fucked over by Baumgartner. And if on the off chance he did manage to make some waves, Baumgartner could always say it was just a mistake. Everything else was handled meticulously. All the expenses were itemized and Duran did endorse the draft from the insurance company."

"You think they forged his signature?"

"I doubt it," I said. "I'd bet that the draft was in that stack of papers that Cardozo brought over to Duran and had him sign. Duran doesn't read English anyway, so why would he bother to even look at it? What interests me," I continued, trying to put it all together in my mind, "is that Duran said all his contact was through Alex Cardozo."

She glanced at me quickly. "The man Diane McClurg had her run-in with at the hospital?"

"The same. Only according to Baumgartner's case file, Nadir Industries was paid for handling Duran's case. Your husband had already kicked Villalobos out of the office by that time."

"You think Cardozo hustles for both Nadir and Villalobos?"

"Maybe. Maybe only Villalobos's physical presence left the office. Maybe Nadir is just a face conjured up by the Wizard of Oz."

"Villalobos?" she asked, catching on.

"I wonder. We'll know about that when I talk to Wayne." I pointed to the next street. "This is it. Turn here."

The houses seemed to shrink and grow dustier with every block we drove. People were moving about on the street now, all with that weary, torpid air that comes with a life of hard labor. Brown-faced children stopped playing among broken-down cars and junk that littered front yards, and stared at us as we went by.

By 11:30, we had eliminated thirteen names from the list. Five of them were gone, no forwarding address; four more refused to talk to us; and the four who did had pretty much the same story to tell as Duran. The numbers changed a bit from case to case, but they had all been royally screwed by their attorney, Baumgartner, and they had the hospital snapping at their heels for payment of their bills. Only one of them had ever had any contact with Baumgartner, and that had been by phone. All the rest had dealt exclusively with either Cardozo or a man named Luis Alesandro.

After smelling burritos all morning, I had a craving for one, so Sharon suggested we stop for lunch at a Mexican joint downtown called Ernesto's. It was crowded and I left Sharon to put our name on a waiting list while I went to search for a phone.

By the time I got back, she was seated in a booth and had a strawberry margarita in front of her. I slid in and said, "Bingo."

"Tell me, tell me," she said, through two straws.

"Nadir was incorporated nine months ago. The principal officers are Luis Alesandro, president, and Albert Dunne, secretary-treasurer. No vice-president. Albert Dunne is also the secretary of Amigos. Not only that. The corporate headquarters are listed as 1134 Fourteenth Street, Suite 34, Santa Ana. That building is owned by Azteca, Inc."

"Then Nadir is a front for Villalobos," she said.

"That's my guess." I signaled to a white-jacketed waiter and ordered a Dos Equis.

Sharon slumped back. "Villalobos never left the office. All that was just for show."

"But for whose benefit? That's the question."

177

She sat up again. "What do you mean?"

"All the cases on our list are Baumgartner's. The fees your husband paid Nadir and Group Associates didn't vary much—usually a flat three hundred fifty dollars, which would be the capping fee. So we can assume he was employing Villalobos as a capper. Then came the trouble and he kicked him out, which put him between a rock and a hard place."

The waiter brought my beer and I dug into the chips and salsa. I was starting to get excited; the whole goddamn mess was finally beginning to make sense.

"What rock and what hard place?"

"He couldn't keep Villalobos around after what had happened, but he couldn't do without him, either. He was in deep financial trouble and he couldn't very well eliminate the source of revenue that Villalobos had been bringing into the office. The only way he could keep his head above water was find another capper. Presto, chang-o, along comes Luis Alesandro who offers him Nadir's services for the same price."

The waiter came back, interrupting us, and asked if we were ready to order. I ordered a chimichanga and a side of flour tortillas and Sharon ordered machaca. We both pounced on the chips and salsa. She was excited now too.

"You don't think Hugh knew Nadir was a front for Villalobos?" she asked.

"Not then. I don't think he knew until a couple of weeks before he died, until he got a call from an investigator from the State Bar who called about a complaint from meddlesome Ms. McClurg about Amigos' little referral operation at the hospital. That call had to get his curiosity up. So what does he do? He starts looking through Baumgartner's case files and he finds that his trusted partner and longtime friend has been working a kickback scheme with both Villalobos and Cassarene and has been defrauding both his clients and Canning of their settlement money."

"You think Ray knew about Villalobos being Nadir?"

"He knew Cardozo was Villalobos's right hand. And Cardozo was the liaison man."

178

Her eyes widened in horror. "Are you saying that Ray killed Hugh?"

"I'm not sure anybody killed anybody at this point. Maybe Canning got so depressed at his discovery that he decided to end it all."

"Then why would Ray send those men to try to hurt you?"

I shrugged. "Maybe he was afraid that my stirring things up would lift the lid on his arrangement with Villalobos."

She shook her head slowly. "I can't believe it. Ray . . ."

"It fits what we have so far," I said, taking a swig of beer. It was ice-cold and cut through the spiciness of the salsa.

"What are we going to do about it?"

"Well," I said through a mouthful of corn chips, "after we take care of business at the bank and UC Irvine, I'm going to drop over to Baumgartner's office, pick up a check for my services to date, and quit."

"Quit?" she said, lurching forward. "What are you talking about?"

"Easy, woman. I'm not really quitting. I'm just going to tell him I am so he'll call off the dogs. I work much better without dodging truckloads of pipe. Also, you might as well stick him with my bill. If we're right, I have a feeling in another week he won't be in much of a mood to pay me, but right now, he should be happy as a clam to lend you the money, just to get me out of his hair."

She ducked her head and winced worriedly. "You don't expect me to be there with you, do you?"

"Yep," I said, nodding. "It'll add to the realism. You're good and pissed that I'm quitting. Also, I'm going to throw in most of the bill for my car as expenses and he'll scream, and I need you to back me up on it."

She shook her head uncertainly. "I don't think I can do it, Jake. I couldn't look him in the eye knowing what I know. . . ."

"Sure you can," I said, squeezing her arm encouragingly. "Look, we can't break up this team now. Where would I be without my trusted Cato?"

"Well, all right," she decided. "I don't know if I can carry it off, but I'll give it a try."

"That's my girl," I said, popping a salsa-dipped corn chip in my mouth.

After a moment, she suddenly looked up from her food. "Cato?"

I nodded. "Drives for the Green Hornet. Don't tell me you didn't faithfully follow their adventures every Sunday."

She shook her head. "I was strictly a Mary Worth girl."

"You're probably better off," I told her.

18

The branch of the Bank of Newport where Harold Cavanaugh kept his safe-deposit box was on Pacific Coast Highway, near Mac-Arthur. The building was new and bright and glassy and surrounded by a lot of tropical-looking plants, and the thick slab of roof that topped it lent it an aura of solidity. Sharon parked in the lot and killed the engine, then turned to me with a concerned expression. "What if you're wrong about this?"

"About what?"

"About Hugh being Harold Cavanaugh?"

"Then I'll close up the box and that'll be that."

"What if you're wrong about him not changing his signature?"

I smiled at her and leaned over and pecked her on the cheek. "Then I'll probably get caught and the people at the bank will probably call the cops and I'll need you for a backup story, so stick around."

"What can they do to you?"

"I guess that depends on how nasty they want to be," I said. "Take my license away, maybe. I don't know if they'd be able to make forgery stick, but they might."

She shook her head. "I can't let you take that kind of risk—"

I silenced her by putting a finger across her lips. *"You* can't pass for Harold Cavanaugh, that's for sure. Look, chances are, it'll work. Your husband probably didn't bank there much. More than likely, they won't know Harold Cavanaugh from Red Skelton. I'll be out in a couple of minutes." I kissed her and got out of the car.

The bank was crowded, which was good for me. The woman behind the safe-deposit counter was busy with a customer as I walked past. I went to one of the counters and pretended to be making out a deposit slip. The fat woman standing next to me must have thought my constant glancing over at the safe-deposit desk was being aimed at her because she turned up her nose and moved a counter away. After a minute or two, the teller took her customer into the vault; while they were gone, I went over to the desk and picked up one of her blank admittance slips and took it back to the writing counter. Out of my pocket, I took the composite signature I'd made up and carefully copied it on the admittance slip, then palmed the slip. The teller was back at her desk now and I walked over, smiling cheerfully, hoping she'd be dumb. "Hi."

She smiled and said hello.

I took a blank admittance slip from the stack on the desk and shielded it from her eyes as I pretended to sign it, then looked up and asked, "What time is it, anyway?"

She glanced down at her watch and I palmed the new slip and substituted the presigned one.

"Ten-twenty."

I handed her the slip and she punched it in the time clock, then went to the file to check the signature. My palms were clammy. She returned without saying anything, took a set of keys from her desk drawer, and went to the stainless-steel-barred doors behind her. I let out the breath I'd been holding and followed meekly.

We passed through a small room containing private cubbyholes where people could go through the contents of their boxes undisturbed, then through another barred door into an L-shaped room filled with small, numbered, stainless-steel doors. She went right to 722. We both put our keys in and she opened it; I pulled out the box and asked her if I could have a private room. She smiled. "Certainly," she said, and led me to the cubbyholes in the other room. I thanked her, picked a cubbyhole and put the box on the counter, then closed the door.

There were only two items in the box. One was a white, blank, business-size envelope, sealed. It was thick with what felt as if it could be money. Ripping it open, I found it was money. I didn't bother to count it, but the denominations seemed all to be hundreds. The second item was a nine-by-twelve manila envelope. It was addressed to Hugh Canning, at his office. The words "Personal" and "Confidential" were stamped, not written, on the envelope, which meant the sender was probably someone who sent a lot of personal and confidential mail. The sender was a McNor Corporation, which meant nothing to me, in San Antonio, Texas. The postmark meant something to me, though. It was also San Antonio, but it was the date that got me: September 5. Allowing three days for travel time, it was possible that the envelope had arrived the day of Canning's accident.

I gathered up both envelopes and buzzed the teller. She came in and together we put the box back. I thanked her and slid past her through the barred doors.

I went out the doors into the sunshine, feeling as if a current of electricity were running up my arm from the things in my hand. The case was there; I was holding it. I don't know how I knew it, but I did. Call it a sixth sense, psychometry, whatever, but I knew everything was going to come together when I ripped open that envelope.

I must have looked rather manic when I opened the car door and got in, because Sharon asked unsurely, "Is everything all right?"

"Fine. Everything went smooth as silk."

"Was it Hugh's box?"

"Here, have some money." I tossed the envelope into her lap and she picked it up and gasped when she looked inside.

"You're sure this belonged to Hugh?"

"I'm sure."

"There must be thousands in here."

"Probably," I said, not paying much attention. I was too busy bending back the metal tabs on the McNor envelope. I looked up long enough to say, "Why don't we get out of here. Just in case somebody decides that those signatures don't match."

The contents of the envelope was a seven-page report on Jackson Meriwether by the McNor Corporation, which was a firm in San Antonio that handled private investigations and security problems. I started to dig into it and Sharon asked, "Where to? UC Irvine?"

I tore myself away from it and looked up. "Huh? Yeah. Right."

I went back to it and she asked worriedly, "Where do you think Hugh got all that money? You think it was from something illegal?"

I kept my head buried in the report. "I don't know."

"Why would he hide it like that? Why wouldn't he want me to know about it?"

"Maybe he was going to surprise you on your birthday and send you on a two-week vacation to Ulan Bator."

She did a double take on that one. "Where the hell is that?"

"The capital of Outer Mongolia. You're an ex-stew. You should know things like that."

"Sorry. That one slipped by me."

She looked over and seemed to notice for the first time that I was engrossed in the report. "What's that?"

"If you'd let me read it, I might find out."

She reared back. "Well, *excuse* me."

She turned left on MacArthur and headed into the hills, away from the coast, and I went back to San Antonio. Five minutes later, I looked up and said, "Well, whatever your husband was going to do with that money, he wasn't going to buy Alicia a fur coat with it."

"Why?"

"Because we just found her." I tapped the report with an index finger. "In here."

"Who is she?" she asked intently.

184

"Not a who. A what. This, my dear, is a report from a private detective agency in San Antonio named McNor Corporation. Your husband apparently hired them quite a few months ago to do some background research on Meriwether, find out what he's really into, where he got his money. In the first report, I guess things checked out pretty much okay. Meriwether is into the same things in Texas he is here—real estate, commodities, stock market, owns part of a minor department-store chain. Your husband paid them their fee and that was that. Until a couple of weeks before he died."

"Cut the dramatic pauses," she said breathlessly. "Let's get to the meat."

"Mr. McNor came across a piece of information, given by an informant, and he wrote Canning asking if he wanted to pursue it. Canning gave him the green light, and what he came up with was Alicia, Incorporated, a company in Beaumont, Texas. And from what McNor says, it's how Meriwether initially got the money to make all those other investments." I paused. "You ever see those inflatable rubber dolls that they advertise in girlie magazines?"

Her mouth gaped and her eyes widened until I could see the white all the way around the pupils. "You've got to be kidding. You don't mean—"

"Jackson Meriwether is the rubber-sex-doll king of the Western world," I read from the report. " 'For Only $14.95, Never Be Alone Again! 37-23-36. You'll love her, she'll love you. Alicia— the bed partner that doesn't talk back—just obeys! Real hair— $10 extra!' Want to see her picture?"

I held up the ad so she could see the wide-eyed balloon with the gaping mouth. Ringlets of brown hair fell across its face, giving it the appearance of an inflated Shirley Temple.

"*That's* what we've been looking for?"

"The beautiful alluring Alicia. Don't blame your husband too much. No man could resist her."

She started to laugh and nearly went off the road.

"Careful," I shouted.

She was howling now, and through the howls, she managed to

say, "Here we all thought he was some mysterious Great Gatsby in a white suit, running guns to Latin America, and all the time, he was making jack-off toys."

"It's funny, all right," I said, "but it sure muddies the water."

Her laughing subsided to a chuckle, and she wiped the tears from her eyes with two fingers. "Why? What do you mean?"

"I was sure we had Baumgartner cold. I was sure he was it. He had motive and opportunity and everything seemed to fit. Now I don't know. Now we've got two people with motive and opportunity."

She stopped laughing entirely now and said, "You mean because of *that*?"

I nodded. "Being accepted by Newport society is very important to Meriwether. He thrives on it—throwing his big parties and having all the hotsy-totsies showing up. The hotsy-totsies would accept a gunrunner. There's some mystery to it, a feeling of adventure rubbing elbows with a man who deals in violence and death. But a man who makes balloons to dip your wick in? Not bloody likely. He'd be a goddamn pariah."

She snapped her fingers. "The phone call!"

"Sharp, Myrna. You might make a detective yet."

"Cato," she said, correcting me.

"Sorry. Cato." I picked up the manila envelope. "From the postmark, your husband could have gotten this the day he died, or maybe the day before. That would explain the phone call and the note—he was probably doodling while he listened to Meriwether sweat on the other end of the line. Hugh could have called him for one of two reasons—blackmail, or just to taunt him, to let him know he was going to make good on his threat to ruin him. It could also explain what they were looking for when they hit your house."

"And the Balboa Bay Club," she said, tight-lipped.

"What about it?"

"We hadn't been there in months, ever since the incident with Meriwether. Hugh had been so embarrassed then, I couldn't

186

understand why he would want to go back there, but he insisted. It would be a fitting place to celebrate a victory, wouldn't it? He would have wound up the victor in the rematch at the same stadium."

"It makes sense," I said. "If it was blackmail, Hugh could have set up a meeting with Meriwether. He did tell you he had a business appointment and we do know it wasn't with any clients on his regular calendar. Maybe he wanted to discuss business or maybe he just wanted to see Meriwether grovel a little." I played the possibilities of the scene in my mind.

"You think Meriwether killed Hugh?" she asked.

"I don't know. It seems like a ridiculous motive for murder, but I've heard of sillier ones. I do know there are too many goddamn suspects in this case and every time I think I have things narrowed down, another one pops up." I thought about what we had. "How far is your bank from here?"

"Fifteen minutes. But it's the other direction."

"You have a safe-deposit box?"

"Sure."

"Turn around. I don't want to drive around with this thing. Let's stick it in your box before we do anything. They already tore up your house once looking for it."

We deposited the report at her bank, then drove over to the U.C. Irvine campus. The university's modern stone buildings looked out of place sitting amid the sun-browned hills, like some stark mirage that had been transplanted from some other time or place. We asked the campus cop in the guard kiosk the way to the Medical School library, and he pointed out a building a few hundred yards away and told us where to park. I stuffed the money envelope in my pocket and we went inside.

A perky little brunette who looked as if she had dressed herself right out of *The Preppy Handbook* was at the reference desk in the library. She told me that the MEDLAR on-line computer banks went back only to 1980 and the charge to pull a reference from those was nine dollars, but that they had five different files that went back to 1979, and she could run those for three dollars apiece. I gave her nine bucks and told her that if I needed the back files, I'd have her pull them later, and asked her to cross-index "Aplastic anemia" and "toxic substances." She came back a few minutes later with a perforated printout about two feet long and we took it over to one of the study tables and started going over it.

There were thirty-four references on the sheet, correlating cases of aplastic anemia with everything from rubber cement and hair dyes to glaze decoration on pottery. For being such a rare condition, aplastic anemia could sure be triggered off by a lot of things. I went down the list, eliminating those substances, like rubber cement, that would require prolonged contact or would obviously be freak reactions, and wound up with fourteen entries. I took the sheet back up to Miss Preppy and she helped me round up twelve of the fourteen journals. She said she could probably get the other two in a day or so, if I needed them, and I thanked her, but said these would suffice, and lugged them back to the study table.

"Educate yourself," I said, counting five off the top of the pile and shoving them in front of Sharon.

"What am I looking for, pray tell?"

"A toxin that would consistently cause aplastic anemia—and notice I accent the word 'consistently.' Preferably one strong enough to get the job done with a single dose."

She picked up one journal and looked at it in disbelief. " 'Mutagenicity and cytotoxicity in V-79 Chinese hamster cells.' That appeared in the March edition of *Blood*, my favorite magazine. I don't know how I missed that issue."

"You wanted to be a detective. This is what it's all about."

In spite of my narrowing down the material, most of the substances mentioned in the journals were either uncertain in their correlation to aplastic anemia, isolated cases, or cases of workers who had come in contact with some toxin over a period of years.

After an hour, my eyes were starting to cross, but halfway into "Autologous Bone Marrow Grafts in Dogs Treated with Lethal Doses of CCNU," they snapped into focus. "I want you to think back, Sharon," I said. "About four or five weeks before the acci-

188

dent. Did your husband have a bout of vomiting or nausea? Any stomach problems at all?"

"Not that I can remember."

"How about a loss of appetite? Maybe a couple of days where he didn't eat?"

Her eyes widened suddenly and she shook her fingers. "Wait. Yes. Hugh came home from work one night—it must have been a month or so before the accident—complaining he didn't feel well. His stomach was upset and he figured he'd gotten something bad at lunch. He'd had fish or something. I gave him a Combid, but he was still in and out of bed all night. He had the runs, too. He was all right in the morning, but for the next couple of days, he didn't eat anything at all. Said he just wasn't hungry. But he was back to normal after that."

"Lomustine," I said.

"Huh?"

"Methyl CCNU," I said, putting the copy of the *Cancer Research* on the table. "It's a drug used in chemotherapy, particularly in the treatment of brain tumors. According to this article, it should only be used by doctors who are used to treating aplasia because one of its main side effects is delayed bone-marrow damage. It's colorless and odorless and a three-hundred-cc dose is fatal."

"But what about the autopsy?"

I shook my head. "That's the beauty of it. The drug is in and out of the system in five hours. Three to six hours after ingestion, nausea and vomiting occur, but the vomiting is triggered from the *area postrema* of the brain, not the stomach, which means that the drug has already done its damage. Anorexia may last one or two days after that, but it usually passes, after which the person would return to normal with absolutely no inkling that his bone marrow had been wiped out and that his life span had been cut to six weeks. If you wanted to kill someone and weren't in a hurry, you'd have about the perfect goddamn murder weapon. Nobody would suspect murder, and even if they did, proving it would be next to impossible."

"Cassarene," she breathed.

I shrugged. "He would be able to get the drug, that's for sure. Maybe he had some left over."

She hunched over the table excitedly. "You mean his wife?"

"It's a possibility. Which is all we need—another possibility. Now all we need to do is find a way to tie in Hugh's secretary, the bartender at the Balboa Bay Club, and the guy who's fixing my car, and we'll wind this thing up."

"Why would Cassarene want to kill Hugh?" she asked. "You think Hugh figured out about Cassarene's wife? Maybe that's where that money came from."

"Even if it did, there would be no way to prove Cassarene's wife didn't die of some disease. Number two, if Cassarene had slipped her a dose of lomustine and your husband knew it, Cassarene wouldn't in all likelihood try using the same stuff on him. As soon as he started developing symptoms, Hugh would have known what was happening to him and gone to the cops. And if Cassarene knew Hugh was terminal, why go to all the trouble and risk of faking an accident?"

"What if Cassarene hadn't been in any hurry for Hugh to die when he gave him the drug, but then something happened to force him to speed things up?"

"Like Hugh discovering that he was up to his eyeballs in an insurance scam to rip off his Chicano patients? Not a bad guess, Myrna. That would possibly drop Baumgartner back into the middle of things. But it could also be that Cassarene isn't involved. Maybe somebody just got the idea from him, or from MEDLAR, for that matter, like we did."

"But the fact is, only a doctor can get the stuff, right?"

That one started me thinking. "Or somebody who has access to a doctor." I stood up and gathered up the journals. "One thing is for goddamn sure: we're not going to get any answers sitting here talking maybes."

We left and drove to Baumgartner's office. On the way, I went over with her how I wanted her to play it as I worked up my expense sheet. She seemed to have it down, although I could see the tension building in her as we neared the Seventeenth Street off ramp.

It was almost five and there was nobody in the waiting room. The receptionist told us that Baumgartner was in conference with a client, but would be able to see us in five minutes, so I took the opportunity to search out Sally Branscomb. I found her alone in her office, putting her IBM Selectric to bed for the night.

"Hi," I said. "Remember me?"

"Hello," she said, glancing up and smiling. "Certainly I remember you, Mr. Asch. How's the investigation coming?"

"That's what I want to talk to you about, Sally. Do you remember a ten-by-twelve manila envelope arriving here addressed to Mr. Canning, either the day or the day before he died?"

Her face scrunched up and she scratched the back of her neck. "Gee, we get so much mail—"

"It would have been from the McNor Corporation in San Antonio, Texas."

Her eyes lighted with recollection. "Oh, yeah, I remember that. I noticed it because it was from Texas. And because Mr. Canning seemed excited when I gave it to him. He said he'd been waiting for it for some time."

"Which day was it, the day he died or the day before?"

"The day he died, I think. I'm not really sure."

"Did you ask him what it was?"

She seemed shocked by the suggestion. "I didn't have to. He told me."

"What did he say?"

"It was a stock prospectus of some oil company he was thinking of investing some money in."

I nodded. "Do you remember Canning going out at all the day he died?"

She nodded. "Just for lunch."

"One more thing: would you happen to remember if Canning had an appointment or received a phone call about four weeks before he died, from a Jackson Meriwether or a Tony Halstead or Dr. Milton Cassarene?"

"You'd have to talk to the receptionist," she said in an offended tone. "I don't answer the phone."

"Thanks, anyway," I said, and slipped out the door, nearly running into Sharon in the process. I touched her arm. It was like petrified wood.

"He's free now," she said, in a brittle voice. We moved down the hallway and she whispered, "I just hope I don't blow it."

"You won't. Just try not to fly across the desk and tear his eyes out."

"It isn't his eyes I was thinking about."

"Just misdirect all that hostility at me."

The lawyer smile was blazing on Baumgartner's face as we entered and he threw open his arms and came around the desk. He first bent to give Sharon a kiss and I could see her visibly stiffen as she dutifully offered her cheek. We shook hands and he said, "Sit down, sit down," then perched himself on the edge of his desk. When we were seated, he asked, "So, what's happening?"

"I'm quitting," I said. From my coat pocket I took my itemized bill, plus the envelope in which I'd sealed my receipts, and handed them to him. "I think you'll find everything there."

He held them, dumbfounded. "But . . . why?"

"Let's just say complications have arisen. Personal complications." I glanced at Sharon, but she refused to look at me. She crossed her arms and turned her head to avoid it. "It is my wish," I went on, "and that of Mrs. Canning that my services be terminated. I've recommended some other investigators that I think might be able to get the job done more objectively—"

"We'll find our own man," she said, tight-lipped. "I wouldn't use anyone *you* recommended."

The corner of Baumgartner's mouth twitched a little, as if he were trying to suppress a grin. "Well, I must say, this is a shock. Have you found out anything?"

"Nothing that's going to make the insurance company change its mind."

"You've written a report?"

I nodded. "Sharon has it."

192

"And your conclusions?"

"I'm not sure," I said, rubbing my chin. "I am pretty sure it wasn't an accident, though."

He lifted a hand from the desk and turned up the palm. "That only leaves suicide."

"No," I said. "There's death at the hands of another."

"Murder?" he exclaimed, sticking his neck way out, as if to get a closer look at me. "You're saying Hugh was murdered?"

"No. I'm just saying it's one of two possibilities, taking into consideration the physical evidence."

"But . . . that's preposterous. On what evidence are you basing that supposition?"

"If by 'evidence' you mean hard facts, I'm not. I've turned up nothing that refutes Transcontinental's version of what happened. But murder can be made to fit the same set of facts." I paused and focused on his eyes. "And then there are the two break-ins, and the fact that somebody tried to have me surgically removed from the case shortly thereafter."

His eyes squinted. "What do you mean?"

"I mean somebody tried to have me whacked." I briefly related the two incidents to him.

He pushed off from his desk and went behind it and sat down heavily. He bit his lower lip and said, "You can't be sure that those were murder attempts—"

"No, I can't, but I'd give odds."

"Why don't you admit that you're scared?" Sharon chimed in. She grimaced, showing some teeth, and glared at me. "That's why you're quitting. Not because of me."

I pointed a finger at her. "Now, look—"

"*You* look," she said angrily. "I was really stupid to have called you in the first place. You're not the same man I knew five years ago." She was laying it on a little thick, but that was okay. It sounded real enough. She turned to Baumgartner and said, "Pay the man off, Ray. Let him go back to L.A. We'll get a *good* detective on the case."

Baumgartner waved placating hands at her. "Now, Sharon,

calm down." To me: "Who would have wanted to kill Hugh? Do you have any suspects?"

He was pumping me. I shook my head. "The next guy you hire will have to come up with suspects. But judging from those two break-ins, I'd say that Canning had something that somebody else wants."

"What?"

I shrugged and took the bill I'd worked up out of my pocket and leaned across the desk to give it to him. "Here's my bill. I'd appreciate a check so I can get back to L.A. tonight."

His face registered disbelief as he went over it. "You can't be serious."

I raised both eyebrows. "Something wrong?"

"It's way out of line, that's what's wrong," he said, snapping it with his middle finger. "Fifteen hundred twenty-eight dollars and sixty-four cents? Give me a break."

"Five days at two hundred a day minus the five hundred retainer—"

"Yes, yes, I know all that," he said impatiently. "But what's the rest of this garbage? Eight hundred fifty dollars for 'car repairs'? What was that, the truck on the Ortega Highway?"

"No. That was a rental. This was the punks with the tire irons."

"My God, it's merely speculation that those men were sent to get you. I'm sorry, but I won't pay that."

"It's a work-related expense," I explained calmly. "I was interviewing a witness in the case when it happened. If I hadn't been on the job, I wouldn't have been in that particular place at that particular time. Look at it like disability."

"I'm looking at it like attempted robbery," he said, leaning back and stroking his mustache.

"Pay him," Sharon said. She wouldn't look at Baumgartner's eyes, but was focusing on a point somewhere around the knot in his necktie.

Baumgartner sat up and said, "Don't be silly, Sharon. We don't have to pay—"

"*You're* not paying him," she reminded him. "I am. This is

just a loan, remember? I made the mistake of not letting you get the investigator, like you wanted, but I'm willing to pay for it. Pay him the full amount and let him get out of here."

Baumgartner shook his head and reluctantly pulled out a checkbook from the desk drawer. "This is against my better judgment." He wrote out a check for the full amount, handed it to me, and I pocketed it.

"You just drop a bombshell like that on us and walk out?"

"It didn't work out, that's all," I said. "That happens in life quite a bit. Good-bye, Mr. Baumgartner."

We started out and Baumgartner called: "Sharon, wait. I'd like to speak to you for a moment, privately."

I continued out the door and went over to talk to the receptionist. With the number of calls she handled, I didn't have much hope of her remembering if Meriwether or Halstead had called Canning a month before his death. She didn't. Cassarene's office had called quite a bit, so whatever she remembered that way wouldn't mean much. Sharon came out, walking briskly, a few moments later. She said good night to the receptionist and walked by me as if I were invisible, and I shrugged and followed Sharon outside.

A few paces down the walk, she started to slow up for me, but I said, "Keep walking like you're pissed. He may be watching from the window."

I followed her two steps behind all the way to the car. When we reached the car, she said, "Well? How was I?"

"Sensational. Better than Jill St. John in *The Oscar*."

"Gee, thanks," she said, making a face, then blew out some air. "I didn't know if I could pull it off. For a while there, I wasn't sure. I wanted to kill the sonofabitch. Then I remembered what you said about displacing all the aggression toward you."

"You were fine. He bought it, didn't he?"

"Hook, line, and sinker," she said, smiling broadly.

"What did he want to talk to you about?"

She turned on Seventeenth and headed for the freeway. "He didn't want me to take too much stock in your murder theory. He thinks it's a bunch of hooey."

"Naturally, he would."

"He wants to do a reappraisal of all the facts and your report before we go to the expense of hiring another investigator. He's starting to talk about cutting our losses. But he promised that if there is a shred of evidence to support the theory that Hugh was murdered, we'll get the best investigator he can find on it."

I nodded. "Ten to one it'll be somebody from Nadir Industries."

She glanced at me quickly out of the corner of her eye and grinned. "He also said that I shouldn't feel badly about your leaving. He's kind of relieved about it. He didn't have much confidence in your abilities from the beginning. He said he'd checked you out with some people in L.A. and they said that as an investigator, you weren't too hot."

"Why, that rotten little prick." I waved a hand at the street. "Turn this goddamn car around. I'm going to go back there and kick his ass."

"Now, now dear," she said. "Calm yourself. Remember your blood pressure."

We got to the freeway overpass. Traffic was bumper to bumper, an infinite procession of cars sniffing each other's exhausts in both directions. The sun hovered over them, a blue-white ball burning through the smog. "No sense fighting that stuff," I said. "By the time we got to your place, we'd just have to turn around and come back again. Select a place where we can get some libation and munchies and by the time we're finished, it should be cool."

"Cool for what?"

"Some more midnight skulking. I want to look around Cassarene's office."

"What do you expect to find? Lomustine?"

"Maybe," I said. "If he used it on your husband, maybe he's got some left. And if he does, we've established two things—how and at least one who. Cassarene's an orthopedist, not an oncologist. Since he doesn't treat cancer patients, he'd have no earthly reason to have any lomustine around."

She turned toward me sharply, ignoring the green Grand Prix in front of her, which had braked suddenly.

"Careful!" I shouted.

She slammed on the brakes and we stopped about six inches from the Grand Prix's bumper. She didn't seem to care about that. "What do you mean, 'at least one who'?"

"If we're right about the lomustine, your husband was a walking dead man. He'd been murdered six weeks before he would have died. But only the person who gave him the stuff would have known that. Hugh himself didn't know."

The Grand Prix started off, but Sharon didn't seem to care about that, either. "You're saying that Hugh could have been murdered twice? By two different people?"

"It's possible," I said.

Angry horns behind us made her aware that we were parked in the middle of a busy boulevard, and she hit the gas. I rested my head against the seat as we took off, and sighed. "In this goddamn case, it seems like anything is possible."

19

The record store was closed, and bars had been drawn across the windows. The ubiquitous congregation of low-riders was standing around outside a nightclub called Helena's Discoteca. They were probably too young to get in, so they just leaned against the psychedelic-pastel walls, smoking cigarettes and bouncing to the live rock music coming through the front doors. Sharon parked half a block down from Helena's.

"Okay. I'll be back in a few minutes," I said, getting out.

"Oh, no," she said, nodding toward the congregation of future low-riders. "You're not leaving me here with these guys."

I looked at them. One of them had already noticed the Mercedes and was pointing it out to the others. "This is breaking and entering, Sharon. It's a criminal offense."

"Only if you get caught."

"The point is, there's no need for you to take the risk. If you want to drive somewhere and come back for me in fifteen minutes, go ahead."

She shook her head. "I'm going."

"It's stupid," I sighed resignedly, "but okay. Let's go."

We locked up the car and Sharon got a couple of catcalls and whistles as we walked away.

"Here," I said, indicating the front doors of Cassarene's building.

The lobby was dark and had that shadowy, unreal feeling that office buildings have at night. Even the hum of the elevator seemed different, somehow ominous. I felt slightly on edge as we rode to the third floor.

The hallway was completely dark. The only light was that from the street, which filtered weakly through the frosted-glass office doors. Something creaked and I froze and listened. The place was dead, yet alive. The empty building had taken on a life all its own, emitting little creaks and moans as it stretched and yawned. I signaled for Sharon to follow me; our footsteps reverberated loudly off the walls.

Cassarene's door was locked, and there were no lights showing behind the glass. I took out my set of picks and selected one, then bent down and started working on the lock. "Wrong pick," I said, selecting another one.

Something cracked loudly and she nearly climbed up my back. "What's that?"

"Nothing. The building is cooling down, that's all."

"This place gives me the creeps," she said in a hushed tone.

"Go back to the car."

"That's all right. I'd rather *have* the creeps than be gang-raped by fourteen of them."

I felt the tumblers kick into place. "*Voilà*," I said, and the bell bonged as I pushed open the door. I shut it behind us and used my pen flashlight to guide us through the waiting room to the inner office. The hallway still smelled of antiseptic. The office was set up like a T, the reception area crossing the longer hallway at the top. There were two open doors in the middle of the hallway and one that was closed on each end. I went to the two open doors first and poked my flashlight in.

They were almost identical examination rooms, containing

tissue-paper-covered examination tables, scales, some cabinets containing gauze and cotton and the usual assortment of medical supplies, but no drugs. I went down to the closed door on the right, and opened it.

My flashlight swept over the shelves of medical books, framed medical degrees, a large desk with a padded leather swivel chair. "We'll come back to this one later," I said, and closed the door again.

I took Sharon by the hand and led her back down the hallway to the other door. It opened into a sterile-white room filled with enameled cabinets suspended above a Formica-topped counter with drawers beneath. Various kinds of surgical instruments were laid out along the counter, along with paper-wrapped disposable syringes of different sizes. The cabinets were all locked. They were probably where he kept his drugs. I pulled open a couple of the drawers. They were filled with more orthopedic instruments, their sharpened, chromed sleekness looking malevolent in the light of my flash.

There was a small refrigerator on the floor at the end of the counter. It wasn't locked. There were a few dozen drug bottles inside, most of them, judging from the labels, anti-inflammatories or antibiotics. I pulled out a half-used bottle of liquid methamphetamine and held it up to Sharon and she nodded. I was putting the bottle back when the bell from the front door bonged, sending my heart jumping into my throat.

"Oh, my God," Sharon whispered in a panicked voice. "Somebody's here."

"Shhhhh." I shoved the meth quickly back into the refrigerator and went to the door to the room, pulling it partially closed. I put my eye to the crack. Sharon was trying to enter my body through my back.

"Who is it?" she whispered.

I turned and put my hand over her mouth then put my eye back to the crack. There was no sound of anyone moving around and no lights were on. I didn't like it. I stepped over to the counter and

200

selected a formidable-looking orthopedic hammer and tested the weight in my hand. It seemed heavy enough.

"What are you going to do?" Sharon asked urgently.

"Just stay here," I whispered and stepped into the hallway, closing the door behind me.

I flattened myself against the wall and edged to the corner near the reception desk. From there, I had a clear view down the hallway to Cassarene's office and part of the stem of the T leading to the waiting-room door. There was still no sound, no footsteps, nothing. Just the sound of my blood pounding. I stood still for a few seconds that seemed like hours, leaking sweat in the dark, wondering what was going on, then said, fuck it, I'd never know standing here, so I moved. I stuck one eye around the corner and peeked out.

The reception area was empty. The door leading to the waiting room was agape, but we had left it that way, and there was nothing but darkness behind it. I looked across the desk through the reception window, but there was just blackness there, too. Nobody had come down the hall, I was sure of that, so whoever had come—if anybody—was still in that room. Somebody was playing games.

I crossed the hall on tiptoe and tried to get a different angle from the other side, but still could see nothing. The stillness was suffocating. I slithered along the wall until I got to the door. I dried my sweaty hands on my pants and tightened my grip on the hammer, then took a couple of deep breaths, and stepped out, facing the front door.

That was a mistake. The cry that shattered the silence came from behind me and to the left, and I turned to see a white blur flying through the air toward my face. I didn't have time to react before what felt like a twenty-pound sledge smashed my head into six hundred fragments and sent me falling backward over a chair, and the hammer flying across the room.

On the way down my head hit something hard, the edge of the coffee table, and the sharpness of the pain somehow cleared the dizziness momentarily. I scrambled onto all fours and looked up in the direction of the attacker, but there was nothing there. Just silent darkness. I shook my head and blinked, but there was still nothing.

I started to get up when I was startled by the scream again, from my right this time, and I tried to turn. A wrecking ball hit me in the ribs, just below the arm, and a hot pain flashed up my side, taking my breath away. I lashed out at the foot with my hand, but I just grabbed a lot of air as the man danced away, then came in again from a different angle.

He yelled some word I couldn't quite get, and the first kick caught me in the middle of the forehead, snapping my head back; then another foot caught me on the right temple, and the room was spinning. I managed to avoid hitting the coffee table on the way down this time and I congratulated myself for that.

The temple shot had completely taken away my equilibrium, and I couldn't get my feet under me. I kept trying, but I knew it was useless as I saw him coming in. The first kick caught me in the solar plexus, and the next three landed flush on the chin. Or maybe it was four. After the first one, it didn't make much difference.

20

Somebody was stroking my hair and calling my name. I opened an eye just to see who it was. I was floating on my back with the other garbage in a Venetian canal. A gondolier was staring down at me from his gondola with a sad look on his face. He looked familiar, which was probably how he knew my name. I reached up for his oar so he could pull me out of the stinking canal and Sharon's face blocked my vision. "Jake, are you all right?"

Then I remembered where I had seen the gondolier before. On a wall. I felt underneath me. I was lying on a couch. "Good question. Am I bleeding?"

"You've got a small cut over your eye, but it doesn't look too bad. I don't think it'll need stitches."

I tried to sit up. That wasn't easy. I hurt in spots I'd never felt before. I held my face in my hands and said, "How long have I been out?"

"Seven or eight minutes."

"What happened to the truck that hit me?"

"The truck is still here," a man's voice said.

I recognized the accent. I turned my head painfully toward the voice. Meriwether was sitting in a chair with his legs crossed, smiling at me. He had on a white V-necked sweater with no shirt underneath, a pair of navy-blue slacks, and hand-tooled cowboy boots. A huge gold medallion on a thick gold rope chain showed just above the crook of the V. Halstead stood beside him, holding what appeared to be a Beretta .380 on me. He was wearing white linen slacks and a black short-sleeved sports shirt. He'd put his shoes back on. They were white loafers and they looked like suede. He was smiling, too. It was a cheerful little group. "Well, well," I said, rubbing my neck. "Your vitamin supply get short, Meriwether? Come by for a little battery charge?"

"Never mind me. *I* think you should explain what *you're* doing here," Meriwether replied.

I rubbed the back of my neck. "Sure," I said, grunting. "We broke in to get some drugs. Mrs. Canning and I are both heroin addicts. We figured Cassarene might have some smack around. I know we did wrong and I want to pay for my mistake, so if you'll call the cops, we'll gladly turn ourselves in."

"After we find out what y'all are doing here. And after you hand over that report."

"What report?"

"Come on, boy. These games are childish and time-consuming. The report on Alicia. The one you got from that safe-deposit box Canning kept at the Bank of Newport."

Sharon gasped. "How did you know that?"

Meriwether looked her up and down and grinned. His eyes glittered like two shiny pebbles. "Let's just say I have my sources, little lady."

"Your sources are misinformed," I chimed in. "I don't know what the hell you're talking about. There was nothing in that box but some stocks and bonds and a little cash."

He leaned forward and said as if trying to be understanding, "Son, let's be adult about this. I *know* you have that report, I don't care what you say to the contrary. And I know what you did

204

with it. So let's just cut out all the horseshit and move on to stage two of the negotiations."

I could tell by his eyes that he did know. And I thought I knew how he knew, which made me angry and nauseous at the same time. Because if I was right, there was only one thing he could do with us.

"You were looking for the report when you hit Sharon's house," I said.

"We had to make sure it wasn't there."

That confirmed part of my theory. But for the time being, the only thing I could do was keep bluffing. I looked at Halstead, who was grinning like a wolverine in heat. I wanted to rearrange the features on both their faces, but the way I felt, I doubted I could manage one.

"You've been tailing us," I said.

He nodded and casually checked out the back of his hand. "I'm a very good judge of men, son. That's how I've managed to make the money I have. I've made money on their weaknesses. I was very impressed with you when you came by the house. Very impressed. There was something in your demeanor that said determination to me. I had confidence that you'd dig up that report. So I thought it'd be a right good idea to kind of stick close to you. And hot damn, you didn't disappoint me. Only you made one move I didn't count on. You dropping the report at Mrs. Canning's bank."

I straightened up and a sharp pain in my side caused me to suck in a breath.

"Are you all right?" Sharon asked, putting a hand on my shoulder.

"Yeah. I should have spotted the tail."

"Don't feel too bad about that, son," Meriwether said paternally. "Tony's good. *Real* good."

"It wasn't you who sent those goons to wail on my gourd, then."

He frowned. "No. I think those were some of George's boys.

205

He and Baumgartner were afraid you were going to stick your nose where it didn't belong and upset their little operation." He chuckled. "Sure enough, you did. Now about that report . . ."

"You're right," I admitted. "It's in Sharon's safe-deposit box."

He nodded and smiled and was about to say something when the shadowy outline of a man appeared at the glass in the door and there was a fumbling of keys. Meriwether nodded quickly to Halstead, who flattened against the wall, gun ready.

The bell bonged as the door opened and Cassarene scurried in and nervously looked around. He didn't seem surprised to see Halstead standing behind him with a pistol. Instead, he pointed at us.

"What are they doing here?" His composed façade had completely disintegrated and his face was pale and waxen with sweat. His spidery hands fidgeted as if trying to spin webs in the air.

"That's just what we're trying to determine," Meriwether said.

Halstead grinned. That seemed to be his favorite expression. "I could find out quick."

Meriwether patted Halstead on the thigh. "Tony tends to think in terms of violent solutions. There's no need for that sort of thing here, Tony. I have confidence that we can resolve this thing to everyone's satisfaction."

"Like you resolved it with Canning?"

"I'm going to check things out," Cassarene said, and went through the door into the back.

"I'm not sure I get your drift, son," Meriwether said.

"Canning called you and told you he had the report on Alicia. You sent Halstead over to get it. What happened? Did he get a little overzealous with his Bruce Lee routine, and you had to arrange an accident to cover up his handiwork?"

Meriwether held up his hands. "Your team is running away with you. Neither Tony nor I had anything to do with Canning's accident."

"He called you that night."

He shifted in his chair. His smile was the confident, self-satisfied smile of a winner. "Sure he called me. He told me he had the report and suggested we talk. Tony and I got to his office about six-thirty, but Canning wasn't there. I just thought it was another one of his cute little tricks, until I read about the accident in the papers."

"What cute little tricks?"

He uncrossed his legs and put his hands on his knees. "The man was psychotic. He had a regular harassment campaign going. Do you know I had to change my phone number three times? He would call up at three in the morning and play the 'William Tell Overture.' Swear to God. He'd send hearses and funeral wreaths to my home, order two dozen pizzas on the phone to be delivered—anything to annoy me."

I turned sharply to Sharon, who looked at me and blinked widely. "I didn't know anything about it, Jake. I swear I didn't."

"Shucks," Meriwether said, shrugging, "nobody likes to admit he's crazy. Even to his wife."

Cassarene came through the door, wringing his hands. Meriwether looked up curiously. "What is it, Milt? You're shivering like a dog trying to pass peach pits."

"They've been in the refrigerator."

I shrugged. "I told you I was a junkie."

"Now, what were y'all looking for in the refrigerator?"

"A Twinkie," I said. "I always get hungry for a snack around this time of night."

Cassarene blurted out, "They must know—"

"Shut up," Meriwether said sharply. Then in a more relaxed tone, "You worry too much, Milt."

I thought furiously, trying to remember if Sharon and I had talked about the lomustine at her house. I didn't think we had. Which meant that there was still a chance he didn't know that we knew, although a slim one. Halstead must have followed us to U.C. Irvine. I had to put up some kind of a smoke screen.

"You really want to know what we're doing here? I wanted to see if the good doctor here had any amphetamines in the refrigerator. I wanted to confirm he was your supplier."

Cassarene took a step toward Meriwether. "You can't think—"

Meriwether turned on him, and said as if trying to get a message across, "It doesn't matter."

I was not sure what didn't matter, but I could guess. It didn't matter what we knew or didn't know. And there could be only one reason why it wouldn't.

"What kind of ideas did Canning have? Blackmail money for not exposing you as King Rubber?"

"I really don't know," he said, and made a clicking sound out of the side of his mouth. "He never said. He just said that he wanted to meet with me, to discuss it."

"And he was gone when you got there."

"That's right."

I shook my head. "You know, Meriwether, for somebody who allegedly has such a love for the female form, you haven't exactly monumentalized it in Alicia."

He sighed sorrowfully. "We're always looking for ways to improve the product."

"Tell me, do you make dildoes and vibrating rubber vaginas, too, or just Alicias?"

He drummed his fingertips on his knees. "We make a little of everything."

"You into screwing Mexicans out of their insurance settlements, too, or is that just Cassarene, Baumgartner, and Villalobos's racket?"

He smiled mirthlessly. "Naw, I leave that stuff to them. They seem to be doing pretty good at it without my help."

"Well, don't worry," I said, trying to sound totally self-confident. "I'll make you a better deal than Canning would have. He was emotionally involved. I'm not. I'm not looking to get even with anybody."

His eyelids drooped and he squinted at me. "What deal?"

"Ten thousand for the report and our silence."

Sharon started to say something, but I nudged her leg with my hand, which was on the couch between us.

"Now why would I want to give you ten thousand dollars?"

208

"Because you only have one other option—kill us. And that wouldn't be too smart for several reasons. Too many bodies in the same family turning up so close together would be bound to get the cops snooping around. Especially after my friend in the D.A.'s office opens the package I mailed to him today. He's supposed to open it the minute he hears that something has happened to me. I didn't want to take any chances after my last near-fatal 'accident.' "

"And what's supposed to be in this mystery package?"

"Tapes," I said. "I put down everything. I made some wrong guesses, but the cops can correct those."

"What do you mean, 'everything'?"

I shrugged. "The accident racket in detail, along with testimony from Baumgartner's clients about how they got shafted. Alicia. And my suspicions about Cassarene here supplying you with redline."

Cassarene had perched precariously on the edge of a chair. His body jerked toward Meriwether. "Jackson—"

"Shut up," Meriwether said, not looking at him. His stare was locked into mine, his little eyes like diamond drills, trying to drill into my thoughts. "You'd make a hell of a poker player, son. You bluff real good."

"Wrong," I said, smiling a little. "I'm a lousy poker player because I never bluff."

He glanced up at Halstead. "Did you see him mail any package, Tony?"

Halstead shook his head. "No."

"I gave it to somebody else to mail. It got mailed, believe me."

Meriwether stood up and began pacing in front of us in tight figure-eights. He rubbed his chin and said, "Let's just say that you're not bluffing and that all that's true. How would I know that after I paid you, you'd keep quiet? Or not come back for more?"

"Number one, I'm not greedy and I'm not a blackmailer. Neither is Mrs. Canning. We've just found ourselves in a situation and we might as well get something out of it. Number two, I don't give a shit how you make your living and I have no reason to ruin

209

you socially. You've never done anything to me. Your man here tried to make an omelette out of my brains, but that's part of the game. As far as Canning goes, as far as I'm concerned, whatever happened to him, he brought on himself."

"And does the little lady here share your sentiments?"

Meriwether turned his drills on Sharon. "Well?"

"Hugh is dead," she said, glancing at me nervously. "I can't bring him back. I have to look out for myself now."

He rubbed his chin again then winked at me. "You're my kind of people, yessir. Show me a man who says, 'It ain't the money, it's the principle of the thing,' and I'll lay you eight to five it's the money, every time. Still, I'd like something else tied in with this deal besides money, just to make sure you don't change your mind or come back pestering me later. Collateral of some kind. Something you'd be giving up if you went back on the deal."

"What kind of collateral?"

"I don't know. I'm gonna have to think about that one. In the meantime, let's all go for a little ride."

Halstead jerked the barrel of the gun up twice, indicating for us to stand, then jerked it twice more toward the door.

"Where are we going?" I asked, taking Sharon's arm.

"To see a friend of mine. He has a place where y'all can do some thinking about this collateral idea and wait until the bank opens at ten o'clock."

"You don't trust us?" I asked as I got close to him.

"Remember what I told you about not liking to be disappointed? It would grieve me deeply if you turned out to be a disappointment to me, Mr. Asch, so I don't think I want to take the chance."

When we got to the door, Halstead told us to stop, then moved around us cautiously to the coffee table and picked up a copy of *Health Today*. He folded the magazine over the Beretta and told us to go on. I thought it was an ironic literary choice.

We went into the hallway and Cassarene locked up the office, and we walked in a solemn procession to the elevator. Halstead made sure I was aware of the gun's presence all the way to the ground floor by periodically poking me with it in the small of the back, and jabbing me harder when the doors opened.

As we stepped out, Meriwether held out his hand and said to Sharon, "Your car keys, please."

"What for?"

"Dr. Cassarene will drive it to where we're going. The keys, please."

She dug the keys out of her purse and gave them to him, and he handed them to Cassarene.

"It's down the block. A Mercedes. You know how to get to the yard."

"I'm no chauffeur," the doctor said petulantly.

"No," Meriwether said, grinning malevolently. "You're an accessory. And I think it's time for you to start thinking like one."

The doctor's spidery fingers closed around the keys as if they were some unfortunate insect that happened to wander into the web, and he went meekly out the front doors.

Meriwether told Halstead to keep us there until he brought the car up, then left. We were only five yards from the street, but waiting in the dark with a gun in my back made the lights seem ten miles away. I touched Sharon's arm. She was trembling.

"Don't worry," I told her. "It's going to be all right."

She nodded, but wouldn't look at me. Maybe she heard the uncertainty in my voice, and didn't want to see it in my eyes.

After a couple of minutes, a gray Cadillac Eldorado, flying Lone Star flags on both sides in front of the windshield, pulled up and stopped. Halstead said in an almost tired voice: "Okay. Let's go."

He moved around me, keeping his eyes on me for any sign of a false movement, and opened the front door. "You. In."

I got in front and he and Sharon got in back. As we took off, I pointed at the flags. "That's a real nice touch."

"I'm proud of my roots, son," he said as I heard the doors lock.

He drove to the freeway and got on the northbound off ramp. Traffic was moving briskly and he edged into the fast lane and let the Caddy unwind.

At the junction for Highway 22, he got onto the Garden Grove Freeway heading west, and after a couple of miles he pulled off at Euclid and turned left. Two blocks down, he made a right and we were on a dark street lined with huge warehouses and industrial buildings.

He slowed and stopped in front of a high wooden wall covered with *placa* and hit the horn in a staccato burst. The gate slid open a bit and a big blond man stepped out and pushed it open the rest of the way. He wasn't picking his nose, but I recognized him anyway. He waved us inside and Meriwether stopped on the way through the gate, and rolled down his window.

"There will be a Mercedes coming in a couple of minutes. Let it in."

The nosepicker nodded and we drove inside.

We were in a morgue. The corpses of dead cars were stacked up by the score, side by side and on top of one another, their front ends all neatly aligned, and the moonlight lived in their chrome and glass, giving them an eerie, glistening glow. We drove past a big mobile crane and stacks of amputated car seats, then pulled up behind the black Lamborghini that was parked alongside a large hangarlike building. A ramped loading dock led up to a door and the sign above it said: ANSALDI WRECKING. SE HABLA ESPAÑOL.

Villalobos and Alex Cardozo stepped onto the loading platform as we got out of the car. They stood looking down on us, back-lighted by the light above the door. They both wore dark blue suits and white shirts, but Villalobos was wearing a dark tie, while Cardozo's shirt was open, the collar flared over the lapels of his jacket. "Well, well, the troublesome detective again," Villalobos said. "And Mrs. Canning. How nice to see you."

Sharon didn't say anything.

The night smelled of grease. I waved at the yard. "Nice place. Your wife own this, too?"

212

He smiled crookedly. "She has some stock."

I nodded. "I must admit, it's a natural, considering your other business interests."

"It does work out rather nicely," he said.

"I'll bet out there somewhere is a 1959 Ford Fairlane with missing license plates."

He looked at me questioningly. "Why do you say that?"

I jabbed a thumb at the nosepicker, who was standing guard by the gate, which he had shut. "Because the car Junior and his friends were driving when we first met was wearing them."

"It's too bad they didn't succeed in deterring you," he said. "If they had, you and Mrs. Canning wouldn't be here now."

I shrugged. "It's just as nice here as in the hospital. Tell me, is Junior on salary, or does he just get paid by piecework? Per head broken?"

"Digby?" Villalobos asked, his gaze drifting almost disinterestedly over to the gate. "He's one of my tow-truck drivers."

"And I'll bet the one he drives has a police-band radio to pick up accident calls and a glove box full of attorneys' business cards to make sure the parties involved get adequate legal representation."

"Choosing the right attorney can be difficult," Villalobos said smoothly. "Especially in times of emotional or physical stress. My people know that and try to be all the help they can."

"I'm sure they do. And it probably works out very well. If they show up at an accident and the victims aren't hurt badly enough, they can always break an arm or two, to build up those settlement checks."

"Bring them inside," he said in a voice as dead as a 1959 Ford Fairlane.

We went up the ramp and Villalobos stood back from the door and motioned us inside with a graceful flourish. The office was small and cluttered and dirty. There were two scarred desks with wire baskets filled with papers, an electric typewriter, and a desk-model calculator. Behind the desks were two old swivel chairs with beaten-down cushions on the seats. The rest of the furnish-

213

ings consisted of red Naugahyde stack chairs, and some battered filing cabinets painted a military green. The floor was badly scuffed linoleum and the walls were a dingy green. Over one of the desks, there was a calendar with a picture of a very stacked black-haired beauty with a coy look on her face, who was sucking the barrel of a cap pistol. She was wearing only a cowboy hat and a holster and a pair of cowboy boots.

Villalobos told us to sit down, then said, "Watch them," to Cardozo and went with Meriwether through a doorway into an adjoining office. They shut the door behind them and I said to Cardozo, "So. Been to any good accidents lately?"

He turned on me with an expressionless stare, but said nothing. Through his half-closed lids, his eyes looked dead and moist, like two steamed clams. His huge head turned to the sound of a car pulling up outside. A door slammed.

"That might be Rodan," I said. "Better go out and see. You wouldn't want to be taken by surprise."

Halstead took one step to the door and opened it and Cassarene came in, trailed by Digby. I hadn't noticed coming through the gate, probably because his beer gut was partially overlapping the handle, but Digby had a .38 police special tucked into the waistband of his grease-stained jeans.

Cassarene looked around, fidgeting with the keys in his hand. "Where's Jackson?"

"In the other room, talking to Villalobos," Halstead said.

Cassarene nodded nervously and said, "I can't—"

Whatever he couldn't was cut off by the opening door of the inner office. Villalobos and Meriwether came out; Villalobos acknowledged Cassarene with a nod.

Cassarene went over to Meriwether and touched his arm. "I can't stay, Jackson. Who's going to drive me back?"

"Relax, Milt," Villalobos said. "I'll have Digby drive you back in a few minutes."

"Sit down, Milt," Meriwether told him in a firm voice. Cassarene obeyed like a whipped dog. He sat down on one of the stack chairs, hunched over nervously.

214

"Jackson tells me you've been a busy boy, sticking your nose into everybody's business."

"That's what I'm paid for."

"He also tells me you want to get paid for unsticking it."

"If you want to put it that way."

Meriwether sat on the edge of one of the desks and watched us. Villalobos stood in front of me and asked, "Exactly how much do you know about my business operation?"

"Enough to send you up from five to ten," I said. "I don't know how much your little operation nets, but I'd say you probably take in a hell of a lot more than any of the attorneys you solicit for. A fact that probably really pissed off Canning, especially after he found out how you and his own partner and friend had been fucking him."

He ran his tongue over his upper teeth. "He was a little irate." He pulled out a package of long, thin, brown cigarettes and put one in his mouth, then offered the pack to Sharon. She took one greedily and he lit it for her with a gold pocket lighter, then lit his own. He exhaled lustily. "What else do you know?"

"Know? Not really that much. I could make some guesses, though."

He bowed slightly and turned up a palm. "Guess away."

"I'd guess that Canning found out about the whole thing a couple of weeks before he died, after he got a call from an investigator from the State Bar, who was calling on a complaint from Diane McClurg."

"That nosy bitch," he said contemptuously. "I should have taken care of her when she first started causing me trouble."

"What did Canning do? Threaten to bring down the whole mess and turn you in?"

"At first. He screamed and ranted and raved. Until Ray showed him how lucrative it was and offered to cut him in. Canning was fanatical in his hatred for me, but when it came to money, he was coldly calculating and quite amoral. I know. I took him in on a couple of deals in Mexico, and I got to experience it firsthand."

"You mean the real-estate deals?"

He exhaled smoke and guffawed. "Those weren't real-estate deals, my friend. They were loads of household appliances we were smuggling into Mexico. People don't realize it, but there's probably more traffic going *into* Mexico in the form of television sets and refrigerators than is coming north in narcotics. And if you have the right connections, it's almost risk-free. *La mordida* takes care of everything."

"I don't believe it," Sharon said dully, shaking her head as if she were having a hard time absorbing all this.

"Oh, you can believe it, Mrs. Canning," Villalobos said, tapping his ash on the floor. "Your husband was a thief, just like the rest of us here. You know what he said when Ray and I offered to cut him in? He said sure, but he wanted 'reparations.' He wanted reimbursement for what he figured he had been screwed out of, which according to his calculations came to somewhere around seventy-two thousand dollars. Not only that. He wanted twenty percent interest tacked onto it. He said he would consider it a loan—that he had loaned us the seventy-two thou for a year, and it was only fair that he should get interest on his money."

"So you and Baumgartner decided it would be cheaper to drive him off a cliff. . . ?"

"I don't know where you get these ideas," he said, as if he really didn't. "None of us had anything to do with Canning's death."

"I'm glad to hear it."

"We agreed to pay the reparations. Why not? Eighty-five grand is a drop in the bucket in an operation like this. Besides, with Canning in, we could up the volume tremendously. As long as he didn't know, we had to be careful, to keep him from being suspicious. But with him in, we could really get the ball rolling."

"So you paid him?"

"Part of it. The trouble was, Canning insisted on being paid off in cash and none of us had that kind of cash lying around. Ray and Milt and I came up with about fifteen grand as a down payment and we promised to get him the rest by the following week."

216

"The money in the box," I said to Sharon. She nodded as if in a trance.

"So who killed Canning?"

Villalobos threw up his hands. "How the hell should I know? I wasn't there. As far as I know, it was an accident."

He sounded sincere. I was sure he always could when he had to. "What about Baumgartner?"

"Ray was with me at Cielo Lindo."

That figured. "Okay."

He smiled, then looked around for a place to put out his cigarette. Cardozo moved from the wall where he'd been standing like the Statue of Liberty and picked up an ashtray from the desk and brought it over. "Okay," Villalobos said. "So now that that's all squared away, how much do you want from me?"

"Nothing. The ten grand should cover both of you. You can share the expense if you want. Two for the price of one."

He looked at me suspiciously. "Why so generous?"

"I told Meriwether: we're not greedy. Canning got greedy, and look what happened to him. Anyway, what's done is done. If we expose you and your operation, we expose Hugh Canning. Sharon doesn't want that kind of a blot on her husband's memory. Besides, there might be lawsuits from clients who got shafted."

Villalobos looked over at Meriwether. "That sounds pretty reasonable to me. What say, Jackson? Divided four ways, it's only twenty-five hundred each."

"Sounds good to me," Meriwether said. He looked over at Cassarene, whose face was the color of sweaty cheese. "See, Milt. I told you we could come to terms."

Cassarene didn't say anything, but his expression told me that he was not pleased. He stood up when Meriwether did.

Meriwether said to us, "George and I are going to drive over to Ray's and talk it over with him. We'll try to come up with some collateral we can bank. In the meantime, you two make yourselves at home. We'll be back in a couple of hours."

Meriwether put his arm around Cassarene's shoulder and

started to lead him to the door. "Now you just go home and mix yourself a nice stiff drink or take one of your own prescriptions and get a good night's sleep, and I guarantee you the problem will all be ironed out in the morning."

"Alex," Villalobos said. "Stay here and keep them company until we get back. Give them a drink if they want it. You know where the stuff is."

Cardozo's big head moved slowly up and down. He was a talkative one. I wondered how he'd done so well selling attorneys in the orthopedic ward.

"Tony," Meriwether said. "Digby here is going to be driving Milt back to his office. You're going to have to lock the gate behind us."

Cardozo closed the door behind them and pulled a chair up next to it and sat down. I felt like a mouse being watched by a cat. A cat patiently waiting.

I scanned the room, searching for something of use, anything. There was the glass ashtray on the desk containing Villalobos's ashes, but it would be too light to do any damage to Cardozo's skull. I considered the sharp metal spindle next to the in-out basket on which were impaled a stack of bills, but I rejected that, too. If I missed a vulnerable spot, I'd wind up wrestling with him and get broken in half. No, quarters. I already felt as if I'd been halved once tonight.

My eyes stopped at the door leading into the back office. Hanging there on a metal hook, like a red bloated sausage in a meat market, was a fire extinguisher. It looked as if it weighed fifteen pounds, heavy enough even to use on Godzilla. All I had to do was think of myself as King Kong.

Cars started up outside and tires hissed on gravel. Halstead and Cardozo would be apart for the next couple of minutes while Halstead was at the gate; I didn't know if I would ever have this opportunity again. Even so, I was still going to have to be goddamn lucky. I wondered if the others had left yet, but pushed it out of my mind. There was no use worrying about that. It was now or never.

I patted Sharon on the hand and said, "You okay?"

She smiled worriedly, and nodded.

"It's going to be all right. Just trust me."

She nodded again and I said to Cardozo, "You got a cigarette?"

He grunted and brought a pack of Camel filters out of his breast pocket. He stood when I did and I went over to him. He shook one out and I turned to Sharon and asked if she wanted one. She shook her head no and I said to Cardozo, "Match?"

He dug out a box of wooden matches with Cielo Lindo's name on it and I said, "Thanks," and took them over to one of the desks and sat down.

The wastebasket under the desk hadn't been emptied. I struck a match, purposely lighting only part of the cigarette, then dropped the match into the wastebasket. Cardozo didn't seem to notice that I hadn't shaken the match out first. I waited a few seconds. Nothing happened. The match had gone out.

I took the half-lit cigarette out of my mouth and looked at the end of it with annoyance. "Damn," I said, and struck another match. Sharon coughed and Cardozo's gaze drifted over to her. I reached under the desk and dropped the lit match very gently into the wastebasket.

The seconds dripped slowly, like water from a leaky faucet, rubbing my nerves raw. I kept my eyes on Cardozo but I could feel sudden, beautiful heat on my leg. I glanced down and saw the orange, flickering glow under the desk. The wastebasket was out of Cardozo's line of sight, but he came forward in his chair and sniffed the air. "You smell something burning?"

"Me?" I asked. "No. But then my sense of smell is pretty bad."

"I do," Sharon said.

I shrugged and sat back, giving the fire a few more seconds to really get going, then jumped up. "Jesus Christ!"

Cardozo jumped up, too, and ran over to see what I was pointing at. The plastic wastebasket was melting and the flames were a foot above its rim, licking the top of the desk. "Holy shit," Cardozo said.

I ran to the fire extinguisher and took it off its hook on the wall and said, "Stand back."

He stood back, looking surprised, and I turned the nozzle at his face and squeezed the trigger. The white powder exploded and he grabbed his eyes and stumbled back yelling. He took in a mouthful of the stuff and gagged, then doubled over in a fit of convulsive coughing, which put his head in perfect position for the extinguisher, which I was bringing around with both hands like a hammer thrower. The metal made a heavy, hollow ringing sound as it rebounded off his head, and he went down like a rock. The only sound he made was when he hit the floor.

I stepped over him and went to the window and peeked through the Venetian blinds. Halstead must have heard Cardozo yell, because he was running from the gate with his gun drawn. He was alone at least, but I still didn't like the odds. That Beretta had a staggered clip that carried thirteen shots. That made it thirteen to zip and no element of surprise to even things up a little. I moved to the door and punched the lock button on the handle and went back to Cardozo. The extinguisher had opened a nasty gash on the side of his head and he was bleeding freely on the linoleum floor.

"Why did you do that?" Sharon said, panicked. "They were going to let us go."

"That was all bullshit they were feeding us," I said as I bent over Cardozo's lifeless hulk and patted him down. "How do you think they knew about everything? When Halstead hit your house, he left a bug behind. That's his specialty. They've been listening to us for days, trying to get a line on that report. They know we know about everything—Cassarene's wife, the lomustine, everything. They were just trying to keep us calm until they got the report and decided what kind of accident to arrange for us. Now we don't have much time. Call the operator, tell her there's shooting and a fire at Ansaldi Wrecking and to send the cops and the fire department. Hurry up!"

Sharon snatched up the phone off the desk and repeated what I'd told her to the operator just as Halstead's footsteps pounded up the ramp outside. I found a sap in Cardozo's back pocket, but no gun. I took it; at least it was something.

"Out the back!" I told Sharon. "Quick! I'll be right behind you."

"Please hurry!" she told the operator and hung up the phone, then went out the back.

I turned the nozzle of the extinguisher away from the fire and kept the trigger depressed until the gauge showed empty. The desk had caught now and the flames were starting to work their way up the wall toward the calendar girl's boots.

My attention was jerked to the door by the sound of the handle rattling and a fist banging on it. Halstead yelled, "Alex? What's going on? You all right?"

I took two quick steps to the other desk and pulled out the wastebasket from underneath it. It was about half full and I emptied the contents onto the blaze. The fire flared higher as two bullets in rapid succession ripped through the door just above the lock, sending a shower of splinters into the room, and me heading out the back.

I moved through the small office where Meriwether and Villalobos had held their conference and out a side door into a darkened hallway. The hallway ran a short way to a back door and I opened it and stepped onto a concrete staircase that led into the main part of the hangar. Sharon was waiting at the top of the steps. "Come on," I said, grabbing her hand and pulling her down the steps. Halstead had to be in the office by now, but he would have to get Cardozo out, which would slow him up, and if he wanted to look around for another extinguisher and try to put out the fire, it would take him even longer. I pulled Sharon along toward the back of the hangar, looking for a door.

"I can't see a thing," Sharon said as we felt our way along slowly.

I bumped into something and there was a tinny crash and I felt Sharon's hand twitch. "Easy."

As my eyes adjusted, I began to carve shapes out of the darkness. We were in a huge dark cavern filled with automobile parts. It was an autopsy room, where hubcaps and car seats and transmissions and carburetors were all stacked up neatly in rows and tagged by type.

The smell of smoke was strong in the air now. If the fire department didn't get there soon, maybe we'd get lucky: instead of being shot, we'd die of smoke inhalation. The adrenaline pumping through my bloodstream had me wound up so tight I felt as if the top of my head was going to blow. The tension was demanding a release and the only thing I could think of to do was laugh, so I chuckled.

"What the hell is so funny?" Sharon demanded as we scurried through the dark.

"Hey, detective work is *fun*, remember? You mean you're actually not enjoying this?"

We reached the back wall and I felt my way along it until my hand hit cold metal. It was a large sliding door, maybe eight by ten, and I ran my hand over it, feeling for the latch. I found it and yanked, but it wouldn't budge. "It must be locked from the outside," I said.

"Asch!" Halstead's voice boomed off the walls.

I ducked and pulled Sharon down.

"You forgot something! Your car keys! How far do you think you're going to get? Come in now and I won't punish you for what you did to poor Alex, but if you make me come looking for you, I'm going to bust you up, piece by piece."

He sounded as if he were somewhere around the stairs.

"Here's a door!" Sharon cried a few feet to my right. I scrambled over as she yanked it open, and we ran out into the night.

The heat from the fire had exploded the windows of the office and the flames lapped the sides of the building, sending an orange flickering glow over the yard. Twenty yards away, rows of dead Volkswagens were stacked piggyback, five high and four end-to-end. I yanked on Sharon's arm and started running for them. I heard a shot and a bullet sing off steel as we rounded the first stack. She cried out in terror as she heard it, too, and I pulled on her arm extra hard and headed for the end pile of VWs.

I had no idea where I was going, but when we stumbled around the end of the last tower of twisted metal, it was apparent that neither of us would stay away from it much longer, not as long as I was dragging her around. Her smoker's lungs were already getting to her, and her chest was heaving in an attempt to make up for the oxygen she owed her body. She collapsed against the pitted side of the car and gasped, "I don't know how much farther I can go, Jake."

There was only one thing to do. I opened up the door of the VW and whispered, "Get in and lie on the floor and don't make a sound."

She clutched at me. "Where are you going?"

"To draw him away. Just stay there and don't move."

She got in and scrunched down under the dash and I closed the door and sprinted to the front end of the stack. I ducked around the corner and stuck my head out, waiting for him. My heart seemed to have detached itself from everything and was just rattling around loose in my chest. I wondered how long it took them to answer fire alarms in Garden Grove.

Halstead was suddenly standing at the end of the row of cars. He stopped next to the window of the car Sharon was in and I shouted, "Come and get us, asshole!" and took off.

The crane looked ominous in the firelight, like some giant prehistoric praying mantis ready to pounce on any bodies it could find even half-alive among the remains.

A bullet zinged by as I rounded its front end, and I cut sharply along its tractor tread and circled around a rusted pile of fenders and bumpers just as another bullet chinked off the tail fin of an old De Soto about a foot from my head.

I was winded now and sucked in big lungs-full of air, but it didn't do any good. The oxygen I was taking in was being consumed by fear. I know guys who can run ten miles, but they couldn't run one with a guy behind them with a knife in his hand.

Not only did Halstead have the knife, but he was in better shape and he was running on meth, which meant that unless the fire department got here pretty soon, it wouldn't be too long before I'd know what a bullet in the back felt like.

I cut around a stack of oil drums and between two more stacks of cars that looked as if they had been tortured before they died, then started doubling back toward the crane. That was when I heard it in the distance. It was the most beautiful music in the world, a symphony of sound. It was somebody coming to a fire—at least three trucks, from the sound of the sirens.

He ripped off two more shots as I cut in behind the front of the tractor and I stopped and shouted, "Hear that, Halstead? They'll be here in a couple of minutes. You're through. You can't get both of us in that time. Better cut your losses. You don't have any murder charges hanging over you yet."

Nothing came back. The sirens were much louder now. I stuck my head around the front of the crane to see what he was doing. He was standing in the open clearing as if paralyzed. His head kept snapping back and forth between me and the sirens, and then he turned and sprinted to the gate. He fumbled with the padlock and finally managed to open it, then started running toward Sharon's Mercedes, which was parked in front of the blazing building.

I should have let him drive away and left him for the cops, but the idea of his getting away unscathed suddenly seemed intolerable. I looked around quickly for something to throw and spied a small, toothed gear wheel on the ground a few yards away. I ran over to it and picked it up by its metal shaft and tested its weight in my hand. Heavy enough to do some serious damage.

Halstead had the Mercedes started and was trying to negotiate a U-turn to get the nose of the car pointed in the right direction, when I started running on a diagonal line toward him. The Mercedes's tires spit gravel as the car fish-tailed and he accelerated just as I came running up on the passenger side and threw the gear as hard as I could through the open window.

He flung up his arm to protect himself and yelled as the gear hit him somewhere, and he lost control of the car. The rear end came around and it spun and smashed into the wooden wall, enveloped in a cloud of dust. I ran to it and yanked open the door.

He was dazed and bleeding from a cut on his forehead. I hit him once, hard, on the temple, to make sure he was good and dazed, then ripped him out of the car and hit him again, just because I liked the feel of it. He slumped to the ground unconscious and I picked up the Beretta from the front seat, then bent down and propped Halstead upright against the body of the car, by the door.

I took his right hand and put it in around the jamb and closed the door until it was pressing tightly against his fingers, then slapped him awake. He opened his eyes blearily. The sirens were only a couple of blocks away now, and there wasn't much time. "Okay, Halstead, we've only got a few seconds until the troops arrive. I want it before they get here. All of it. Who arranged the accident for Canning?"

"Fuck you," he said, and coughed. Flecks of blood and spittle appeared on his lips.

I put the gun between his eyes and cocked it. He just smiled.

"You aren't gonna shoot me."

"You're right, I'm not. I'm going to break your fucking fingers," I said and leaned on the door.

He screamed, and I said, "And after the right, then I'll do the left and if we have time, I'll maybe do a foot."

I leaned on it harder and he screamed again and said, "Baumgartner and Villalobos set it up! Jackson and I were going to meet Canning that night, like we said, but we got there too late. We saw Alex and the other guy, Digby, taking him away. He was already out and they were taking him to his car. Cardozo drove Canning's car and Digby followed in his, and we followed them up the Ortega Highway and saw them do it. They didn't know we were tailing them."

"And you didn't try to stop them. Why should you? It solved

your problem a little early, that's all. You didn't figure it would be that big a problem finding the report once Canning was out of the way. Did you bug Baumgartner's office, too?"

"Jackson wanted to know who knew about that report. He figured whoever stumbled onto it would probably try to put the bite on him, too."

"Did they know Canning was dying from the dose of lomustine you slipped him?"

"Loma-what? I don't know what you're talking about."

I bumped the door with my knee, and he shouted: "No! No! They didn't know."

"I'll make the next one easy for you. A true-false question. Meriwether claims he had cancer, so he probably did a lot of research on chemotherapy drugs and their side effects, which was probably how he knew about lomustine. Since Cassarene is his redline connection and Meriwether is the kind of guy who likes to know who he's dealing with, he does some checking and finds out about Mrs. Cassarene's symptoms. When Canning starts making his threats and playing his little pranks, Meriwether decides to use a little of the doctor's methodology and uses his knowledge about his wife to make sure Cassarene comes across with the drug. Right so far?"

He didn't answer, so I was forced to do the bump with the door. "Yes! YES! Jesus!"

"How did you slip it to him?"

His face was sweaty and his eyes were squeezed shut against the pain.

"I told Canning I wanted to sell him some dirt on Jackson. He fell for it and we set up a meet at a bar—"

I leaned on the door. "What bar?"

"Jesus, ease up, will you? The Tropic Winds. I gave him some bullshit about wanting fifty G's for the info, knowing he couldn't come up with that much."

"And he left a very sick man." The sirens were very close. "One more question: You put a bug in Sharon's house, didn't you?"

226

"Yeah, yeah, I planted one there."

I thought about him and Meriwether listening to Sharon and me making love, chuckling over every moan and groan and I rammed my shoulder hard into the door and he screamed a long scream as the small bones in his hand splintered. I released the pressure on the door and stood up and he fell over, rocking back and forth and holding his hand to his chest.

The first fire engine was pulling through the gates, its sirens dying. I pulled the keys from the ignition of the Mercedes and went to find Sharon. She was curled up in a fetal ball on the dirty seatless floor of the Volkswagen when I opened the door, and she looked up and sucked in a startled breath. "God, you scared me," she said, grabbing her chest. "I thought it was him." She saw the gun in my hand. "Is it over?"

"All over."

She uncurled stiffly and I helped her out and she grabbed me and held me tightly and started to cry. Her hair smelled like smoke and grease and crankcase oil. "I died every time I heard a shot," she said in jerky sobs. "I thought he'd killed you."

"No chance. We detectives are indestructible types. Like were-wolves, only with a little bit more compassion."

The sirens were dying as the fire engines rumbled into the yard and the voices of men were shouting instructions. I put my arm around her and said, "Come on, let's go socialize."

Flames were jumping from the roof of the warehouse now and the firemen were training their hoses up there, the streams of water like blood in the engine's lights. The air was thick with the sweet smell of burning wood and little bits of ash floated through the air like snowflakes.

A blue-and-white patrol car was parked by the Mercedes with its doors open and its running lights on. Two uniformed cops were outside the car, talking to Halstead, who was holding a compress against his head; his broken hand had been bandaged. I started to wave a greeting, but stopped dead when both cops drew their service revolvers and went into the police firing stance. "Freeze, both of you! And drop that pistol!"

227

I had forgotten the thing was in my hand and I dropped it as if I'd picked it out of the fire.

The younger, smooth-faced cop waved us over, his gun still trained on us. "Step over here to the car."

"I think there's been a mistake here, officer," I said. "We're the victims, not the perpetrators."

"We'll have plenty of time to determine that later," he snapped. "Right now, just assume the position."

Halstead watched with amusement as we followed orders and the older cop patted us down. He pulled the sap out of my back pocket and said, "For a victim, you're pretty well armed."

"The gun is his," I said, jerking my head at Halstead. "I took it away from him."

"You can tell your story downtown," he said, and snapped the cuffs on my wrists. He started to read us our rights and Sharon screamed, "Wait a minute here! What are we being arrested for? What are the charges?"

"This man is a private detective," the younger cop said, waving at Halstead. "He says he was hired by Ansaldi Wrecking to check out security because of recent thefts. He says he caught you two in the office trying to get into the safe and you assaulted him and another man who we've just called an ambulance for, and to cover up your work, you set fire to the building."

"He *what*?" Sharon shouted shrilly. "He's lying. He kidnapped us at gunpoint. He tried to kill us."

"*I'm* the private detective," I said. "You can check my I.D."

He gave me a bored nod and said, "We'll sort it out downtown. In the car, please." He opened the back door and as he helped her in, she noticed for the first time her car, and horror contorted her features. She looked up at me and cried, "My car!"

"Relax," I said. "I'm not going to charge you for it."

"Officer," she said urgently, "that's my car."

"We'll tell you where you can pick it up later," he said, and put me in next. He turned to Halstead. "You, too."

Halstead slid in next to me, holding a bloodstained compress against his head and Sharon said, "Why the hell don't you hand-cuff him, too?"

The cop slammed the door without answering her and she leaned over me and said, "I hope you bleed to death, you sonof-abitch."

Halstead took the bloody towel off his wound with his good hand and grinned at her. In the red light of the fire, with his Vandyke, he looked like one of those devil masks they sell at Halloween in the five-and-dime.

Sharon threw her head back against the seat and exhaled in frustration. "I don't fucking believe this."

"Don't worry," I told her. "Once they find out you're Cato and I'm the Green Hornet, they'll know right away who the bad guys are."

21

It took some time, but they finally sorted out who the bad guys were. "It's like a fucking Agatha Christie novel," one of the investigating detectives remarked after we had managed to get across to him that Canning had been murdered twice by seven people. "I hate fucking Agatha Christie."

The Assistant D.A. assigned the case expressed similar thoughts, but neither his dislike of Agatha Christie nor his doubts of ever getting a jury to follow it all prevented him from indicting the crew for murder one, among other things. The strength of those indictments convinced Transcontinental to loosen its grip on Sharon's two hundred thousand dollars, and rule Canning's death "at the hands of another, or others."

Me, I loosened my grip on myself. I spent the next week hanging around Newport, soaking up the sunshine and Sharon, and it was sometime during that week that the futility of trying to deny what I was feeling struck me. I broke down and confessed to her that I loved her and probably always had, and once I'd told her, I couldn't seem to stop telling her. The fear dissipated. I *knew* the timing was right this time. I could feel it. I began to make plans in my mind.

The following Wednesday, I tore myself away from her long

enough to take care of some business I'd been ignoring in L.A. I'd planned to be there for four days, but when I got there, all I could think about was getting back to her, so I worked extra hard to clear up everything so I could squeeze in a few extra days at the beach. I was packing to leave when the letter arrived for me by express mail. It was in her handwriting and postmarked Boston, and I knew before I opened it what it was.

Dear Jake,
    I know what you're thinking, and part of it may be true. I don't know, but try not to judge me too harshly. I'm just a screwed-up little girl.
    A man I've known for some time called last night and asked me to go with him to Jamaica for two weeks. After giving us a lot of thought, I agreed. I hope you understand, but I just can't handle the commitment of a heavy relationship right now, not after everything that's happened. I'm so confused, I don't know which way is up anymore; I'm not sure I know what love is. I do know you mean a lot to me.
    I'll be back in two weeks. Call me if you want to talk about it. I hope you understand and don't hate me.
                    Love,
                    Sharon

"I understand," I said, watching the letter burn in my ashtray. "And so did P. T. Barnum. There's one born every minute."
I spent the next four days driving the freeways from San Diego to Carmel, with the windows rolled down and the radio tuned in full blast to the sounds of hard FM rock, as if the jamming of my auditory senses would somehow block out the pain. I would stop at night and buy a couple of pints of Old Granddad and take them to the motel room and kill as much of them as it took to put me out, then start off again in the morning. After that, I drove back to L.A., made two phone calls, and took the next plane to Boise.
It wasn't as cold up there as I'd thought it would be.